Gerard's Descent

The Mountain Mama Series

Blue Deco publishing
BlueDecoPublishing@gmail.com

Gerard's Descent
The Mountain Mama Series

Cover by Colleen Nye
Editing by Genevieve Scholl
Formatting by Colleen Nye

Published by Blue Deco Publishing
PO BOX 1663 Royal Oak, MI 48068
BlueDecoPublishing@gmail.com

Copyright © 2018 Blue Deco Publishing & Marianne Waddill Wieland
Printed in the United States of America

All rights reserved.

No part of this book may be reproduced or transmitted in any form or by any means, electronic or mechanical, including photocopying, recording or by any information storage and retrieval system, without written permission from the publisher.

The unauthorized reproduction or distribution of a copyrighted work is illegal. Criminal copyright infringement, including infringement without monetary gain, is investigated by the FBI and is punishable by fines and federal imprisonment.

This is a work of fiction. All characters and situations appearing in this work are fictitious. Any resemblance to real persons, living or dead, or personal situations is purely coincidental.

I would like to dedicate this book to the late Richard Dana Diakun for all the help and music he suggested. The songs he gave me were perfect for the situations going on in the book and they pulled the story lines together nicely. I had told him that I needed a name for a particular character and he asked if the character could be him. He wanted to be part of the book. Thus, the character of Dr. Richard Dana, conductor of the New York Symphony Orchestra and professor at Julliard, was born.

Richard was able to read and approve the storyline for his character and the major parts of the book before he passed away. He loved it. He gave me several personal situations that had happened to him in college and a few conversations about different subjects that I was able to incorporate into the story line at his request. His character will remain alive in the rest of the book's sequels just as he wanted. Rest in peace, my good friend. You will be forever missed.

One

What was that smell? He slowly opened one eye and took a deep breath. He started to gag. Urine, vomit and sweat. Sweat despite the chill in the air and the bad breath of six other drunks in one of Chicago's many jails. He had dozed off as the only one in the cell and woke up to a throbbing headache and sick stomach.
What am I doing here?
The last thing he remembered, he was partying with two hot chicks that he hoped to take back to his apartment in the Gold Coast area of Chicago.
What happened? How did I wind up in here? Why can't I think straight?
Gerard closed his eyes again and tried to think back. First things first. What day was it? That would give him an idea of how long he had been here. He looked up at the others in the room and his head started to spin. He was moving too fast. He could feel his pulse throbbing in his ears.
Must be dehydrated he thought.
He moved his head slowly to the side to try to see the others in the cell. He could see two Chicanos that were maybe eighteen or so, one very old white man that was shaking from head to toe, two young white males hugging each other, and one very large black man with some kind of

skin condition. He had white patches on his arms and hands and Gerard noted that he only had a short- sleeved shirt on with a small blanket draped over his shoulders.

He needed to pace. Pacing was how he came up with his best ideas. Maybe it would help him piece together the events that had caused him to end up in this hell hole. He slowly sat up, shutting his eyes to stop the spinning. He took another deep breath and gagged again.

"Okay," he said outloud. He took a step and slid in something that was on the floor, almost falling. He looked down to see vomit all over his shoes.

"Hey! Who did this?" He yelled to the others in the cell. When no one answered, he spoke again.

"I said, who did this?!" He was yelling louder now. The two Chicanos continued to sleep. The two white males continued to ignore him. The old man tried to say something but his teeth were chattering so much that no words came out. So, it was the large black man that answered.

"You did, man. Can't you see that's why we all crowded over here? You been puking and thrashin' around all night. I don't know what you be doin' or how much, but I hopes I never gets hold of any of that shit."

"I did this?" He wiped his hands down his face. "Damn!" He had dried vomit on his chin. He wiped his hands on the legs of his pants even though he was still in one of his best designer suits.

"Give him yo' jacket." The big black man said as he nodded his head toward the old man.

"Me?" Gerard looked offended. "You give him your blanket, Uncle Ben."

"I will, man, but yo' jacket will help keep his body heat in."

Gerard took off his jacket and handed it to the black man who gently placed it around the old man's shoulders. Then he placed his own blanket over the old man as well. The old man tried to say something but the words would not come out. Gerard could see the appreciation in the old man's eyes. The fact that he could tell this was somewhat disturbing to Gerard. He rarely gave a second thought to what anyone else felt.

He sat back down. Soon the old man stopped shaking. When he did he looked at Gerard and the black man.

"Thank you."

Gerard felt even more uncomfortable, but nodded his head at the old man.

"Why are you in here?" Gerard looked at the black man and could tell he had spoken in too sharp a manner. The Chicanos looked at the black man like they were expecting a fight to break out.

"Wrong place, wrong time. Least I has a warm place fo' the night. God provides," answered the black man. He stood up and came over to stand next to Gerard. He was at least five inches taller than Gerard's six-foot, one-inch height and double Gerard's size. Gerard was proud of his physique but next to this guy, he felt like the size of an ant. Probably best not to piss him off.

The black man stuck out his hand.

"I'm Ben."

Gerard looked startled. "I'm sorry for calling you Uncle Ben but you don't have to rub my nose in it. My head feels like it may burst at any minute."

"I'm not kiddin'. My name is Ben Carver and believe you me I been called worse things than 'Uncle Ben'. I ain't nobody's uncle, but if I could make money at it, I be glad to sell rice." He smiled at Gerard. Gerard shook his hand and sat back down. Ben sat next to him.

"My name is Gerard."

"So, what be bringin' you here, Gerard?"

"I don't know. That's what I'm trying to figure out. I've never gotten so drunk that I.." Gerard paused.

"I guess that's not true. I have landed in jail before when I was younger. The last thing I remember was being in my club on Thursday night telling a man that he can't do drugs in the bathroom and if he didn't get that shit out of my club, I would call the cops. I don't remember being brought in here or what I was booked for."

Ben hesitated, then looked at Gerard. "I might be able to help with dat. Two cops practically carried yo' ass in. You be mumblin' somethin' about the 'Amish' and sayin' 'bad blood' every few minutes."

"Don't I at least get a phone call?" Gerard was rubbing his bloodshot eyes.

"You had yo' phone call. I was sittin' on the bench next to the phones. You be callin' somebody name of 'Nick' and I gotta say, man, you was a real bastard to him."

"Oh...God," cried Gerard. "I called my brother on his honeymoon. He is in Greece. No wonder no one has shown up."

"I thinks you was booked for 'drunk and disorderly'," said Ben.

"I guess it could have been worse," said Gerard as he looked around the cell like he was looking for an escape route.

"It be worse," said Ben shaking his head. "You be also charged with possession. Crack was found in yo' pocket."

"Great. Just great." Gerard slapped his hands on his knees as frustration just about got the best of him. "I haven't used that since my college days. I haven't used any drug. I only started drinking again recently."

"You looks like you gots a good job…and money. What you go back to drinking fo' anyway?"

Gerard stood up and walked a few paces, then turned around to look at Ben. "It's a long story."

"Look like we gots time." Ben stood up and leaned against the wall. "If yo' brother is comin' all the way from Greece, he gon' be a while yet."

"If he comes."

"Yo' brother a lawyer?"

"No. He's a pianist." Gerard stated this in a matter of fact way.

Ben scratched his chin and aimed a look in Gerard's direction. He seemed to be thinking hard before he spoke again.

"Now, I knows I don't gots the best education in the world, but how's a pianist gonna get yo' ass out of the slammer?"

"His new father in law is a lawyer." Gerard seemed to be weighing his words. "If you must know, so am I."

"Get outta here! You a lawyer too? Can't you just post yo' bail and leave?"

"I'm guessing they found priors and are holding on to me until *my* lawyer gets here."

Gerard started pacing. "I have a mother and father who never wanted any of their own children. I grew up at a boarding school in England. My brother, Nick, was raised by our aunt, Bess, and my younger brother and sister were raised in the same penthouse as my parents, but never knew them. They were raised by the maid and butler. They didn't even know each other."

"Dat's a damn shame, Gerard. I's sorry to hear dat, man." Ben started to pace as well.

"Anyway, a few weeks ago, we had reason to visit the West Virginia town in which my brother is building a tourist resort. While we were there my father revealed he was born in West Virginia into an Amish family and not the good kind of Amish. He was abused every day and finally escaped with his life when he was twelve."

"Let me gets dis straight, Gerard. Yo' daddy is Amish? How comes you ain't gots on a straw hat and suspenders? I's confused, man. So, yo' younger brother is building a playground in the West Virginia hills?" Ben was pacing like Gerard now.

"No. No. No." Gerard was emphatic. "You are not listening! The Amish family my father was born into was not your usual Amish family. He was beaten every day and finally had the good sense to get out of there. So, somewhere in the world, I have some Amish aunts and uncles. He was never able to locate the rest of his family after he became an adult and tried to find them. And my brother, Nick, is building the resort. My younger brother, Rod, is a manager and a pilot."

"Chill, man. I don't be meanin' no harm. I's just having a hard time following this... I don't even know what you call it." Ben had stopped pacing and had a worried look on his face.

"You and me both," replied Gerard. "It turns out my mother's family was worse. My grandmother died with my mother's birth and my grandfather used her as a punching bag all her life. He even used my aunt Bess as a substitute wife, if you know what I mean. I thought my mother was addicted to plastic surgery but it turns out that my grandfather crushed her hands with a hammer and set fire to her face. And my Aunt Bess was murdered."

"Yo' granddaddy murdered yo' Aunt Bess?"

"No! She was murdered at a teller machine in New York," answered Gerard harshly.

"Who murdered her? Yo' mother?" Ben's face was scrunched up and he was scratching his head.

"No, you cretin! Can't you understand anything I'm trying to tell you?"

"Hey man, they is no need fo' name callin' here. I's trying to follow what you be sayin' but it don't make no sense."

"No, it doesn't make any sense, so I started drinking to dull the pain. I'm sorry for calling you a cretin. My nerves are shot," said Gerard. "The gist of it is, I grew up thinking my mother never wanted me and my father was an ass. Turns out my grandfather was a rich, sadistic, sociopathic, rapist, so my mother was afraid to raise her own children. My father, on the other hand, was at every school event, graduation, and was in communication with my teachers my whole life. I just never knew it. He was raised Amish so he went along with my mother and kept his distance so she didn't take all the blame."

"Dat's why you came in mutterin' 'Amish' and 'bad blood'". Ben started pacing again. "Man, dat's too much fo' anybody. I want to be goin' out and getting' wasted just hearin' 'bout it."

Gerard sat back on the bench and changed the subject. "What are you really in here for, Ben?"

"Like Asher, here," he pointed to the old man. "I'm homeless too. No one be wantin' to hire a polka dotted black man my size. I was tryin' to keep the cops from takin' Asher in. He'd been sick, you see, and instead they took me in too. I spends time on the street playin' my harmonica and takin' handouts. I tries to protect some of the weaker homeless people. I does what I can. If I gets food, I shares it. I goes into libraries and looks on the internet. I tries to learn as much as I can."

Gerard looked Ben up and down. "You look like you eat well and you've got muscles to spare."

"Yeah. I gots a connection in Chinatown and a baked goods store near there. I lifts the heavy boxes and they gives me food. I looks in dumpsters. You'd be surprised what you can find. But not all the homeless are poor. Some make a pretty good livin' on the streets and it's they choice rather than a necessity. Sometimes they causes trouble for the homeless who don't got no choice. That's when I steps in to help protect them."

Gerard looked over at the old man who seemed to be sleeping. At least he was not shaking any longer.

"I don't see why you couldn't get a job as a body guard if nothing else. Where's your family?"

"My family died in a house fire when I was eighteen years old. I's the only one that got out. I tried to get my granny and baby sister out but smoke got them first. That be fourteen years ago. My mother left us with my granny when I be ten and my sister be two. Never knew who my daddy was."

Ben was looking at the floor and Gerard could see he was trying to hide the fact he was tearing up. "What happened to you after that?" Gerard hoped he wouldn't cause more bad memories for Ben.

"I spent a long time in a burn unit so I have some idea of what yo' mother went through." Ben kept staring at the floor.

"So those are scars on your arms and hands and not a skin condition." Gerard thought too late that he might have insulted Ben.

"Yep," was all Ben said.

They were silent for quite a while. The guards came and went releasing the Chicanos and the white males.

Ben got up to look at Asher. "Gerard, I don't think Asher is breathing."

"No. He's just sleeping," said Gerard as he barely glanced Asher's way.

Ben got up and felt for his pulse. "Help!" Ben yelled as loud as he could. "Help! This man's dead!"

The guards came running and drew their guns while the cell door was opened. It was determined that nothing could be done and the medical examiner was called in. He was pronounced 'dead' and hauled away in a body bag. Gerard had never seen someone die and he was starting to feel queasy again. He and Ben continued to watch until the group rounded the corner and could be seen no more.

"He was a good Christian man." Ben put his hand over his heart. "He's with the Lord now. A better place."

Gerard considered this. "My brother just married into a Christian family. Now he's gone all 'Christian' too."

"I think God be the only reason I be still here today." Ben said this as he walked back over to Gerard. He lightly put his hand on Gerard's shoulder. "It sounds like the same thing is true for you too."

Gerard shook Ben's hand off his shoulder. "I don't know what to think these days, but I feel bad about the old man being homeless and dying in this dump. Any family to bury him?"

"None that I ever heard about," Ben responded.

"I want to see my son!" Gerard heard Andrew Wallace yelling down the hallway.

"Hey, that's my father. I didn't want him to know!"

Gerard heard the clerk reply. "Sir, only his lawyer is allowed at this time."

Jim Dennison was hurrying down the hall as fast as he could. "Thanks for coming, Jim, but I've got to say, what in the hell took you so long?"

"That's another story."

Jim consulted some papers he had been given. "Gerard, I've seen the charges and your father is posting bail now."

"I'm sorry for interrupting Nick's and Jill's honeymoon, Jim," said Gerard with genuine emotion he realized he rarely displayed.

"It's not a problem. They were packing to return home when your call came in," said Jim. "Nick is here. Rod flew us all in. We got hung up in traffic."

"Jill's not here too is she?"

"No, but not for lack of trying. She and Brenda Montgomery both wanted to come."

Gerard pretended to pound is head on the wall. "Great. So, Brenda knows too. I'm sure she just wanted to have a good laugh. No offense, but I think I'll stay away from your neck of the woods for a while."

"Sit tight and we'll have you out of here in no time." Jim shook Gerard's hand and went back down the hall.

"Sounds like you been sprung, man. It was nice doin' time with you," said Ben.

"Good luck, Ben." Gerard shook Ben's hand. "If you are in the downtown area, I own the Grand Wallace Chicago and also The Club."

"You don't want to be seen with me," said Ben not meeting Gerard's eyes. "We come from two different worlds, but I wish you well. I be hopin' you get that drinkin' and whatever else you got goin' on under control. If you done it befo', you can do it again. Godspeed, Gerard," Ben said as Gerard was released.

At the checkout desk, Gerard received his personal belongings. He could hear one of the officers talking about the old man, Asher.

"He has no family. We'll just cremate him and dispense with the ashes."

"No!" Gerard startled his family and the officers present with his outburst. "He's family to me. I'll pay for the burial."

His family and Jim were shocked, but Andrew had a smile for is son.

"Yes," he said. "My daughter will get in touch with you to arrange the burial. Come on, son. Let's get you home."

"Before I leave, I would like to post bail for Ben Carver," said Gerard looking back toward the cell. "He's a friend, too." Gerard did so and left with those he felt, at least, cared for him a little. He made a silent promise to himself to try hard to get his life back in some kind of order.

.

Marianne Waddill Wieland

Two

Gerard and his brothers returned to Gerard's apartment in the Gold Coast, while Jim and Andrew elected to stay in the corporate quarters of the Grand Wallace Chicago. Gerard barely said a word to Nick and Rod as they arrived at his home. He went straight to the shower. He vaguely noticed his place smelled like alcohol and was a total mess.

After his shower, he found his brothers emptying his stash of rum and tequila down the drain.

"What do you think you're doing?" Gerard yelled across the room.

"Helping you clean up your act and your living room," said Rod as he held up some female bras.

"You can't just waltz in here and take over like you own the place." He grabbed the underwear from Rod.

"I think that's the last," said Nick. "I think it would be wise to get some sleep and discuss this further in the morning."

Gerard looked unhappy but he pointed out two of his four bedrooms in which Rod and Nick might sleep, but said nothing else.

"By the way, Gerard, you're welcome," Nick said sarcastically as he shut the bedroom door a little too hard.

He got the feeling his brothers were not finished with this conversation but was too nauseated to care. He took two over the counter pain killers and a couple of antacid tablets and retired to his own room to try to get some rest.

~

Gerard woke up the next morning much later than usual. He still had a slight headache, but not nearly the pounding one that had been present when he climbed in bed. He downed a couple more pain pills and went to the kitchen. There he found Rod and Nick unpacking a few grocery items and opening a box of donuts.

"Help yourself," said Nick.

"I don't know how you live in this filthy place and without any food," said Rod.

"I live here just fine and you can keep your comments to yourself," snapped Gerard in a nasty tone of voice that had both brothers staring him down.

"Time out," yelled Nick while he pointed his finger at Gerard's face.

"I want you to listen and listen good. We came all this way to bail you out of jail. We put our own lives on hold for you. I left my new wife and Rod was good enough to fly all of us out here to help you because you are our brother and Dad's son. As for Jim, he didn't have to come, but did so out of the goodness of his heart. At the very least, you should be civil to us."

Nick softened his tone a little. "Man, you have a family that cares about you. I know you have been really struggling with the revelations about our mother's past and the Dennison's part in it, but you might have to face the fact that you need some help dealing with it all, and not in this way." Nick waved his arm at the trash cans filled with alcohol bottles.

Gerard took a deep breath and was grateful that he didn't smell urine and vomit.

"I'm sorry," he said to his brothers. "I've spent the last thirty- six years thinking one way about my life. Then we find out most of what we knew wasn't true at all." He looked at the trashcans and around his dirty kitchen and living room. He shook his head.

"I just tried to block out the pain. Sometimes my head is not as level as I pretend it is." He grabbed a donut and closed his eyes at the pleasure the sweet treat brought him. He couldn't remember the last time he had eaten.

"This has hit us all hard," said Rod. "I grew up in the same penthouse as mother and dad and didn't pick up on any of this. I feel like a blind idiot or an ostrich with it's head in the sand. Gwen feels the same way, but at least she had an idea there was more to the story than we were allowed to see."

"Let's all get cleaned up. We need to meet Jim and Dad at the hotel for brunch in an hour," said Nick who was making a call to Jill as he spoke.

Rod started picking up the living room until Gerard stopped him. "I'll call my cleaning service. They will have this cleaned up in no time." They could both hear Nick leaving a voice mail on Jill's phone.

"I miss you so much. Sleeping without you last night was torture. I love you so much, babe..."

"I hope I find that kind of love someday," said Rod to Gerard.

"I think some people are cut out for wedded bliss and some are not," said Gerard. "I can't imagine having only one woman in my life. The more, the merrier I always say."

"And I feel just the opposite," replied Rod.

The cleaning service arrived just as they were leaving the apartment. Gerard gave some quick instructions while Nick hailed a cab. The trip to the hotel was short and they could have walked, but fatigue had remained with all three brothers.

Gerard closed his eyes and tried to remember the events that led to his arrest. All he could remember was what had taken place after he woke up in jail. He felt bad for the old man and was glad he could be of some help with the burial. He also thought of Ben and hoped he had found some place warm and dry. He usually didn't connect with many people except for loose women, but some how he found he was at ease talking with Ben. He could be himself. He wouldn't have to try to impress someone like Ben.

Stop it!

Ben would never fit into his world, so why he was even thinking about it, he couldn't imagine.

He thought about his real friends and had a major revelation. He didn't have any! He had employees, a lot of 'yes' men, lots of women, and a couple of vague acquaintances with whom he played tennis. Try as he might, he couldn't think of anyone with whom he could have a real conversation. He'd had a couple of nice conversations with Jill.

She was a beauty all right. Too bad Nick had gotten to her first, the lucky devil.

He'd had conversations with Jim but they were always situational conversations. He had enjoyed the few times he had spent with Nick in West Virginia and the short time he had spent with Rod in Pennsylvania. He had felt he had been able to be himself with his brothers during those times. They didn't require anything else of him.

Most everyone in his world wanted something. His money, his connections, sex. But most of the time, his money. Then there was Brenda Montgomery. She didn't seem all that impressed with him. In fact, she went out of her way just to show him how un-impressed she was. Her sharp, sarcastic tongue seemed to draw him in, shake him up, and toss him to the curb.

There had been that time at Nick's that she had thrown herself at him, or rather, on him. She was much smaller than he, but she had managed to overpower him and had...well, everyone knew what she had done. He had been so shocked that he hadn't tried to stop her. Well, that, and he really hadn't wanted to. And it had felt so good. Usually, he was the aggressor. This had been a little outside his comfort zone.

Then she had done it again under the stairs at Nick's and Jill's wedding. He had been more than a little agitated with that encounter. Anyone could have seen them.

What had she been thinking?

And any conversation with her was always one sided on her part. He could never get a word in before she was bashing him for something.

His thoughts stopped short as he felt the cab come to a halt. They all climbed out and Nick stopped to try to call Jill again. Rod went into the hotel but Gerard hung behind with Nick dreading the coming conversation with his father and Jim.

~

Brenda and Jill sat together at a table in the studio's kitchen at Mountain Mama's Restaurant in Beaumont, West Virginia. Jill was checking her phone for messages from her new husband, Nick. Brenda sat with her chin resting on her hands. Jill's Aunt Gladys came over to the table with some of her homemade bread and jam.

"Try this, gals. It's a new bread recipe I'm testing along with what I call 'Valentine Jam'".

Gladys sat the basket, butter, and jam in the middle of the table. When neither girl seemed to notice she tried again.

"There's also honey butter as well as margarine."

When there was still no response she put her hands on her hips.

"I also added arsenic to the whole lot just in case. If you don't like it, well, it won't matter long anyway."

Gladys kept staring at them until finally Jill looked up.

"Oh, sorry, Aunt Gladys. I'm sure this is delicious. I'm just wondering why I haven't heard from Nick this morning."

Gladys looked at Brenda with her eyebrows raised.

"Yeah, thanks Gladys. That addition of the arsenic is a big selling point with me this morning. How 'bout you give me some to go."

Brenda looked back at Gladys with a wink. Gladys just shook her head and went on about her business.

Brenda helped herself to some of the bread. She chewed for a moment, took another bite, chewed and swallowed. The bread had the taste of sour dough with a touch of what? Hot pepper? She added some jam and took another bite. Her eyes widened in surprise.

"Oh my gosh! Jill, this is unbelievable! I can taste cherry and cranberry for sure. Maybe some concord grape and possibly some hot sauce too!" Brenda continued to eat.

"Jill, snap out of it and try this." Brenda put jam on a slice of bread and tried to get Jill to take it.

Jill was texting as fast as she could with a worried look on her face. When she stopped, she looked at Brenda.

"Yes, you're right. That last ingredient Aunt Gladys mentioned will be a big selling point right off, I'm sure."

Brenda playfully smacked the back of Jill's head.

"Ouch! What did you do that for?" Jill rubbed the back of her head.

"You just said the best ingredient in Gladys's Valentine jam was arsenic," said Brenda.

Jill stared at Brenda for a minute and then started to laugh. "I'm sorry, friend. I'm just wanting to hear some kind of news from Nick. I have no idea what is really going on and I'm worried. I should have tried harder to be included in the trip to Chicago."

"Yeah, me too," said Brenda leaning back in her chair.

"Brenda," said Jill. "Answer me this. Why would you even want to go to Chicago with the guys to bail Gerard out of jail? You're barely civil to him on a good day and on a bad day you...well, you know what you did. What gives with that anyway? You barely know the man."

"I don't know, Jill," Brenda replied. "Something about Gerard makes my blood boil. I want to wipe that arrogant, self- satisfied look off his arrogant self-satisfied face. It's like he's looking down on us as being so much better than we are."

Jill put her phone down and looked at Brenda. She had jam on her cheek and looked really young at that moment but Jill felt Brenda needed to hear a few things.

"It sounds like a control issue, Brenda. If you can't control him one way, you try to control him with another."

Jill's brother, Matt, and Nick's daughter, Anika, came in the room, grabbed the bread and jam, and sat at the next table.

"Any word from dad about Uncle Gerard?" Anika spread jam on a piece of bread as she asked.

"Nothing yet, honey," said Jill. "I'll let you know as soon as I do."

"I don't feel a bit sorry for him," stated Matt. "He is rude and he is arrogant. But I think his biggest problem is that he suffers from low self- esteem."

"Low self- esteem? Are we talking about the same person?" Brenda asked as she left her seat to grab some more bread, this time with honey butter instead of the jam.

"Sure," said Matt. "Think about it. He was devastated about his family background. He started drinking again. He keeps his distance with everyone and is rude and obnoxious before anyone can start a conversation with him. To me, that sounds like someone who wants to hurt others before they can hurt him first. He pretends to be in control but I think it's all a cover due to low self-esteem."

"Resident genius," Jill said nodding her head toward Matt. "But I think you're on to something."

"Of course, Matt's right. He's always right." Anika looked sideways at Matt to gauge his reaction to what she said. She quickly changed the subject before Matt could offer comment.

"This jam is really good."

"I guess," Matt said off-handedly. "You've had, what, five pieces? You won't fit into those size two jeans for long."

"Matt!" Brenda and Jill spoke at the same time.

Brenda continued. "What a mean thing to say!"

"It's okay," said Anika unfazed. "He's entitled to his ridiculous opinion. He's been saying for some time that I'm too skinny." Matt just rolled his eyes.

Jill finally gave up and pulled up some pictures of Greece on her phone for the kids to look at. When they were engrossed in the pictures, Jill turned her attention back to Brenda.

"So, I think you and Gerard have some common ground. I think you use your sharp words and your body to cover up low self-esteem as well."

Brenda started to protest, but Jill cut her off. "You were determined to conquer Gerard with your mouth in more ways than one."

Jill took a long drink of her iced tea while Brenda started tearing her napkin into small pieces, all the while avoiding Jill's gaze.

"I've noticed that about you, Brenda, and I'm only saying this because I love you. You dive in for the kill without giving anyone the chance to get to really know you without all the 'extras.'" Jill used air quotes when she said extras.

"That's not it at all," protested Brenda. "I'm just more out-going than most people."

Matt gave a loud exaggerated sneeze.

"Under the stairs."

He had the reflexes to move faster than Brenda as she chased him out of the room.

Just then Jill's phone rang. Anika, seeing her father's number, answered it.

"Hey dad! We were just talking about you. Yes, she's here. I love you too!" Anika handed the phone to Jill.

"Nick! I've been so worried!" Jill stood up and walked toward the window.

"We're getting ready to meet Jim and dad for brunch. It was a very long night and I can't wait to get back to you."

Jill responded. "I can't wait to kiss you all over."

Anika jumped up, covering her ears, and ran from the room. Jill turned to watch her and just shook her head.

"We might be here another day getting Gerard's arraignment taken care of so he can get to New York to handle a possible legal matter concerning Alphonse

Laurant. One of his female staff members may try to slap him with a harassment charge."

Jill laughed. "Are you serious? I think he just suffers from 'little man syndrome'. I don't think he means any real harm." She walked back over to the kitchen counter and jumped up to sit.

"You're probably right, but until Gerard can get there to sort it out, that's where it's at. I'll keep you updated on the situation here."

They said "I love you" several times, but before they hung up Gerard grabbed the phone from Nick and spoke to Jill.

"I am so sorry for interrupting your honeymoon. I'll try to make it up to you some way."

"Don't worry about it," said Jill as she jumped down from the counter. "Just take care of yourself and come by here as soon as you can. We all miss you and I know Brenda would love to see you."

"Really? What, so she can laugh at me?" Gerard asked in is trademark snotty tone.

"No," said Jill as patient as possible. "I think she's interested in you, but she has a hard time getting that message across."

They said their 'goodbyes' and as Gerard entered his hotel with Nick, he had a big smile on his face.

Three

Gerard stood in the atrium, near the children's museum, on the second floor of the Navy Pier. He was staring out into the icy waters of Lake Michigan. He could hear the birds chirping in the background, the spray of the water arches, and the children laughing. It had been nearly three weeks since his father and brothers had bailed him out of jail and Jim Dennison had managed to get the charges dropped. He smiled to himself. Maybe family wasn't so bad after all.

Not too many people were out at the Navy pier today. Must be the foot of snow that had covered the city last night. Chunks of ice were floating in the lake and he could see a Coast Guard cutter in the distance. A few couples were in the atrium and he could see families with their children at the museum. He wasn't sure why, but the Navy Pier had always been one of his favorite places, no matter what time of year. He did a lot of thinking here. Even with the crowds of people on the lower level, he could manage to feel alone. He liked that feeling.

He walked a few paces to sit at one of the wrought iron tables near the edge of the atrium. He had a good view of the whole atrium, the lake, and the few people braving the walk down the pier. He thought back to the funeral his sister, Gwen, had arranged for the old man, Asher, who had died in jail. It had been about a week after his release. Nick and Jill had made the trip to attend as well as Jim, Rod,

Gwen, and Jill's Aunt Shirley who had sung 'Amazing Grace' during the service. There had been flowers and an organist. His sister was truly gifted at making last minute arrangements and doing a bang -up job.

He had hoped that Ben Carver would have been there, but Gerard had been unable to locate him even though he had tried. He hadn't found as many homeless people as he had thought he might. He had gone into Chinatown when he had remembered that Ben had told him of a connection of his there. The few homeless he did meet had not heard of Ben or had not seen him in a few weeks.

His father said that some people pass through our lives for only a short season. Maybe Ben and Asher had been there for him. He had done something for two other people without any benefit to himself. He couldn't remember a time in his life that he had ever done that. Jill had called it 'a selfless act' on Gerard's part. She even said she was proud of him and he got a big hug out of the deal.

Man! Was his brother ever a lucky son of a gun!

They'd all had to leave shortly after the funeral, but did manage to have lunch together at one of Gerard's favorite places. Very fancy and expensive. A far cry from Mountain Mama's in the West Virginia mountains.

Occasionally, well, more than occasionally if he were truthful, his thoughts turned to Brenda Montgomery. Her short, blonde hair, almost platinum blonde, he would say. Her big blue eyes. Soft full lips, and her…he stopped that line of thought. That was better thought about when he was home, alone or in the shower.

He would be going to Nick's and Jill's in a week or so for a Valentine's Day party and celebration of the new format of Jill's cooking show. It would be launched with Nick and

Jill as the chefs. *Bor...ing* thought Gerard, but he had promised to attend.

He put his hands in his coat pocket to warm them up and felt a piece of paper. He pulled it out and remembered that Nick had handed it to him before he left on the day of the funeral. It was a scripture.

"Greater is he who is in you than he who is in the world." 1st John 4:4. *What? What does that even mean?*

He started to throw it in the nearest trashcan, but something stopped him. He folded it up and put it in his wallet.

He took his time and slowly walked down the stairs into the main lobby area of the Navy Pier. He doubled back through the food court and out a side door. He could see that the city was on top of the snow removal but so much of the pier was still under construction that walking to the end was not worth the effort. A real shame, too. That was one of his favorite things to do. Even though the construction was annoying, the end result would be worth it. He thought of taking in a show at the Shakespeare theater about halfway down the pier, but decided against that too. He decided to just go home and quickly turned toward the street and the ever- present cabs that were parked there.

After the short ride home, he opened the door to his apartment to find he was a little disappointed, for once, that he was alone. Hopefully there was a game on that he could watch to help ease the last of his anxiety. Anxiety he had been feeling since his arrest. He would also like to turn his mind off a certain young lady about six hundred miles to the east. Lady? Could he really call her that? He turned the TV on and decided he would have to think about that later.

Brenda was helping Jill set up one of the banquet rooms for a group of seniors celebrating a fiftieth wedding anniversary for a couple of their own. They were in one of the larger rooms and were putting up decorations for a Hawaiian themed luau. Brenda and the twins, Marlene and Darlene, cousins of Jill's, were the entertainment for the night. Brenda would be playing the piano and along with the twins, singing a bunch of 'Golden Oldie' songs. Later, after the dinner, they would be doing a hula dance they had been rehearsing.

Jill had a buffet of Polynesian foods and Brenda had to say, she had out done herself this time. Brenda was looking forward to the meal as she and the twins had been invited to eat with the guests.

"Brenda, why don't you go ahead over to the apartment and get dressed. The guests will be arriving in half an hour. Nana will greet them as Mountain Mama and do her thing until the celebration begins."

"Okay, you talked me into it," said Brenda as she headed over to Jill's former apartment humming one of the 'Golden Oldie' tunes.

"Speaking of 'Golden Oldies'," she said to herself, "I wonder how Gerard is doing?"

She pulled out her phone and sent a text to him.

"Hey, 'Grandpa', how's it hanging. It's been a while and I'm having trouble remembering. LOL."

She started dressing herself in pink shorts and a pink, blue, and yellow flowered shirt. She got her hula skirt and top all ready to go for later on and had just about given up on hearing back from Gerard when her phone rang. She saw

Gerard's name and leaped onto the sofa to grab it before it went to voice mail.

"'Grandpa'! I thought you had forgotten me by now," said Brenda in her sexy voice.

"I don't think that's possible," replied Gerard. "What's up with the 'Grandpa' thing?"

"You keep making remarks about how much older you are than me, hence, 'Grandpa'. Besides, I like it. It's sexy."

"Sexy? Grandpa?" Gerard couldn't keep the disgust out of his voice. "You are sicker than I thought the last time we met."

Brenda just laughed. "You might not say that if you were here where I am." She explained what was going on.

"Wow. I'd like to see the hula show. Explain it to me in detail so I can have a happy ending to this day."

"No time. I go on in ten minutes," said Brenda while she was gathering up her clothing.

"It won't take that long," Gerard replied drily.

"Oh," said Brenda. "Been doing without the ladies, have we?"

"Let's just say I've been slowing things down. Trying to understand the family I was born into and find some peace without any outside help."

"Sometimes we all need a little extra help. We just have to be wise in the way we get it. Take Jill and the Dennison's. They rely solely on God," said Brenda. "I believe in God, but haven't been able to sustain that walk except for short periods of time."

"Me neither," replied Gerard. "There's no way I'd ever be good enough for that lifestyle." There was a slight pause.

"Hey! I'll be down there in two weeks for the Valentine's Day party. How about we get together and toss down a couple...or you know..."

"I do know, and what was that you just said about doing without outside help?" Brenda was speaking in a teasing tone of voice.

"I can control the drinking. I'm not an alcoholic, you know. I haven't had a drink since I was arrested."

Brenda thought for a minute. "Didn't you have a possession charge as well? How did you get out of all that?"

"They didn't find any fingerprints of mine on the bag of crack they found in my pocket," he said smugly. "So, Jim managed to get the whole thing dropped. He brought up the whole family drama and how I have been a successful businessman in the city of Chicago."

Gerard continued to pat himself on the back. "After all, I am a stellar attorney myself and as they say, bada bing, bada boom, the rest is history."

"Bada bing, bada boom?" Brenda put as much emphasis as she could on the two words. "Yeah, I was right with Grandpa. Hey, I've gotta go. I'll see you at the party."

As Gerard hung up, he settled back in his recliner with a smile on his face. He pulled one of the afghans some girl had crocheted on to his lap. He knew he would have a happy ending to the day after all.

"Wait," he said out loud as he quickly sat up. "I'm in a damn recliner with an afghan on my lap. Maybe she's right calling me grandpa."

He thought a minute and then smiled. "I'm still sexy, though. You can't refute that! Some people got it, some people don't, and I've definitely got it in spades!" He settled once again into the recliner to finish watching the game and thought of the shower he would take when it was over.

Four

The week before Gerard was due to visit the town of Beaumont, West Virginia, the weather was unseasonably warm for Chicago. He stood on his second story balcony and breathed in the cold, refreshing air. He was very proud of himself. Another weekend behind him without a drunken orgy.

He had taken a business acquaintance to dinner the evening before, female of course, and he had not even tried once to hit on her. He wasn't sure if he was really trying to make changes in his life or just too old for all the bull. Then maybe it was his desire to get back to Mountain Mama's place and to see Brenda again.

He went back inside and picked out one of his more expensive suits and dressed for the day. He looked good. Really good, and this was most important to him. He was planning to represent a couple of clients to close the deal on a piece of property that had been in limbo for several months due to city ordinances and yada, yada, yada, he thought to himself.

At the last minute, he decided to walk to his office, in his hotel, six blocks away. It was good to be alive, he thought to himself. He was about to enter the side door to his hotel when he ran into something that felt like a brick wall. Too late, he realized he had walked into someone waiting in the shadows.

The man stepped out of the doorway just as Gerard started to speak.

"Look, asshole, if it's money you want, then name your price." Gerard's hands were in his pockets and he felt for his cell phone.

"As much as you want if you just take the money and leave. All I have to do is push one button on my phone and you'll wish you had gone in another direction today."

Gerard hoped his bluff would serve him well, because he did not have 911 on speed dial and couldn't get his phone turned around in order to dial it. He started to pull the phone out of his pocket hoping the intruder would think he was pulling out a gun. So far, the intruder had not threatened him with one.

Just then the phone rang and he saw Brenda's name on the screen. He wasn't about to answer it, but knew his bluff had been called. He held his hands up and slightly backed away.

"Hey, look man..."

Just then a huge arm reached out and pulled him into a hug. "Gerard! Man, it's me, Ben. You done gone and forgot me this quick?"

Gerard was stunned. Ben! He had thought he would never see him again. He hugged Ben back.

"Ben! Man, where have you been? I looked all over for you to let you know we were having a funeral for the old man, Asher. I couldn't find you anywhere."

They stepped back from each other. Gerard continued.

"I thought you might turn up here, if for nothing else to at least say 'thank you' for bailing you out last month. By the way, you just scared the piss out of me!"

Ben looked down at the ground feeling very uncomfortable. "Oh, man, I be so sorry. 'Bout as soon as I gots out, I comes down sick like Asher was. I gets myself to the free clinic and they puts me in one of they beds fo' 'bout ten days. I thought I was leavin' this world."

Ben stopped staring at the ground and finally looked at Gerard. "It be good to see you, man. I comes over to the side entrance so you wouldn't have to be seen with me in front where most of the employees are."

"Ben, Ben...I've probably never said this before in my life, but I don't feel embarrassed to be seen with you. I am so glad to see you," said Gerard grabbing Ben's gloved hand. "Come on in. We can talk in my office and I'll order us some breakfast."

Gerard held the door open for Ben and they headed up a few short stairs into the hotel's main lobby. He could see the street from the main entrance and what he saw stopped him short. Crossing the street, headed for his hotel, was none other than Brenda Montgomery. Right here in Chicago! That must have been why she was calling.

"Ben, don't go anywhere. I see someone who could be important headed this way." Gerard pushed open the main entrance door and jogged out onto the street. He caught up to Brenda before she got to the corner. He grabbed her from behind, wrapped his arms around her, turned her around, and planted a big kiss on her shocked face.

"Hey, gorgeous. There's more where that came from."

Without missing a beat, Brenda stepped on his foot and slugged him in the face.

"I don't know who you think you are, but nobody grabs me that way and gets away with it."

She reached in her purse to grab the pepper spray when a big, black arm caught her hand.

"I wouldn't do that if I was you, young lady."

"Then it's a damn good thing you're not me."

She turned the can of spray toward Ben and sprayed. Ben was quick enough to turn his face and took the shot of pepper spray in the ear. Ben let go of her arm. She took off running to the next empty cab and jumped in. The cab took off, leaving Gerard standing next to Ben in the snow-covered sidewalk of Michigan Avenue rubbing his jaw.

He looked at Ben. "Are you okay, man?"

"Yeah. I be turnin' my face and shutin' my eyes just in time," said Ben wiping his ear off with his glove. "Took a good shot in the ear, though. It be stingin' like a bitch!"

"I don't know what just happened," said Gerard still staring after the cab. "That girl has always been feisty, but I thought we were on better terms than that."

Ben put his hand on Gerard's shoulder. "Come on, man. Let's be gettin' you inside and puttin' some ice on that jaw. And I needs to wash that spray outta my ear 'fo I goes deaf." Ben looked at Gerard's face.

"Man, that be gonna leave a mark." Gerard led Ben back into the hotel, limping all the way to his office.

~

Brenda stood at the cell phone counter located in the Five and Dime store on Main Street in Beaumont, West Virginia. Her cellphone had died and she had hoped to get Gerard on the phone to let him know she would be unavailable for a few days at this number. She contemplated buying a track phone but figured that was a waste of time and money. She would see Gerard soon enough at the Valentine's party this coming weekend.

As she was leaving, she ran into Jill and Anika entering the store.

"Hey, friends." Brenda gave them both a hug.

"Hey, yourself," answered Jill with a smile.

"Are you here slumming now that you're rich beyond belief?"

"Not at all," said Jill testily. "Just because I'm married to Nick doesn't mean my lifestyle will change. I plan to continue my shopping habits as usual."

"Sorry," said Brenda a little testy herself. "I didn't mean anything by it. It just seemed like the thing to say at the time." She looked around for a graceful way to exit the store and not offend her friends.

"So," she changed the subject. "Anika, where's your better half?"

"Better half of what?" Anika rolled her eyes as she spoke.

"Matt, silly girl. You two are always together," said Brenda.

"Not always." Anika turned around and headed to the back of the store, ignoring any reaction from Brenda.

"What did I say?" Brenda looked at Jill and then back in the direction Anika had gone.

Jill stared in the direction that Anika went as well. "Well, there seems to be trouble in River City as the song goes. Matt has been thinking more and more about leaving for college in the fall and he is busy with Nick a lot. I think Anika just feels left out and a little jealous of Matt's time."

"I thought they were just friends," said Brenda.

"That's on the surface. I think it goes much deeper than that, at least for Anika," Jill replied. "I think we're better off not bringing up the subject."

"Hey, I can dig it," said Brenda snapping her fingers and swinging her hips.

"Nineteen seventy- two called and wants it's 'dig it' back."

"Funny. Ha ha," said Brenda flippantly.

"By the way," said Jill. "Your sister, Bonnie, called me earlier. She said she can't get you on the phone."

"True," said Brenda. "My phone died right after I tried to call Gerard to tell him my phone was dying."

"Any way," said Jill, "she said she was walking down the street this morning and a strange guy with a big, black boyfriend, grabbed her and kissed her right there on Michigan Avenue. By Gerard's hotel."

Brenda ruffed up her own hair. "Wow! I should try to call her. There are some real weirdos in Chicago." She was thoughtful for a moment. "Must be why Gerard lives there."

"Maybe it was Gerard," joked Jill.

"No way. Even though he seems to be staying away from his loose ladies..."

"Present company excepted," interrupted Jill.

"Ha ha, again," said Brenda. "Anyway, I don't think he's taking up with men of any color. He'll be here on Saturday."

"Is Rod flying him in?"

"I have no idea." Brenda replied to Jill. "Who knows if he will really show up, or if he will show up alone." She thought for a moment. "At least we can be sure he won't be showing up with a big, black boyfriend." They both laughed.

Anika had returned. "I hope he does show up with a big, black guy. Maybe I can use him to make Matt jealous."

Gerard and Ben sat in Gerard's office eating the breakfast Gerard had ordered. Ben had first aid cream on the side of his face and ear. Gerard had ice packs on his face and foot.

"This is the best food I've eaten since...since...since my granny was alive. Before the fire," said Ben, struggling to get the words out.

"This is just plain old food to me," said Gerard, a hint of his haughty tone creeping in. "It does hurt to chew, though."

"Just goes to show how diff'rent our lives is," said Ben.

Gerard's phone rang and he had to put down the ice pack to answer it.

"You've got to be kidding, Victor. That rat bastard! What else is he going to get into? Can't he stay out of trouble for two days without someone, somewhere threatening to sue him for something?" Gerard put the phone on speaker and picked up the ice pack, placing it back on his cheek.

Ben and Gerard could hear Victor talking to a female in the background. His sister, Gwen.

"I'll be flying down to Beaumont for the weekend."

"Will that be on the wide angle O'Cedar or the heavy-duty push style?"

Gerard put all the attitude into the statement he could while trying to keep the ice pack in place.

"Hello to you too, Gerard. I've missed you so much." Gwen put just as much attitude into her return statement.

Ben started to laugh. Gerard tried to gesture for him to knock it off before his sister heard.

"Who is that with you, Gerard? Some punk ass 'yes man' you seem so fond of?" Gwen was on a roll now, and Victor could be heard laughing in the background.

"I be sorry, miss," said Ben trying to cover his laughter with a cough.

"Gwen, who I'm with is none of your business," said Gerard in his nastiest tone. "All you need to know is that I will be there in two days, on Wednesday." He punched the speaker button and hung up the phone.

"I'm sorry, Gerard," said Ben looking at the floor. "I didn't mean to make her mad. Was that one of yo' girlfriends?"

"No, for God's sake," spat Gerard. "That was my sister. She can be a royal pain. Now I have to get to New York City to settle yet another dispute with Alphonse Laurant. He can't stay out of trouble with the women."

Ben looked at Gerard. "Is he related to you, too? Does this sort of thing run in yo' family?"

"Quite the comedian, you are," replied Gerard. "And, no. He is most certainly not related to me. Alphonse can be a major Jack Ass. He causes a lot of trouble."

"New York City. Always wanted to go there," said Ben with a faraway look in his eye.

"Hey, that's not a bad idea," said Gerard putting the ice pack down again.

"Look, man, I won't tryin' to get a invitation to go," said Ben looking startled.

Gerard interrupted him. "With you along, it'll scare the crap out of Alphonse. It could slow his trouble making down if he thinks you are my bodyguard." Gerard got up to pace. "That's what we'll tell him."

"Ahhh...no, man. I can't be goin' to New York City," said Ben as he got up to pace too. "I don't be havin' the right clothes, the right shoes, ain't gots no phone...no, man, fo'get it." Ben was backing toward the door as he was protesting.

"Ben, you have to. You owe me," said Gerard as he grabbed his jacket. "Those things are incidental. Come on, we have a make-over to do. You're coming with me to New York and you will look like my bodyguard. I won't take 'no' for an answer." Gerard grabbed Ben by the arm and pulled him out of the office door with Ben continuing to protest all the way.

By dinner time, Gerard had fixed Ben up with a suit, black cargo pants and jeans, black tee shirts and a black leather jacket. Ben was still protesting.

"Forget it, Ben. If I am to pass you off as my bodyguard, then you have to look the part."

"Okay, if you gon' do it, you gon' do it. But it don't feel right when you bails me outta jail, buys me stuff and takes me to New York. I be findin' some way to pay you back, man." Ben kept shaking his head back and forth.

"Well, it feels right to me." Gerard was still rubbing his jaw now and then. "You saved me from that witch, Brenda, by stepping in to keep me from being pepper sprayed."

"Yeah, I guess I done did that for you," said Ben rubbing his ear.

Gerard continued. "I've never done much for other people, but for some reason, with you, I can talk and be myself. And to top it all off, you really don't want anything from me." He was looking at his phone for messages.

"Do you have any idea when I had a real friend?"

Ben tried to say something, but stuttered some incoherent answer.

"Don't even try to guess. I've never had one. But, Ben, you seem like you could be a real one, but if you tell a soul, I'll deny it."

The cab they had been riding in stopped in front of Gerard's apartment and he paid the driver. Both men got out and entered Gerard's home, with Ben carrying most of the packages.

"I have my bad boy rep to protect, you know," said Gerard. "How would it look to my siblings if they found I have a very tiny soft spot, maybe not for everyone, but for the homeless."

"You buried Asher, man, they gots to have some idea you ain't all bad," said Ben looking around the apartment nervously. "What can I be sayin'? Thank you, man. I'll see you on Wednesday and I promise I be ready to go."

"Stop right there."

Gerard put his hand on Ben's arm. "You're not going anywhere. You are staying with me now. You have to practice the part of a bodyguard."

Gerard pointed to a room just off his kitchen. "You take that room over there. Help yourself to anything you need. There should be new toiletries in the bathroom. I have frequent overnight guests, if you know what I mean."

When Ben didn't move, Gerard gave him a gentle shove in the direction of the room he had pointed out.

"Mi casa es su casa."

Ben wiped tears from his eyes. "I doesn't know what that means, but I promises to do the best job I can pretendin' to be yo' bodyguard." He gave Gerard a hug and went to the room Gerard had provided.

Gerard watched him go and felt a strange feeling in his gut. He rubbed the spot.

"Must be heartburn."

He retired to his own room all the while wondering why Brenda had treated him as she had. All of his calls went straight to voicemail. He finally gave up.

"Oh well, her loss." Then he headed to the shower.

Five

As soon as the private jet taxied to a stop at the private landing strip belonging to the Wallace family, Ben was out the door. He fell to his knees on the ground, raising his hands in the air and yelling as loud as he could.

"Thank you, Lawd! Thank you! Thank you! You gots me back on the ground, Lawd!"

Rod and Gerard stood by the nose of the jet staring at him.

"You said he was your bodyguard?" Rod was shaking his head at Gerard.

"Yes, he is my bodyguard," stated a frustrated Gerard.

"Let's forget the fact that I have no idea why you need a bodyguard, but are you sure of who is guarding whom? Did you hear him scream when we took off? How many times did he 'yak' while we were in the air? I'm going to have to have the carpets cleaned."

Gerard continued to watch Ben and his antics which had changed from praising the Lord on his knees to running in wide circles and yelling praises.

"Thank you, Jesus! Hallelujah!"

"It's his first time in the air," said Gerard looking at Rod. "Just saying."

Rod watched as Ben bent over with his hands on his knees to catch his breath.

"Nah, not buying it, Gerard. Out with it."

"Oh, all right, if you must know. He's not a real bodyguard."

"No shit." Rod was looking Gerard straight in the eyes. "What kind of game are you playing now?"

"He is pretending to be my bodyguard to scare the crap out of Alphonse," said Gerard with his nose in the air. "There, now you know."

Rod took another look at Ben, noting his height and build. "Okay, then. That works for me. Let's get this show on the road."

After unloading the jet of their luggage, Gerard and Ben said goodbye to Rod and watched as the jet taxied back down the runway and took to the skies.

After an hour's ride in the limo, Gerard and Ben were unloading the luggage at the front entrance of the Grand Wallace New York.

"Well, well, well. What do we have here?" Oscar the doorman for the hotel was looking from Gerard to Ben.

"Well, well, well," said Gerard as snotty as possible. "I see you're still here. My sister must still have a soft spot for unfortunate cases."

"I thought we had seen the last of you, Gerard, but I guess not as long as Alphonse is around." Oscar moved toward Ben. "I'm Oscar. And you would be…?"

"He would be none of your damned business," said Gerard taking a step toward Oscar.

"Hold on brother," said Ben stepping in the middle. "I'm Ben, Gerard's main man…what's up…get back wit yo' bad self…" Ben was doing a foot shuffle while he was nervously trying to diffuse the situation.

"I've seen enough," said Gerard opening the door for himself. "Ben, get the bags…now!"

Oscar moved closer to Ben. "Now who are you really? I've been working here for twenty- five years and I haven't seen you before."

"My name be Ben Carver, from Chicago." Ben stuck out his hand and Oscar shook it. "I's Gerard's bodyguard."

Oscar motioned for Ben to bend down to his level. "That's a good thing 'cause somebody gonna kill his ass sooner or later."

Ben straightened up. "Not on my watch, brother, not on my watch." Ben picked up the bags and followed Gerard into the hotel.

"Must be new," Oscar said to himself.

Ben caught up to a very angry Gerard. "Take those bags to the concierge and meet me in the bar in two minutes. We have to set some ground rules." Gerard stalked off mumbling to himself.

Ben found Gerard sitting at the bar with two drinks in front of him.

"I'm sorry, man. I be just too far outta my comfort zone."

"I'm over it," said Gerard not looking at Ben. "But if you ever act like that again, you're fired. Number one rule. Be professional at all times."

Gerard swigged down one whole drink. "Look scary and don't talk to the people unless I tell you to do so. Is that understood?" Gerard swigged down the other drink.

"Another one, Andre' and one for my bodyguard."

"What will you have, sir?" Andre' was waiting for Ben's order.

Ben put his hand to his mouth trying not to laugh his excitement out and leaned to Gerard.

"Ain't nobody called me 'sir' befo'."

"Get it together and order a drink!" Gerard was swigging down the third drink when Ben spoke to Andre'.

"Umm… do you have Coke or Pepsi products?"

Gerard choked on his drink and Ben ended up slapping him on the back to help him gain control. When Gerard could breathe again, he told Andre' to bring a Rum and Coke over to the corner table along with another drink for himself.

"Listen, Ben. You're in my world now. You do as you're told or you're out," said Gerard with a slight slur to his voice.

"You know what, man?" Ben sat down and leaned toward Gerard. "I's had just about enough of yo' nasty mouth. I can live on the streets of New York just as well as Chicago. Now I didn't ask to come here. That was yo' idea and just 'cause I comes from the streets don't mean I be any less of a human bein'. So, if you can't treat me no better than this…"

Ben looked at Gerard's haughty face and said, "Fo'get it…I be outta here." Ben stood to leave.

"Okay, okay." Gerard stood as well.

"I apologize. I'm not used to being nice. It's why I have no friends." He deflated a little. "You're right. Let's have something to eat and talk this over. Will you forgive me, Ben?"

"Ain't nothin' to fo'give, man, but I be needin' some food in my stomach if I gotta drink hooch."

With that said, they both laughed and sat back down to make a game plan.

~

Brenda and Jill were working in the studio kitchen on recipes for the Valentine show that would be done on

Thursday before the party on Saturday. Brenda was trying hard to follow Jill's recipe for heart shaped cherry cakes with cherry icing.

"Damn!" Brenda had dropped the bag of confectioner's sugar she was trying to measure into a bowl.

"Don't sweat it," said Jill looking more worried at Brenda than anything else. Jill motioned for one of the kitchen crew to clean up the mess.

"What's up with you today? You're as nervous as a fox with a hound on his tail."

Brenda threw down the recipe card she was working with and covered her eyes with her hands.

"I don't know," she whined. "I keep thinking about Gerard and what I want to do to him when I see him. He is such a hunk."

"He's a hunk alright," said Nana as she came into the room leading Margaret by the arm. "A hunka what, I ain't a gonna try to figger out. How 'bout you, Maggie?"

"He is my son. He is good looking. That is all I can say," replied Margaret in a flat tone.

Nana led her to sit at one of the studio tables that had some homemade bread and jam made by aunt Gladys.

"Now Maggie, I want ye to hep yerself to some 'o this and gimme yer opinion. Gladys made it. She might be a sellin' it in our new bakery store." Nana left Maggie to it and went over to Jill and Brenda.

"How's she doing?" Brenda looked skeptical.

"Still a wantin' to jest be by my side," said Nana. "I go ever where with her. I don't know how long it's a gonna be before she snaps out of it. She won't eat much and she can't afford to lose no more weight."

"She's still wearing those gloves," said Jill. "Poor thing. She still doesn't talk much to anyone but you, Nana. Do you think she will come to the party?"

"If'n I'm there, she'll be there," said Nana looking at Margaret. "I'm a gonna try to get her to eat some jam and bread..."

"That will bring us back to Do, oh, oh, oh..." Brenda, feeling ignored, sang as she walked over to the table and sat down by Margaret.

"Do, a deer, a female deer...Re, a drop of golden sun...Mi a name I call myself..."

Maggie sat up straighter and interrupted. "Fa, a long, long way to run..." she half sang in a cracked voice.

The others were silent and staring at Margaret. She looked back at them.

"So, a needle pulling thread..." she sang.

"La, a note to follow So..." continued Brenda when Margaret stopped.

"Ti, a drink with jam and bread..." sang Nana an octave lower than the others. She looked around at everyone present and noticed that Jim, Andrew, and Dr. Weir had joined them. She quietly nodded to everyone.

"That will bring us back to Do." They all sang in unison then stopped, all looking at Margaret.

Margaret looked at each one standing around her and slowly sang.

"Do...Re...Mi...Fa...So...La...Ti...Do."

Margaret looked at Brenda. "You started this, young lady, so you can keep it going."

She picked up a piece of bread, spread some jam on it and started to eat with gusto. Brenda just stared with her mouth hanging open until the others were all looking at her to do something.

"Go ahead," said Dr. Weir.

Brenda began to sing.

"Rain drops on roses and whiskers on kittens, bright copper kettles and warm woolen mittens…"

The others joined in with the rest of the song and as Margaret finished her bread, she stood and sang along with the others.

When the song was over, Nana gave Margaret a big hug and Margaret hugged Nana back so tight that Brenda thought Nana's bones might snap.

Margaret was smiling. She went over to Andrew and gave him a hug, then to Dr. Weir, and so on around to everyone present. Then she sat down and began to eat more of the jam and bread.

Matt and Anika had joined the group by the end of the song, but not being as close to the situation with Margaret as the others, didn't see what a breakthrough this was for her.

Matt went to the old upright piano in the corner, sat down, and made an announcement in jest.

"Hey, I'm Nick." He began to play some runs up and down the keys while the others watched.

Anika joined in.

"Hey, yourself." She sat on the edge of the piano bench and wiggled her bottom closer to Matt.

"I'm Jill's guitar. Play me." She said this with as much sexiness as a seventeen year- old girl could muster.

Matt looked at her without missing a note on the piano.

"I don't play Jill's guitar. I only play with my own instrument."

Everyone stopped talking and stared at Matt who had stopped playing. He was beet red in the face realizing what he had said.

"What I meant to say was..."

"It's always the young 'uns ain't it?" Nana was shaking her finger at Matt and Anika.

"Annie, I love ye, but ye got to stop throwin' yerself at Matt."

"I am not throwing myself at Matt. He's not that lucky!"

She stood with all the dignity she could manage in her tight jeans and body hugging tee shirt. She marched out of the studio area only looking back once to see if Matt was following. When she saw he was ignoring her, she picked up the pace and ran up the stairs.

~

Gerard and Ben were finishing up their meal and discussing the day's events. Ben was laughing at Gerard's interpretation of himself after he was back on the ground.

"I thought we be all gon' die befo' we be settin' foot on the ground again," said Ben. He was looking out the window at all the lights and people.

"Other than the lights, I be almost thinkin' I was still in Chicago, man."

"New York is nothing like Chicago. The people aren't as friendly here," said Gerard stretching his legs under the table.

"I need another drink. Andre!" Gerard shouted across the room. "Another for my friend, too."

Ben looked worried. "Are you sho' you wants another drink, Gerard? I knows I don't need one."

"Man, you just had your first jet ride and you're in New York City for the first time. We're celebrating." Gerard slapped Ben on the back. "Now shut up and drink your hooch."

Andre' set the drinks on the table and Gerard tipped him with a fifty- dollar bill. Ben's eyes nearly popped out of their sockets, but he decided to keep his remarks to himself. He continued to look around the bar and out the window sipping his drink, while Gerard downed two more drinks.

"Hey, Gerard, man, ain't that the Brenda chick that bitch slapped you in Chicago the other day," said Ben as he stood to get a better look at the girl standing on the sidewalk near the entrance to the bar. "Yeah, man. I think that be her."

Gerard jumped up so fast, he knocked over his and Ben's drinks.

"That is her. Is she following me? Or is she looking for me to apologize? Should I ignore her or give her another chance?"

"Gerard," said Ben. "You done spilled yo' drink all over yo'self. You looks like you done wet yo' pants."

Gerard vaguely looked down and swiped at the fly of his pants. "No one will notice that. Come on. I'm going to pretend nothing happened and surprise her again."

"I don't know, Gerard." Ben was reluctant to follow.

"Bodyguards go with their charges, so, move it, before she leaves. I think it was all in the delivery. I think I scared her before."

Gerard went out the side door, walked up behind Brenda, and slowly moved his hands over her shoulders. He pulled her against him and ran his hands down her arms turning her around as he did so. Ben was keeping his distance.

"Hi again, baby. Let me entertain you." Gerard was rubbing his cheek against her head and preparing for a kiss.

"Hello, sweetie. Let me entertain *you*." She took his face in both of her hands and kicked him in the groin as hard as she could.

"Next time you want a happy ending, don't be so quick to think I'm the one to give it to you."

She pointed at the crotch of his pants where he was holding himself and groaning. "Consider that one a freebie." She turned and ran for the nearest cab.

"Gerard, you gots to get yo'self some better friends." Ben helped an almost incapacitated Gerard back to their suite in the hotel to recuperate, once again, from an attack by Brenda.

Six

Gerard and Ben were sitting at a table in the hotel's signature restaurant, Marcel's, talking to Gwen and Alphonse. It had been two days since their arrival and each day they had worked hard to diffuse the situation between Alphonse and two women of his kitchen staff. At least Gerard and Gwen had worked hard. Ben had sat silently and stared at Alphonse with a scary look on his face.

Alphonse was adamant that he had not made any inappropriate gestures to either of the women, however, he was reluctant to admit that he may have done so prior to meeting Marlene, Jill's cousin, at Mountain Mama's.

"Alphonse is highly sought out by the women of all ages and races. He is not about to let down the women who have worked so hard to gain his attention," said Alphonse in a heavy French accent as he looked at himself in his pocket mirror.

"Oh, puh...lease!" Gwen was quite put out with Alphonse. "Don't make me gag. I have had about enough of your high and mighty attitude. You are damn lucky that I even keep you on here."

"Alphonse, I have to leave to go to Mountain Mama's as soon as the limo arrives to take us to the landing strip."

Gerard was pulling out some bills to leave for a tip and noticed Alphonse perk up when he said 'Mountain Mama's'.

"I am afraid to leave you here unattended for fear you can't stay out of trouble. Do I need to leave my bodyguard here to keep you in line?"

Ben perked up at this news. He had spent two days keeping his mouth shut around this little 'Napoleon'. That was what Ben called him in his own mind.

"Why don't he be comin' with us to the mountains?" Ben asked innocently noting Gwen and Gerard were making silencing motions to him behind Alphonse' back.

Alphonse stood up with a pleased look on his face. "It is settled. Alphonse will go to Mountain Mama's to see his mountain family." He quickly left calling his agent, Victor Deville, on his way to pack his bag.

"Thanks a lot, Ben," said Gwen with a scowl on her face. "Now we have to deal with him all weekend." She got up to go.

"I have to grab my bags and get together some more clothes to take to mother. I'll be back in about fifteen minutes. Don't you dare leave without me." She stalked away.

"I think she gon' get her broom while she upstairs," said Ben. "She gon' fly there faster than we are, man."

"Don't I know it." Gerard ordered one more drink before heading to the front door.

"Whatever made you suggest Alphonse join us at Mountain Mama's?" Gerard signaled for the concierge to bring their luggage.

"I be sorry, man. I just be sittin' here keepin' my trap shut and he be all runnin' off at the mouth...I just be thinkin' it might help."

Ben held the door open for the luggage rack being pushed by one of the hotel staff.

"It's too late now and maybe in the long run, keeping him away from the kitchen isn't such a bad thing." Gerard stretched and took one last swig of his drink. "That way the women in question can have time to think about dropping their lawsuit without him hanging around. Victor and I both think they are just a couple of women scorned, and trying to get back at Alphonse."

The limo pulled up just as Gwen and Alphonse met them at the entrance of the hotel.

"Miss Gwen, I'm going to miss you as always," said Oscar. Gwen gave Oscar a kiss on the cheek.

"Hold down the fort, will you, Oscar? I'll be back on Monday by noon." Gwen allowed Oscar to help her into the back seat of the limo.

He looked at Gerard and said nothing as he shook Ben's hand. Ben loaded the luggage and tossed down a pill for motion sickness so that Rod would allow him back on the plane.

~

Two hours later, they all entered Mountain Mama's restaurant stomping their feet from the six inches of snow that had fallen overnight. Despite the snow, the restaurant was in full swing with the lunch crowd. Nana met them at the door, for once, without Margaret.

"Land's fire! That there is a big 'un you got with y'all" said Nana staring up at Ben. She walked slowly around looking him up and down. Apparently satisfied with his looks, she held out her hand. "I'm Lena, or you can call me Nana, which ever floats yer boat. I figger not too many folks mess with you, do they boy?"

Ben took her bony hand in his huge one. "I just tries to keep the peace fo' Mr. Gerard. He gots problems with the ladies and I handles it fo' him, yes'm I do."

Andrew came into the foyer and was introduced to Ben. "I'm glad to see you doing alright for yourself. Gerard looked all over for you after he was released from the pokey last month."

Ben explained a little of what had happened to him after his release and Nana, being Nana, led him by the arm into the restaurant. Gwen said hello to her father and followed Nana.

"Did you fly commercial or did Rod fly you in," asked Andrew.

"We came with Rod. He'll be here soon. Alphonse is with him closing up the plane," said Gerard. "Rod insisted on keeping Alphonse with him, I think, to give Gwen a break. The two bickered all the way here. Never heard anything like it."

"That's pretty common for them," replied Andrew. "They have had a volatile relationship for years. I am really surprised to see that she kept him. I thought he was a goner after Margaret showed up here."

"He invited himself, just so you know. That little shit can't stay out of trouble," griped Gerard.

"Watch your language, son. They don't take kindly to the kind of talk you are used to."

Andrew led Gerard away from the door and into the studio area where they met Jill and aunt Gladys setting out baskets of bread on the tables. Andrew left Gerard there and headed back into the main restaurant area.

Jill went over to Gerard and gave him a big hug and a kiss on the check. "Gerard, I am so glad you came! You just made my day and Brenda can't wait to see you!"

"You keep that little bitch away from me," spat Gerard. "If I never see her again, it will be too soon." Gerard turned around and headed for the door passing Ben on the way back in.

"What was that about?" asked Gladys. Then she noticed Ben. "I'm sorry, but have we met?"

Ben saw that both women were staring at him and realized they had no idea who he was. "I'm Ben, Gerard's bodyguard."

Gladys and Jill looked at each other.

"Bodyguard?"

"Yes'm. Mr. Gerard, he be real good to me and I tries to keep him safe." Ben shook hands with each.

Jill got a look of recognition on her face. "You were in jail with Gerard. He tried to find you for the funeral for the old man."

Ben explained again what had happened and Jill gave him a big hug. "God love you, Ben. I'm glad you could be with us this weekend."

"I know he love me, Miss Jill, and I know he love Gerard, too," said Ben looking around to see if Gerard was around to hear what he had to say. "But Gerard, he don't understand God's love. He be tryin' to find the answers in a bottle, but don't tell him I told you. He be havin' my hide."

"Oh, dear," said Gladys. "We won't tell a soul, but we'll keep an eye out for signs of trouble."

Just then, the others came into the room followed by Rod and Alphonse. They heard a 'girly squeal' and Josie came running into the room and jumped into Rod's arms.

"I'm so glad to see you," she jumped down. "Social media just doesn't do you justice Rod Wallace." Rod was pleased but very red in the face.

Introductions were made all around and the tables set with family style platters of country ham, potato salad, baked beans, and cole slaw. Gladys had made the homemade bread and jam that had been added earlier.

Ben was almost crying he was so overwhelmed. Gerard elbowed him to get back into professional mode. The table talk was about the party tomorrow and where everyone would stay. Gerard and Ben would stay with Nick and Jill. Gwen would bunk there with Anika as well.

Rod took up the offer to stay at the Dennison's home, more than likely to be near Josie. Alphonse, being Alphonse, elected to stay in Jill's old apartment at Mountain Mama's. He said he could be of some help in the party preparation if he was on site.

After the meal was over and the housing arrangements had been made, they all departed to their destinations. Alphonse found Marlene and Darlene and when the others left, he was trying to figure out who was who.

Seven

By six o'clock the next evening, everything was in place for the festivities to begin. The guests were starting to arrive and Nana was at the door greeting them as had become her custom. Tonight, she was decked out in a red dress and jacket, trimmed in white instead of her usual Mountain Mama clothing.

Margaret was sitting on the bench just inside the doorway also dressed in red with her ever present gloves that came up to her elbows. She was rocking a little bit and was not making eye contact with anyone. When she was spoken to, she blankly held out her hand and stared forward.

Jill came to the front with Nick close behind, just as Gerard and Ben entered the building.

"Hoo wee," said Ben as he shook Nana's hand. "It get cold in Chicago, but they's somethin' 'bout this mountain air that be chillin' my bones."

Gerard gave him a scathing look. "Ben, time and place. Time and place."

"Sorry, man, I fo'gets." Ben straightened up and put a blank face on.

"Move on along, young'uns. Yer a blockin' the doorway," said Nana as she pushed Gerard forward out of the way.

"Watch it, you old biddy. This is an Armani original," said Gerard as snotty as he could.

"Old biddy? Did I just hear you refer to my Nana as an old biddy?" Jill was steamed. "If that is the attitude you plan on having this evening, you can just leave right now."

"Leave? Are you serious?" Gerard was looking around for someone to back him up. "I just got here from Nick's in this cold weather and I'm not going back now. How do you propose that I return to his house?"

"Ride Shank's mare," said Margaret still with her blank expression.

Everyone stopped to look at her. She rarely said much, but to make that 'hillbilly' statement...that was new. But it was Ben who spoke.

"What she say?"

Jill answered him as she placed her hand on his arm. "That's a West Virginia term for 'you can walk'.

"Oh, I get it. Mother." Gerard leaned over and said the latter in her face. "I can also forget it just as quick. Come on Ben." Gerard stalked off with Ben following.

When they entered the main dining room, there were already quite a few people in attendance. There were buffet tables along the outer edge of the room and a drink table set up with coffee, tea, pop, and lemonade.

Gerard headed to that table before bothering to look around any further. He poured himself a cola and looking to see if anyone was watching, he removed a silver flask from inside his jacket. He added a generous amount of rum to his drink.

"Gerard, man, you sho' you wanst to be drinkin' here at this place?" Ben was tugging at the collar of his black suit.

"You want some in your...lemonade?" Gerard was looking at Ben's drink with a foul look on his face.

"No, man. I'm just not into hooch like you are, 'specially here in yo' family's place," said Ben, continuing to tug on his shirt.

"Hey, man, look who it be. It be that gal what been followin' you from Chicago to New York. I better be keepin' her away from you."

"Great," said Gerard looking to move to another area of the room.

"On the other hand, I think I'd like to have a word with her. I don't know what kind of game she's playing, but I've had enough. Put on your scary face, Ben. I'm going to have my say."

As he walked in Brenda's direction he vaguely noticed some of the other family members standing along the edge of the room seemingly watching him.

Strange, he thought to himself. *Weird bunch, the whole lot of them.*

He slugged down the rest of his drink and prepared to tap Brenda on the shoulder when she turned around and pulled something out of her pocket.

"Back for more, I see." Brenda aimed a small can of pepper spray at Gerard and Ben.

"What the..." Gerard jumped back and Ben stepped in front of him to catch the pepper spray if he had to.

Brenda laughed and bounced off into the studio area.

"I thought you gon' give her a piece 'o yo' mind," said Ben trying hard not to laugh.

"Shut up, Ben." Gerard stalked back to the drink table where Alphonse was talking himself up to a small group of middle aged ladies.

"Alphonse has all the good ideas," he said. "It was good that I came when I did, otherwise, this could have been a disaster."

Ben was getting a little tired of this rooster in the hen house.

"How the weather be down there, Napoleon?" He accidentally spilled his lemonade over Alphonse's head. "I's so sorry, Napoleon. I knows that be feelin' cold and sticky."

Alphonse was trying to catch his breath and sputtering. His mouth was moving, but no words were coming out.

Gerard threw him a towel. "Looks like you could use a shower."

Alphonse tried to save face. "It is true. Alphonse needs to clean up. Would you ladies like the pleasure of helping?" He and the ladies moved off to the stairs leading to the apartment on the second floor.

"I be sorry, man, but I had enough 'o his bull," said Ben.

"Hey, man. There she come again." He pointed to Brenda coming back into the room.

"Okay, this time, I'm going to confront her to her face and not sneak up on her." Gerard carefully walked straight to her. She saw him coming. He opened his mouth to speak when...

"Are you here for more? Then let me entertain you again." She made a knee-jerk move before skipping out of the room.

Gerard and Ben looked at each other. Ben spoke first. "Bitches be crazy. You really do be needin' a bodyguard, man."

"Attention, everyone." Jim was on the stage area getting ready to make an announcement.

"We have a few different groups for your entertainment here tonight. I know our family band usually does the music, but we thought we'd take a break tonight and have some of our other area groups perform. Out first group is well known to most of you as being regulars here several years ago. Sadly, two of the group have moved to other cities and we only have them here together a couple of times per year, but here they are now. Please give a warm welcome to the Montgomery Sisters, Brenda, Bonnie, and Georgia!"

The three triplets jogged onto the stage area and each struck a pose.

"I'm Brenda".

"I'm Bonnie".

"And I'm Georgia and we're here to entertain you!" All three girls pointed at Gerard.

Gerard choked on his drink. He had cola dribbling out of his mouth and down his Armani suit. Ben started slapping him on the back while he was trying to stop giggling.

"Looky there, Gerard. They be three 'o them bitches." Ben doubled over he was laughing so hard. "Man...the look...on...yo' face!" He was trying to catch his breath.

"Shit!" This was all Gerard could get out. Nick came up behind him and guided him to a table reserved for family.

"You all were in on this weren't you." It was a statement, not a question.

"Sorry, brother of mine," Nick said in his most saintly voice. "When Bonnie and Georgia arrived, and talked with Jill about Bonnie's strange phone call, Brenda figured out what had happened. Now, quiet, they are really good."

Matt joined the girls on the stage at the piano, Jill with the guitar, and Mark on the drums. They sang four songs about love, the typical songs you hear on Valentine's day.

Gerard heard them, but had a hard time letting this turn of events register. It didn't help with Ben swatting him on the back, giggling, and nodding his head toward the triplets. He felt like a real ass. Obviously, the girls he had accosted in

Chicago and New York, had not been Brenda. It was a flipping miracle he had not been arrested.

Ben was right. He did need a bodyguard just to keep himself out of trouble. But, damn, it wasn't his fault. Brenda never said she was a triplet. She did say she had a sister in Chicago and another in New York.

Look at them, he thought. *They are identical. I have no idea which one is Brenda. This is unacceptable!*

"Hey, man," said Ben slapping him on the back yet again. "They good, ain't they? Which one is yo' Brenda, man?"

Gerard looked at him with a look of disbelief on his face.

"How the hell should I know? They look exactly alike and have the same clothing on."

Ben started laughing again. "They be windin' down, man. I think they done singin'. Here she come, man, you better gear up."

"Will you please shut up!" Gerard stood up and crossed his arms in a defensive position. He could see the other two sisters talking to members of the Dennison family off to the side.

Brenda sashayed up to Gerard and Ben, and lifted her sassy face.

"How's it hanging, handsome? Who's your friend?" She tipped her head in Ben's direction without taking her eyes away from Gerard's.

Gerard stared her down. He refused to be the first to speak. Eventually, Brenda looked at Ben.

"So, are you the boyfriend I've heard so much about from my sister, Bonnie?"

"Boyfriend?" Ben looked very confused and turned to Gerard. "I ain't nobody's boyfriend."

Brenda sat down and began to pick at her nail polish. "Bonnie said some man grabbed her and that man had a big, black, boyfriend." She looked Ben up and down. "You're big. You're black. Reasonable question, I think."

Before Ben could respond, Gerard sat down angrily, and scooted his chair closer so that he could lean over to Brenda.

"You played me. No one plays me." He had his finger pointing at her nose.

Brenda started to get angry herself. "No one 'played' you." Brenda used air quotes for 'played'. "I tried to call you to let you know my phone was out of commission. You didn't pick up."

Brenda could see her sisters, Jill and Anika heading their way. She stood back up with a scathing look at Gerard.

Anika jumped in before the others could speak. "Uncle Gerard. You do have a black boyfriend. See, Jill? I called it!" She started to do a happy dance swinging her hips around with her hands in the air.

She suddenly stopped and spoke to Ben. "I'm Anika. Gerard is my uncle. Would you please be my date to the school dance?"

"What?" Ben stood up. He towered over all the others. "She serious?" He looked to Gerard.

"She be jail bait, man." He looked at Anika and then Jill. "She jail bait, ain't she?"

Jill spoke first. "Pay no attention to my step daughter. She is following through with a crazy statement she made earlier in the week. She does not really expect you to be her date at a school dance."

"I would like to offer an apology to Gerard and Ben," said Bonnie. "I would also like to get an apology for being man-handled in broad daylight on Michigan avenue."

"And you would be?" Gerard was not going to let this drop easily.

"I would be Bonnie in this matched set." She lifted her chin and crossed her arms.

"And I am Georgia. You met me in New York. Sort of." Georgia was a little pink in the face. "I am sorry for kicking you where the sun don't shine."

"Come on, Gerard," said Brenda lightly touching his arm. "The subject never came up about me being a triplet. No one meant to deceive you."

"You tell him, Miss Montgomery," said Anika earning herself a look from Jill. "Okay, I'll go now, but Ben, think about it. School dance. It could be fun." Anika trotted off, more than likely to look for Matt.

"I suggest you all have a seat and discuss this matter like normal adults." Jill was looking at all of them. Slowly, one by one, they sat at the table and Gerard relaxed just a little.

"Ben, why don't you come with me. I want to introduce you to some of my family."

"Okay, Miss Jill, but I doesn't has to go to a school dance with jail bait, does I?"

Gerard and the triplets sat staring at each other. Up close, he could see very minute differences in the girls. Brenda had more freckles than the other two. Bonnie was, maybe, an inch taller, and Georgia's look and hair was more refined than mussed.

Finally, Gerard broke the silence. "Okay. I messed up. I shouldn't have just grabbed you even if you had been Brenda." Gerard directed this to Bonnie.

"No, you should not have," Bonnie replied.

"You are quite strong, I might say. As are you, Georgia," said Gerard.

"Thank you," they all said in unison. As Jim announced the next musical act, the four continued to discuss the unfortunate situation of another case of mistaken identity.

~

Jill and Ben had made the rounds with her family making sure everyone met Ben and that he felt comfortable on his own. Ben was tasting some of the homemade bread and jam Gladys had made and listening to Shirley discuss him joining them for church tomorrow when he felt a tug on his shirt. He looked down to see Margaret Wallace trying to get his attention.

"May I speak with you, young man?" Margaret was having to look almost straight up to see Ben's face.

Ben looked around like he needed permission to speak with her. But to be fair, he had heard a lot of horror stories about her from Gerard.

Margaret continued. "Let's have a seat, shall we?"

"Okay, Miss Margaret," said Ben still looking nervous. "I guess it be okay if I does."

"If you do," said Margaret.

"If I does what?"

"If you do what."

"What I be doin'?" Ben was clearly very confused. "I just be watching Gerard."

"Never mind," said Margaret changing the subject. "How did you get all those scars on your arms and hands?"

"You be the first to see them is just scars, Miss Margaret." Ben was looking pleased. "Most folks ask if I has a skin disease."

"I think you have been in a fire. I think we have that in common," said Margaret with a raise of her chin, a coping mechanism she had developed.

"You be right," replied Ben.

He told her of his plight to try to save his grandmother and little sister. "I spent about seven months in a hospital burn unit, so I knows how you must 'o suffered for two years in the same kind 'o place. I be sorry, ma'am, but Gerard told me 'bout what happened and I be real sorry you had to go through that."

"I'm not here to discuss that," said Margaret sharply. "I have questions about how you cope when others look at your scars."

"I ain't had a problem with it. They's part of me now. I remembers how hard I tried to save my family, and that makes me sad, but I knows I'll see them again when I gets to Heaven."

"I won't discuss Heaven with you either," said Margaret less sharply than before. "I refuse to let my scars be seen. I wear these gloves always, so that I don't have to be reminded of what happened to me."

"Does those gloves make you fo'get what happened?" Ben leaned closer to her. He noticed a couple of people standing near, out of Margaret's line of vision, trying to look like they weren't listening.

"No. Of course not. What happened is permanently seared on my brain," she replied.

"Then hows that be helpin'? Forgive me, Miss Margaret, but I's just tryin' to understand why you thinks you needs them gloves."

Ben could see more people had gathered just out of Margaret's line of vision. He saw Nana and a bald man push themselves into the front.

"Is yo' arms and hands so scarred they can't move no mo'?"

She looked down at her hands clad in red colored elbow length gloves and flexed her fingers. A rousing piano tune could be heard in the background.

"You know, before all this happened, I was a piano virtuoso. I would have become famous, like my son, Nick." She kept looking at her hands.

"So, I's askin' again. Is yo' hands so bad that you can't play no mo'?"

"I can't play." Margaret hung her head sadly.

"So they is a bad, nasty mess and you can't move yo' fingers no mo'"

"Of course not," Margaret snapped her head up. "The scars are barely visible now."

Ben scratched his head. "Then take them gloves off and see what you can do." Ben could feel, more than see, that the others in the background seemed to be holding their breath.

Margaret looked down and very slowly, she removed her gloves, one at a time. She flexed her hands and fingers. She held out her arms, inspecting them. She looked up at Ben with a question in her eyes.

"Yo' arms and yo' hands is beautiful," he said. "I doesn't see no scars. But I would loves to hear you play somethin' on the piano."

Margaret looked over at the upright in the back of the studio. She purposefully stood up and marched to the piano with Ben behind her. She sat down on the bench and motioned for him to set next to her. She flexed her fingers again and played a couple of notes. She suddenly stopped and looked at Ben.

"Miss Margaret, they be nice notes, but can you plays a song?"

Very slowly she played the intro to an old hymn. It was rusty, but she was doing it. The others had moved closer to where she and Ben sat and Nana put her hand on Margaret's shoulder. Margaret jumped up, and seeing the others, ran out of the room, grabbing her gloves as she went.

Ben stood and started to follow.

"Son," said the bald- headed man. "I am Dr. Nathan Weir, Margaret's psychiatrist, and I have to say, you just did more to help her in ten minutes than I have been able to do in twenty years."

He shook Ben's hand. Nana gave him a hug and left to follow Margaret. Ben found himself starting to tear up until he saw Gerard in the background with that look on his face that said, 'what the hell?'

Eight

Sunday evening, Ben and Gerard sat at Jill and Nick's kitchen table along with Brenda and Matt, finishing the leftovers from lunch. Anika was upstairs having 'girl time' with her aunt Gwen about issues with Matt. Earlier in the day they had all attended the Dennison family's church and followed that with lunch at Mountain Mama's.

"I wish my sisters could have visited for a while longer," said Brenda despondently. "We rarely see each other anymore and I miss it so much." Brenda sighed and continued to pick at her cherry pie.

"Are you going to eat that or play with it?" Matt was eyeing the last of the cherry pie that Brenda had grabbed after dinner. "Because if it's the latter, I would be glad to take it off your hands."

Brenda shoved the pie over to him and heaved another heavy sigh.

"I don't need it anyway. I've put on weight since I've been hanging around the restaurant more than usual." She sighed again. "I really wanted to spend more time with Bonnie and Georgia."

"What's the big deal?" Gerard was showing Ben something on his laptop.

"All you have to do to see them is look in the mirror."

Brenda gave him a dirty look.

"Just saying... maybe you should take some time off and visit them." He and Ben started laughing and Matt joined in as well.

"I bet I know what you're watching," said Brenda in a bored voice.

"I had thought about going with Bonnie to Chicago for a few days, but I promised to babysit for Mamie Gray this coming week."

"Ms. Gray? The new principal?" Matt's interest changed quickly from the laptop to Brenda's news. "Why would you be babysitting for her? I didn't know she had any children."

"You? Babysit?" Gerard laughed. "This woman obviously has no idea what she's getting that child into."

"Gerard, that's not nice." Ben was still laughing at the show on the laptop. "Brenda be doin' a good deed jest like you did fo' me."

"Shut up, Ben," said Gerard. "I'm not incarcerated anymore. I don't have to do any good deeds for anyone. I have fulfilled my quota of 'incarceration' good deeds."

"You don't have to be behind bars to be incarcerated," said Matt suddenly very serious. "Your poor mindset and sin in your life can keep you there until you get an understanding of what the Kingdom of God is all about."

"Oh, are you still here?" Gerard directed this to Matt. "Why don't you go somewhere and fondle my niece? Everyone knows that's what you really want to do."

"Is that right?"

Jill stood in the doorway with her hands on her hips, Nick right behind her with a scowl on his face.

All eyes turned to them and the guests that stood slightly behind them. Just then, Ben burst out laughing at the laptop.

Nick spoke first in a bored voice tone. "Don't even tell me you're still watching that old show of me making a fool of myself."

Ben was still laughing even when the others had stopped. He slapped Gerard on the shoulder and nearly knocked him out of his seat. With that, Gerard shut down the laptop.

"Sorry, man. Oh, and sorry, Nick. I don't means no disrespect," said Ben looking down at the table.

"No offense taken," said Nick. "Now it's official. Everyone has seen it."

"I haven't seen it," said a small boy who had pushed his way around Jill.

"Oh, sweetheart, forgive my manners," said Jill. "This is Mamie Gray and her son, Xander."

Jill took Mamie's arm and pulled her into the foreground with the boy. She was a beautiful young woman of mixed race with light caramel colored skin and soft, dark, hair with a few golden highlights. She was casually dressed in a black and white thigh length sweater with black leggings and a black tee-shirt. She had on worn, black, lace up combat style boots, the only thing that was a little out of place in her stylish outfit. The boy was tall for a 'just turned six' year old and was light in color as well.

Jill introduced those at the table and Ben happened to be the last one introduced. He stood up with a gaping look on his face and walked around the table to shake Mamie's hand. He grabbed it and began shaking it like a dog with a new toy.

"I's very pleased to meet you, Mammy. You is the best lookin' thang I's seen in so long..."

Ben dropped her hand and smoothed back his almost non-existent hair. He started his foot shuffle, moon walk, nervous dance.

"Hoowee! Look at yo' fine self standin' there right here with the rest o' these nice people. They be plain lookin' standin' next to yo'..." Ben paused looking her up and down. "Yes'm. Mammy got back."

Mamie interrupted Ben's tirade. "Did...did..he just call..." She took a deep breath and tried again. "Did he just call me...Mammy?"

"He did, Mama, he did just call you Mammy," said Xander looking from Mamie to Ben.

"Why did you call my Mama that name?" Xander walked over to Ben.

Ben had broken out in a sweat and started to mop his forehead with his napkin. He was looking from person to person for someone to help him out of this jam. He saw Gerard's face and knew he had gone too far again. He tried to back track to a more professional manner of speaking.

"Well, I be much obliged...or I be appreciatin' it if you be forgivin' my unprofessional 'tude here befo' you all, and I mean all yo' friends and yo' kin folk." He kept wiping his head until pieces of napkin stuck to it. "I be sorry, Manny."

"Manny?" Mamie was starting to get an attitude. "Now, it's Manny?"

Ben started to back away into the living room and away from what he realized was a very embarrassing situation for everyone.

"Marnie? Mable?" Ben ran into an end table.

"He's funny, Mama. Look at his head," said Xander following Ben. "I want him to baby sit me. Can he Mama, can he?"

"You, little man," said Brenda pointing to Xander. "Come here and give me a hug. You know you want to stay with me. We have too much fun. I have a lot of plans for us this week."

"Are we going to get ice cream? And go to the movies, and eat out every day?" Xander had stopped pursuing Ben and had turned his attention to Brenda.

"You know it," she answered giving him a hug.

The others had moved into the living room where Ben was sitting with his head in his hands. Matt joined him on the couch.

"Forget it Ben," he said. "Anyone can make a mistake when they get nervous. You haven't been in the public eye as long as the rest of us. Shake it off, man."

"I'd like to shake it off him," said Gerard moving to sit in the chair across from Ben.

Mamie took Brenda and Jill to the side. "Is he, you know, 'special'?

"No," said Jill and then she explained a little of Ben's circumstances.

"I understand. That makes a little sense now." Mamie went into the living room and stood in front of Ben.

"My name is Mamie," she said in a slow -paced voice as if she were talking to a child with learning disabilities. She held out her hand. "I am pleased to meet you."

"Mamie." Ben repeated the name then took her hand and started to giggle, earning him another look from Gerard.

"What do you do, Ben?" Mamie sat down on the other end of the sofa. Everyone looked to Gerard for an answer.

Gerard returned their looks with a haughty stare. "He's my bodyguard."

"Of course he is," said Mamie giving Gerard a knowing look.

"Brenda, I have Xander's things in my car. Let's go put them in yours and then we can visit a little before I have to leave."

By the time they reentered Nick's house, everyone had relocated to different groupings. Xander sat with Matt and Nick at the piano with Nick showing him some notes. Ben was nowhere to be seen and Anika and Gwen had joined Jill in the kitchen.

Gerard sat alone texting on his phone and drinking from a silver flask. Mamie joined the girls in the kitchen while Brenda chose to sit on the arm of Gerard's chair.

"Are you still upset with the triplet thing?" Brenda lazily started running her fingers at the base of Gerard's hair.

"I guess not," he replied while putting his phone in his pocket.

"Want some?" He handed her the flask and she took it, sniffed it and returned it to him.

"No, I would rather have something else. Wine, maybe? I'll see if Jill has any."

She left for the kitchen and returned with a wine glass filled with white wine. She drank it almost straight down.

"Hey, girl. Go easy on that," said Gerard.

"Look who's talking," Brenda replied. "How much of... what you're drinking have you had...boy?"

"Don't call me boy," said Gerard in his arrogant way. "You, of all people, know better than that."

"And you, of all people, know that I am much more than just a girl," said Brenda in her sexy voice.

"The rest of us know that as well," said Matt from his location by the piano.

"He never misses an opportunity to get under my skin," said Gerard. "Let's get out of here and go someplace where we can...talk." Gerard gave Brenda a wink.

"Xander, come here," said Mamie from the doorway. "Mama's got to leave. You know I'll call you every day and bring you home something special."

"I know, Mama," Xander replied. "I'll miss you." He gave Mamie a big hug and sloppy six -year old kiss.

"I'll miss you, too, baby boy," said Mamie as she gave Brenda a hug and retreated out of the door.

Brenda had joined the girls in the kitchen while Xander had returned to Nick and Matt at the piano. Ben had returned to the living room and sat near Gerard.

"Think you made enough of a fool out of yourself tonight, Ben?" Gerard casually leaned back in his chair and stretched.

"'Bout as much as you did, man," answered Ben wiping his hands over his face and finding bits of napkin as he did so.

He saw Gerard's face and backed off. "Just sayin." He watched as Gerard pulled a second flask out of his jacket and downed about half.

"I think I needs a drink, too, after makin' a ass out myself. It's just...I ain't seen no fine lookin' girls that close befo' and I doesn't know how to act when I does see 'em."

Jill brought Ben and Gerard mugs of hot cocoa.

"Thank you, Miss Jill," said Ben. "That's the ticket."

As Jill returned to the kitchen, Ben and Gerard watched her backside and the sexy swing of her hips. "She be fine lookin', too, man. You surrounded by fine lookin' women. Even yo' neice and yo' sister, man."

"Time out." Gerard took another drink from his flask, emptying it. "Don't even think of making any moves on my niece or my sister, and I say that for your own good, Ben. My sister will chew you up and spit you out. As for my niece, I think she's following the same pattern."

"Gerard, are you going to drink that cocoa or let it get cold," asked Matt from across the room.

"Don't you even think of touching my hot cocoa, genius boy, or my niece. Am I making myself clear?" Gerard stood up and looked toward the kitchen.

"Speaking of touching something hot..." He left to join the women in the kitchen.

Brenda was gathering some cookies and kid friendly food that Jill had made for her at Mountain Mama's earlier. She was no cook, especially for children, and she would have Xander for the whole week.

"Thanks for the help, Jill. I know Xander will love it." She saw Gerard enter the kitchen and her demeanor changed instantly from 'one of the girls' to 'sexy siren.'

Gwen noticed. "You had better rein that in before the boy notices and has no idea how to react."

"Trust me, Aunt Gwen, Matt won't notice," said Anika. "He barely looks at me anymore."

"Not Matt. The child, Anika, the child," said Gwen.

"Roger that," said Brenda looking up at Gerard and winking.

Gerard noticed and proceeded to help Brenda finish gathering the food and offered to take it out to her car. As he left, Brenda said her goodbyes and got Xander into his coat for the trip to her house.

Brenda faced Gerard after getting Xander into his seat belt. "How about you follow me home, big boy? I could use some...entertainment." She brushed up against him.

"Great minds think alike," he responded. "I'll borrow a vehicle and see you there."

Fifteen minutes later, they were putting away food in Brenda's small kitchen. Xander was getting ready for bed in Brenda's extra bedroom.

"The child seems to know his way around here," Gerard stated.

"He has been here a few times while Mamie honors her commitment to our country," Brenda replied.

"What does that mean?"

"Mamie is in the Army reserves," said Brenda nonchalantly. "She has to go away every so often to fulfill the requirements for which she is obligated. She does something with computers, I think. She doesn't talk much about it. Her husband was killed a little over six years ago when they were both on active duty. He never even knew he was going to be a father. Anyway, she left the Army to have her baby and signed up for the reserves. She's been the principal since this term started in September. We hit it off right away."

"Speaking of hitting it off..." Gerard moved in and started kissing Brenda on the neck.

"Why are you doing that?" Xander had come into the kitchen unnoticed.

"I'm being friendly to Miss Brenda," replied Gerard rubbing his forehead.

"She doesn't need that kind of friendly," said Xander. "Will you read me a story so I can go to sleep?"

"Of course," said Brenda leading him to his bedroom. "Gerard, help yourself to anything you want."

"I plan to," he said winking twice.

When Brenda returned to the kitchen, she found Gerard had poured himself a drink and one for her as well. She took it and downed half.

"You know, we've had a couple of good times in the past, but we have never even kissed."

"Well, then, let's rectify that right now," he said pulling Brenda onto his lap.

She sat straddling his legs, as close as she could get and pulled his face to hers in one of the sexiest kisses he had ever had. She kissed him, running her tongue over his bottom lip, then drawing him into her mouth giving new meaning to the act of kissing.

After a few minutes, he pulled back. "Wow! Amazing! I have to catch my breath. You have no idea what you are doing to me, young lady."

"Oh, I know exactly what I'm doing to you. There's no room for error on that point. No pun intended," she tacked on at the last minute.

"You, also, can stop with the 'young lady' crap. There might be ten years between us in age, but I can handle every inch of you, and you know it. Pun intended that time."

"Yes, I do know it, so I think it is time to get a few things straight." Gerard lifted her off his lap and sat her in one of the other kitchen chairs.

"I have enjoyed the couple of times we've gotten together and I am sorry there was nothing reciprocal on my part. Well, there was when I was home alone, if you get my drift."

"Oh, I get your drift alright," said Brenda with a wink.

"To continue," said Gerard. "I am not looking for a relationship, marriage, love, or anything remotely close to any of those. I am looking for a good time, some fun, maybe some sex, but nothing on a permanent basis. I do not want to be tied down to anyone. Ever."

Brenda slugged down the rest of her drink. "Ditto, baby."

She stood up and slipped her bra off without removing her shirt and returned to slowly lower herself back on Gerard's lap. She had never felt this much lust for anyone before. She was on fire and proceeded to tug his jacket and tie off.

I haven't felt this hot for someone in forever, she thought.

Gerard let her remove his jacket while he had another drink. He was feeling very mellow, but with an edge that needed a release. He could see how excited she was through her shirt. He picked her up and she kept her legs wrapped around him.

The deep kissing started all over again and Gerard gently put Brenda down on her bed, never removing his lips from hers. He lost control at that point and so did she. He all but ripped his shirt off and was sliding his hands under Brenda's shirt when...

"Why did you take your shirt off?" Xander was standing just outside the door. He continued in without waiting for an answer. "Miss Brenda, I can't sleep."

Gerard felt he had been doused with a bucket of cold water. He helped Brenda up and picked up his clothing. He looked at Brenda with a great longing and she returned the same.

"I don't think I'll be getting any sleep tonight either," said Gerard. He gave Brenda a quick peck on the cheek and quietly left to return to Nick's home and yet another night with only himself for entertainment.

Marianne Waddill Wieland

She stood up and slipped her bra off without removing her shirt and returned to slowly lower herself back on Gerard's lap. She had never felt this much lust for anyone before. She was on fire and proceeded to tug his jacket and tie off.

I haven't felt this hot for someone in forever, she thought.

Gerard let her remove his jacket while he had another drink. He was feeling very mellow, but with an edge that needed a release. He could see how excited she was through her shirt. He picked her up and she kept her legs wrapped around him.

The deep kissing started all over again and Gerard gently put Brenda down on her bed, never removing his lips from hers. He lost control at that point and so did she. He all but ripped his shirt off and was sliding his hands under Brenda's shirt when...

"Why did you take your shirt off?" Xander was standing just outside the door. He continued in without waiting for an answer. "Miss Brenda, I can't sleep."

Gerard felt he had been doused with a bucket of cold water. He helped Brenda up and picked up his clothing. He looked at Brenda with a great longing and she returned the same.

"I don't think I'll be getting any sleep tonight either," said Gerard. He gave Brenda a quick peck on the cheek and quietly left to return to Nick's home and yet another night with only himself for entertainment.

Marianne Waddill Wieland

Nine

Three days later, the family was gathered at Mountain Mama's restaurant for a feast made by Alphonse Laurant who still had not returned to New York. He said his Sous chef, Henri, had everything under control so he could spend more time helping out with things in Mountain Mama's restaurant. What he really had been doing was spending time with Marlene.

Ben and Gerard were still in Beaumont as well. Gwen and Rod had returned to their respective homes, Gwen to continue business as usual and Rod to prepare to take over duties as CFO of the Wallace hotel empire.

Brenda and Xander had been at the feast as well. Gerard had not had any real contact with Brenda since he had been at her house a few days ago. They had played phone tag a few times, but with school and taking care of Xander, Brenda had been unavailable.

Ben leaned back in his chair rubbing his stomach. "I don't think I's ever had this much to eat in my whole life."

"I'm so full I could take a siesta," said Brenda.

Xander looked confused. He looked at Ben, then Brenda and finally Gerard. "What's a siesta?"

Brenda started to answer. "Xander a siesta..."

"Let me handle this", said Gerard. "Xander, when you have a whole lot of food to eat and you can't possibly eat any more, what do you feel like you need to do?"

"Take a crap," said Xander.

The whole table started laughing. Nana was slapping her leg and even Margaret was smiling. Ben was laughing so hard he was almost on the floor. The other table turned around to see what was so funny when...

"Make way. Make way! Alphonse is bringing one more surprise to all his mountain family." He strutted in carrying a large square package wrapped in brown paper that he had received earlier in the day. He presented it to Jill and Nick.

"Alphonse!" Jill took the package and had to have Nick help her hold it. "What did you do?"

"Is the least Alphonse could do for all the many things you have done for him," he said a little less haughty than usual.

Jill began to remove the wrapping and found that inside was a portrait of Alphonse, himself, dressed in hillbilly clothing. It was big. It was ugly.

Xander and Ben started laughing. Jill and Nick were speechless. It was Nana that came to the rescue.

"Now ain't that somethin'. Alphonse, you good lookin' feller, you." She went over to Alphonse and gave him a big hug.

Jill mouthed a 'thank you' to Nana behind Alphonse's back.

"That's the ugliest thing I've ever seen," said Brenda. She went over to Jill to get a better look and received a hug from Alphonse.

"Alphonse knows you have been eyeing him, beautiful Brenda Montgomery. But I am afraid my heart is taken for now," said Alphonse. "If that changes, I will make sure to make you aware." Alphonse gave her a kiss on both cheeks and left to go help in the kitchen.

"Good Lord," said Nick. "What on earth are we going to do with that?"

"Why don't you put it in the guest quarters upstairs?" Brenda reached out to touch the ugly painting like it might bite her if she got too close. "After all, that is where he likes to stay when he visits. Why on earth he thinks I would look at him twice, I'll never know!"

"Not a bad idea," said Nick. "What do you think, babe?"

"I hope he wasn't planning on it being hung here in the restaurant. We could give it a try upstairs and see what he says," said Jill.

"How about Gerard and I take it upstairs and try to hang it," stated Brenda looking at Gerard.

"Hey," he said. "Don't drag me into this mess. I know exactly where I'd hang it. Right over his French head, with a boot to his ass while I was at it."

"Gerard," said Brenda slowly, like she would to a child. "Help me hang the painting upstairs."

"Take Ben with you. He can hang it."

Gerard felt a tug on his sleeve. He looked to the side to see Xander trying to get his attention. "Mr. Gerard, I think Miss Brenda wants you to go upstairs with her."

Brenda rolled her eyes. "Out of the mouths of babes."

"How dense can you get, man," said Ben.

"Oh, all right," said Gerard. "Let's get this over with."

He stood and grabbed the painting from Nick and headed for the stairs. Brenda followed at a slower pace.

"No funny business in my old apartment," yelled Jill after them. "And there are some nails and a hammer in the kitchen closet."

As soon as the door closed on them upstairs, Brenda grabbed the painting and chucked it to the side and pushed Gerard down on to the sofa.

"Yes, Mr. Gerard." She imitated Xander. "How dense can you get."

"Oh," was all he said. He got up to look in the refrigerator for some wine and was not disappointed. He was sure Alphonse kept some handy.

Yeah, the good stuff, he thought.

He poured himself and Brenda a glass, then turned the bottle up and drank at least a quarter of the bottle himself. He, also, pulled yet another silver flask from his jacket and downed half of that. The alcohol had an immediate effect on him. He was feeling no pain when he rejoined Brenda in the living room.

"Where's the hammer?" Brenda met him mid room.

"In my pants," he laughed and handed Brenda the wine glass.

She downed the glass as fast as he did. When she was done, he picked her up over his shoulder and carried her to the bedroom. He threw her down on the bed and she pulled him down on top of her.

"This could be really good, Gerard, if you let it," said Brenda.

"What's that supposed to mean?"

"It means you have to shut your yap for a change and let me work my magic." Brenda managed to get on top of him and she slowly unbuttoned his shirt, removing it along with his jacket. She ran her perfectly manicured nails down his chest, teasing his sensitive parts as she started to unbuckle his belt laughing in that sexy way she had.

"You think that's funny, do you?" Gerard sat up and rolled Brenda over on her back so that he was in the dominant position once again.

"I was thinking 'it's hammer time'." Brenda pulled him down into a very deep kiss.

Gerard pulled back slightly and ran his hands over her, paying special attention to her breasts, making her moan his name. The laughter was gone. This was serious business. He drank more from his flask.

Brenda shamelessly pulled her shirt over her head and tossed it to the floor. She arched her chest upward and Gerard took the hint. He removed her bra and gasped. She was beautiful beyond words.

Brenda reached up for him, but he stopped her.

"I owe you one or two," he stated looking deep into her eyes. "Let me show *you* this time."

She lay back as he removed her jeans. She closed her eyes and gasped as he had his way with her, kissing and licking parts of her that she had fantasized about. He took her to new heights of awareness with his fingers that she had only imagined in her dreams and when she had exploded, nearly screaming his name, she reciprocated as she had done in the past.

As they both lay exhausted they heard a faint knock on the door.

"Brenda. Gerard." It was Matt. "The family needs you to come back to the studio. Now."

They looked at each other. Matt's voice held a sense of urgency that they both recognized even in their slightly inebriated state. They began to hurriedly dress and made it back downstairs in record time.

Brenda noticed Jill's brother, Mark, standing in the middle of his parents, siblings and Nana. He was sobbing and the others were trying to comfort him.

"What's going on?" Gerard asked of the room in general.

Ben walked over to him. "Somebody name o' Nancy jus' lost her baby. That man, over there gots to be her husband."

"That's Mark, Jill's brother," said Brenda as she went over to Jill and gave her a hug. Then she went to Mark and did the same, tears running down her cheeks.

Gerard did the only thing he could do. He turned around and headed back upstairs to finish the rest of the wine.

Maybe I'll hang the damn picture while I am at it."

Ten

Almost a month had passed since the news of Mark and Nancy losing their baby had touched the lives of the Dennison family. Gerard had felt so uncomfortable with the situation that he and Ben had left the next day to return to Chicago. Nancy had gone to stay with her parents and was pushing Mark away, encouraging him to go to Beaumont to stay with his family for a while. Jill had arranged for Lance, her cousin and Sous Chef, to take Mark's place at the Mountain Mama's restaurant in Blacksburg, Virginia, and Mark would stay in her old apartment and work with her.

Brenda and Mamie were sitting at a table in the restaurant on a Saturday, discussing plans to go to the Saint Patrick's Day festivities in Chicago at the invitation of the Dennison's.

"They turn the river green? Really?" Xander was getting excited over the prospect of going to Chicago.

"Yes,' said Brenda. "And they have parades with marching bands where the men wear skirts."

"No way," said Xander getting even more excited. His lunch arrived at the table and he wrinkled his nose at the broccoli on his plate.

"Mama, why did God put all the vitamins in broccoli and spinach instead of candy and ice cream?"

"So you could complain about it," said Mamie as she continued looking at her calendar. "Are you sure the Dennison's are putting us all up in Gerard's hotel?"

"Yes, but Gerard doesn't know we're coming. I spoke with Ben yesterday and he said Gerard gave him the day off and said not to bother him all day."

Brenda took a bite of her sandwich while Mamie cut Xander's burger in half so he could eat it.

Mark came into the room and headed toward their table.

"Hey, doll," said Brenda. "How's Nancy?"

Mark just shook his head. "It's like I not only lost the baby, but Nancy too. She has shut me totally out. Barely speaks to me. Her parents are no help. I only get a few words from the whole lot. She won't even consider letting me visit. I feel like she thinks I had something to do with her miscarriage."

Mamie chimed in. "You don't really believe that do you?"

"How can I not? I still have nightmares that I will never see Nancy again," said Mark with his head hung low.

"Believe me, it wasn't your fault." Mamie had spoken before she had put any real thought to what she had said and she tried to back paddle. "I mean, how could it have been your fault?"

"I don't know anything anymore. At least Lance is taking good care of Mountain Mama's over in Blacksburg," said Mark. "I know he misses it here, but he seems to like the freedom he has there as well."

"Are you going to Chicago with the family?" Brenda asked as she piled up the dishes on the table.

"No. I'm going to stay here so that Jill and the others can go. I don't really have the party spirit in me right now."

Brenda got up and gave him a hug and a kiss on the cheek. "Too bad Nancy got to you before I did. You'd be in so much trouble, you gorgeous hunk."

"Brenda," said Mamie. "There are children present. Watch your mouth. One of these days you're going to say or do something that you can't take back"

"It's okay, Mama. Miss Brenda just likes to speak her mind," said Xander in a matter of fact way.

"I guess that's my cue to exit," said Brenda. "I'll call you when I have more details."

She left to head home where she had a ton of papers to grade before the trip to Chicago that would take place in a week.

~

"Gerard, man, I doesn't need the day off. What does I have to do except be yo' bodyguard?" Ben had had this same conversation with Gerard at least once a day for the last two weeks.

"Find something else to do on Saint Patrick's Day besides trot behind my butt all day. I don't care what it is, but stay away from downtown and the apartment." Gerard was adamant.

"Everything will revert to normal on Sunday morning, but you can return to the apartment on Saturday afternoon and continue with business as usual if you have to."

Gerard looked at Ben's confused face. "It's none of your damned business why I need time to myself."

"Okay, then," said Ben. "I guess that settles it." He went to his room to call Brenda so she could let the others know Gerard still did not want them to visit.

The following Saturday, the Dennison and Wallace families were at the airstrip getting ready for takeoff to

Chicago. Brenda, Mamie, and Xander had joined them, but Nana, Margaret, and Mark preferred to stay behind.

"Has anyone been able to reach Gerard?" Jim asked as he helped Rod load the last of the luggage.

"As far as I know, all of us got the same message on his voice mail," said Jill.

"I will not be home on Saint Patrick's Day. If you have a problem, call Ben. I will return on Sunday."

The others agreed they had heard the same thing.

Xander was so excited, he couldn't sit still. He would be sitting in the cockpit with Matt and Rod and had been warned by his mother that if he did not behave, he would have to move to the back with her.

Two hours later, they were all in the Grand Wallace Chicago getting situated to go to the parade. Ben had met them there, because, as he said, he had nothing else to do.

Matt spoke to Anika first for a change, which was a shock to Anika. "How about we hang together after the parade? Look around Chicago a little."

"So, are you calling a truce?" Anika was a little skeptical after the way he had been avoiding her the last couple of months.

Matt laughed. "I guess I am. No funny stuff, though."

The Wallace's had a private box reserved for their party near the judges stand. They could see the green river and had the best view of the parade. Nick picked Xander up to sit on his shoulders for a better view.

"Nicky," said Andrew who, for reasons no one knew, had started calling his son, Nicky. "You are going to make a fine dad one day."

"Thanks, Pappy, I think." Nick looked at Jill and rolled his eyes, making her laugh.

"Hey! The parade is starting," shouted Xander from his prime seat on Nick's shoulders.

Most of the group stood up to get an even better view and could see a Celtic band leading off the parade followed by a huge float with a well- known Celtic group waving to the public. The Celtic band consisted of powerful drums, bagpipes, men in kilts, and...Gerard. Ben saw him first.

"That be Gerard! What he be doin' out there?" Ben was shielding his eyes from the sun to get a better look.

Rod and Nick looked at each other. "He's playing the bagpipes!" They said this in unison and high-fived each other. They remembered their conversation at Family Band Night back in the fall when they made a joke about Gerard playing the bagpipes.

The others were just as shocked. Even Andrew did not know this about Gerard.

"That is why he doesn't want any of us here. He wants to keep it a secret," said Josie. "Nice legs, though."

"I hasn't seen any sign of those bag things anywhere in the apartment," said Ben. "I wonders where he be practicin' at."

"He hasn't said a word to me," said Brenda.

The band stopped in front of the judges stand and played for a few minutes before moving on. The float behind them was advertising a Celtic concert at the symphony hall later in the evening.

"We have tickets to see them. I love Celtic music, especially this group," said Lorraine.

The parade continued for the next hour down Michigan avenue. Xander had managed to collect quite a bit of candy assisted by the adults in the group. Mamie put most of it in her backpack, giving him only a couple of pieces.

When the crowd started to disperse, the family decided to separate as well and meet again for the night's concert. Matt and Anika took off for the Navy pier, followed by Brenda, Mamie, and Ben. Rod and Josie went to Water Tower place and to walk along the river, and the adults went to the museum campus to see the Shedd Aquarium and Xander went with them after much discussion.

~

They all met later in the lobby of the hotel, all except Xander. Mamie had hired a babysitter that came highly recommended and ordered pizza to eat while they watched movies. All in all, he was happy to be left behind.

The limo took them the short distance to the concert hall and they were ushered into a private box that Ben figured must be the best seats in the house. Even in his suit, he felt under dressed. The other men had on tuxes and the women, shimmery gowns. He thought Mamie was beautiful in her beige colored dress with pink and yellow accents. She even had a flowery thing in her hair that matched her dress. He had a hard time taking his eyes off her until she caught him. She gave him a look that made it clear she was off limits.

As they glanced through the program waiting for the concert to start, they noticed an insert announcing a substitute drummer for the evening.

Andrew said it first. "Do you all see what I see?"

"Gerard is the substitute drummer!" Lorraine stood up to get a better look at the stage. "Did any of you know about this?" They all looked at each other and shook their heads.

"Well," said Ben. "I sees some drumsticks on the dinin' room table once. I axe him if he play the drums. He say 'no, he didn't' and that he use them as chopsticks to practice eatin' Chinese food."

"And you bought that?" Rod was giving Ben his best grimace.

"I ain't sees no reason to question him," said Ben scratching his head.

"Quiet," said Josie taking hold of Rod's arm. "It's about to start."

The conductor came out and made some announcements making mention of the substitute drummer, Gerard Wallace, who on occasion, travels with them.

Gerard and the other drummer joined the four girls and the violin player on the stage. The first number, 'The Call' had a powerful intro, especially the drums.

"Look at him go," said Ben.

"Yeah, look at him go," echoed Rod.

The songs continued with the family mesmerized by Gerard and his talent. And every so often Ben would say, "look at him go," and Rod would echo with, "yeah, look at him go."

Nick made comment that Gerard was good enough to play on one of his concerts, but Matt had stated that they didn't allow 'rat bastards' in the symphony hall. Jill just rolled her eyes and messed up Matt's hair.

"Stop messing his hair up, you're ruining his look," said Anika. She leaned into Matt and batted her eyes at him. He moved away from her causing unrest and very soft ugly remarks that the others couldn't hear.

After the concert, they were ushered backstage to meet the Celtic group. Anika and Matt spent time with the violinist and she even allowed them to play for her. She was very impressed. The girls were so impressed that Nicolai was there for their concert, that he ended up giving autographs to them.

Ben turned around just in time to see a shocked Gerard come out of a dressing room.

"What in the name of all that is Holy are you people doing here?" Gerard's words were slurred and his eyes dilated.

Brenda went over to him and put her hand on his arm. "Gerard, we had no idea you had such talent. The bagpipes and now, the drums."

"Don't even tell me you saw the parade this morning." Gerard looked at Ben. "I gave you a simple task. Just keep away from the apartment and field any family calls away from Chicago."

"Son," said Andrew. "This is not Ben's fault. He tried to keep us away, but we wanted to be here with you in Chicago for the holiday."

"Don't any of you say one word." Gerard stalked off calling for Ben to follow, but when he looked behind, the whole group was following.

"Damn! I guess you all might as well come too. The cat's out of the bag." Gerard continued to stalk away just assuming the others were behind him.

Later, after the family had finally left Gerard's apartment to return to the hotel, Brenda sat with him on his sofa. Ben had retired to his own room. Brenda leaned into Gerard and sipped her wine. Gerard had downed most of the bottle while his family was still there. She looked up at him to see that his eyes were drooping.

"So, are you going to make me leave too?" Brenda proceeded to run her nails over his leg.

"Not on your life," he slurred, looking at her, maybe for the first time tonight. She was beautiful in a mint green slinky dress he really wanted her to take off. He stood up and weaved slightly as did Brenda when she stood. Gerard tried to pick her up and carry her to his room, but lost his balance causing both of them to fall to the floor.

"What be goin' on out here?" Ben was looking out his door and rushed to help them up. Both were totally drunk. He carried Brenda to Gerard's room and put her on the bed, then assisted Gerard to walk to the room and fall into bed as well. Both were asleep before Ben left the room.

"Idiots," said Ben, and he closed the door.

Eleven

Brenda woke up the next morning lying on the bathroom floor. She was using the small trash can for a pillow and when she lifted her head, the nausea hit her like a punch in the gut. She leaned over the toilet and...nothing. She had no more to throw up. It was on her dress, her hair, the floor, and...and...she tried to slowly get up.

What if she had thrown up on the bed? On Gerard?

She couldn't stand, so she crawled back into the bedroom. Gerard was still asleep. She pulled herself up on the bed. Good. No vomit on the bed or Gerard. He looked out cold. She could see the sky just starting to lighten out the window. She would try to clean up before he got up.

Forty- five minutes later, she had managed to shower, and clean up the mess in the bathroom. She had put on a bathrobe of...someone's... she found behind the bathroom door. She felt a little jealous of whose it might be, but they had agreed neither wanted anything but a good time.

She wandered out to the kitchen to find something for her raging headache and found a bottle of over the counter pain killers. She downed a couple and went to sit in a recliner. She fell back asleep until someone gently touched her arm.

"Wha... What." Brenda tried to sit up but was confused. She saw Ben standing next to her with a hot cup of coffee.

"Miss Brenda, I thoughts you could use this." Ben handed her the coffee. "You been 'sleep in that chair fo' three hours now. Mr. Gerard, he not up yet and I be a little worried. He always up by now, even when he be drunk the night befo'."

"Thanks, Ben. You're a good man. You didn't have to take care of us, but you did anyway. I know we were a mess." Brenda got up and stood on her toes to give him a hug.

"Maybe we better check on Gerard. Make sho' he okay."

Ben entered the bedroom to see Gerard half off the bed with his head hanging down to the floor. He rushed over and put him back up on the bed. Gerard was still out cold.

"Ben, something is terribly wrong. He should be waking up." Brenda started calling his name and smacking his cheeks but there was no response out of Gerard. "Ben, call 911, now!"

Ben did as he was told and while they waited for the ambulance, he called Jill and Nick to let them know what was going on.

~

Brenda paced in the waiting room frantic to hear something about Gerard's condition. She nor Ben could get any information because they were not family. She had been drinking a steady flow of coffee since they arrived. Her head was still aching, but more like a dull throbbing behind the eyes.

"Brenda, Ben!" This from Andrew barging through the ER waiting room door. He was with Rod and Nick. Rod had not planned to fly the family out last night and they had not been far away at Gerard's hotel.

"How is he?"

Eleven

Brenda woke up the next morning lying on the bathroom floor. She was using the small trash can for a pillow and when she lifted her head, the nausea hit her like a punch in the gut. She leaned over the toilet and...nothing. She had no more to throw up. It was on her dress, her hair, the floor, and...and...she tried to slowly get up.

What if she had thrown up on the bed? On Gerard?

She couldn't stand, so she crawled back into the bedroom. Gerard was still asleep. She pulled herself up on the bed. Good. No vomit on the bed or Gerard. He looked out cold. She could see the sky just starting to lighten out the window. She would try to clean up before he got up.

Forty- five minutes later, she had managed to shower, and clean up the mess in the bathroom. She had put on a bathrobe of...someone's... she found behind the bathroom door. She felt a little jealous of whose it might be, but they had agreed neither wanted anything but a good time.

She wandered out to the kitchen to find something for her raging headache and found a bottle of over the counter pain killers. She downed a couple and went to sit in a recliner. She fell back asleep until someone gently touched her arm.

"Wha... What." Brenda tried to sit up but was confused. She saw Ben standing next to her with a hot cup of coffee.

"Miss Brenda, I thoughts you could use this." Ben handed her the coffee. "You been 'sleep in that chair fo' three hours now. Mr. Gerard, he not up yet and I be a little worried. He always up by now, even when he be drunk the night befo'."

"Thanks, Ben. You're a good man. You didn't have to take care of us, but you did anyway. I know we were a mess." Brenda got up and stood on her toes to give him a hug.

"Maybe we better check on Gerard. Make sho' he okay."

Ben entered the bedroom to see Gerard half off the bed with his head hanging down to the floor. He rushed over and put him back up on the bed. Gerard was still out cold.

"Ben, something is terribly wrong. He should be waking up." Brenda started calling his name and smacking his cheeks but there was no response out of Gerard. "Ben, call 911, now!"

Ben did as he was told and while they waited for the ambulance, he called Jill and Nick to let them know what was going on.

~

Brenda paced in the waiting room frantic to hear something about Gerard's condition. She nor Ben could get any information because they were not family. She had been drinking a steady flow of coffee since they arrived. Her head was still aching, but more like a dull throbbing behind the eyes.

"Brenda, Ben!" This from Andrew barging through the ER waiting room door. He was with Rod and Nick. Rod had not planned to fly the family out last night and they had not been far away at Gerard's hotel.

"How is he?"

"We have no idea," said Brenda. "We aren't family, so we have no news. HIPAA laws, you know."

"I'll go and find out what is going on," said Andrew hurrying over to the desk and pounding his fist. "I want to see my son!"

Rod was looking around the room and seemed to have a nervous edge about him. When Nick questioned him, he just shrugged.

"I hate hospitals."

Ben spoke up. "Rod, why don't you come with me to the cafeteria, so the rest of yo' family can get to the bottom of this." The two of them left the area leaving Nick and Brenda alone.

"Brenda, I thought something was wrong when we left. I had a bad feeling we should not have left him alone when we did," said Nick anxiously.

"It's my fault," said Brenda as she started to cry. "I knew he was drinking way too much and it didn't help when I joined him in it. I spent the night on the bathroom floor...anyway, it wasn't a pretty sight."

"I know how persuasive he can be, and I can see the two of you have an interest in each other," said Nick. He stood up and saw his father being escorted through some doors into another area of the hospital.

"It's easy to be drawn into someone else's problems, especially if you are trying to impress them."

Brenda continued to cry. "I haven't been in this kind of situation before. I don't follow. I always lead. I don't know what is happening to me! My good judgement seems to have left me." She jumped up when she saw Andrew coming through the doors.

"Andy," she cried. "What did you find out?"

Andrew looked at them both before moving to sit on one of the chairs. He put his face in his hands, then ran his hands through his hair.

"He has alcohol poisoning, but he also has some sort of tranquilizer in his system as well. I'm guessing that when he saw us at the concert and found we were at the parade as well, he must have taken something to calm his nerves. I don't know if you realize it, but he has had problems in the past with substance abuse."

"He's mentioned it, but never explained anything from his past," said Nick as he sat next to his father. "Listen...Pappy...I am having a hard time calling you Pappy. Can I just call you Dad?"

"Son, right now I'd just as soon be called a jack ass", said Andrew. "I knew he was going to have the hardest time with our family history. I should have made a better effort to help him through all this."

"Dad, we are all struggling with this in our own way, so don't even try to take all the credit for what Gerard has been going through." Nick stood up and started to pace. "Jill and I have even discussed how we might make things easier for him."

Brenda stood to join Nick as he continued to pace. "I've just made the problems worse," said Brenda. "I have to find a way to help him, too. Are they giving him any treatment?"

Andrew stood up to join them in their pacing. "They have pumped his stomach, done an EKG, bloodwork, and constant monitoring of his vital signs. The next hour is critical. The doctor will let us know as soon as any test results come back. Until then, I'm the only one allowed to see him."

Rod and Ben returned from the cafeteria and were given an update on Gerard. Ben looked like a man that had been through some kind of private hell.

"I's shoulda tried harder to keep him outta the hooch, but he don't listen to much I gots to say. But he been so good to me, I would go through any kind of torture, do anything fo' him," said Ben.

Rod jumped up, cold sweat on his forehead, white as a sheet, and he looked like he might throw up.

"Son, are you ill, too?" Andrew put his hand on Rod's shoulder drawing the other's attention.

"I hate hospitals," said Rod in a shaky voice. "I think I will go back to the motel, but you have to promise to let me know when you hear anything."

Andrew promised and gave his son a hug. Rod left at a good clip out the doors and into the parking lot where they watched him bend over with his hands on his knees, then stand up taking big gulps of air before getting in a waiting cab.

"I wonder what is going on with him," said Brenda.

Just then, the doctor came through the double doors and straight to Andrew. He nodded to the others and Andrew made sure he knew they were family as well and could hear anything he had to say about Gerard.

"It has been touch and go, but he has started to stabilize. We are going to put him in the intensive care unit. He has developed a heart arrhythmia and we want to monitor that, at least overnight. We have given him medication to correct it, but close monitoring is necessary."

The doctor explained it would be best if they went home to rest and came back in the morning. He promised to call if anything new developed. The doctor didn't think any visitors right now, especially family, would be good for Gerard.

~

They had taken the doctor's advice even though neither Andrew nor Brenda wanted to leave the hospital and Ben felt it was his place to guard Gerard. However, the intensive care unit was having none of that.

The next morning, they were called to the hospital for a care conference to decide what needs to be done for Gerard. He had tried to get out of bed during the night and pulled all his tubes out. He was a bloody mess from pulling out the two IV sites. He was also demanding to be released. He had brought two nurses to tears.

They sat around a conference table in a comfortable room and had been served coffee and donuts. They were quietly talking about the situation and waiting for the doctor, nurse, and Gerard, as well as the case manager. Brenda was feeling much better but Ben had not slept much due to his great worry over Gerard.

"Ben," said Rod. "There was nothing you could do, so stop beating yourself up over it."

The others noticed how pale Rod was, but before they could say anything, the hospital personnel they had been waiting on, as well as the nurse pushing Gerard in a wheelchair, arrived.

"Thank you all for being here this morning," said Dr. Jones.

"Don't thank me," said Gerard in his snotty manner. He was looking everywhere in the room except at his family and friends. "I just want out of this insane asylum. There is nothing wrong with me. I just made an error in judgment. It won't happen again."

"Bloody damn mess," said Diane, the one nurse who was not afraid of him.

Gerard had the good grace to look a little ashamed of himself. He proceeded to grab a donut and was silent for a while.

The case manager spoke about why Gerard was in this predicament and what could be done to manage the health problems that had been caused by his behavior.

Dr. Jones spoke to Gerard. "Mr. Wallace. Gerard." The doctor cleared his throat like he was nervous to say what needed to be said. "You arrived here last night in a very serious condition. We were afraid at one point you might not wake up. Because of your drinking binge, you have developed a slight heart problem that, for the moment, has been corrected with medication. You will need further evaluation to determine if there will be any lasting damage."

"Like hell, I will." Gerard made to get up out of the wheelchair he was in.

Diane and Dr. Jones gently sat him back down. "You listen, and listen good," said Diane. "You are on a narrow road to destruction. You might not be so lucky the next time you do this. You are an alcoholic and you need help. I suggest you wipe that smug look off your face and admit it."

"Now wait a minute," said Brenda. "You can't talk to a patient like that."

Nick joined the conversation. "Why not? You talk to your students that way every day. Straightforward and to the point. That is what he needs right now, not a bunch of 'kiss ass' comments because everyone is afraid to tell it like it is."

"Couldn't have said it better myself," said Dr. Jones. "Gerard, you need help. I would suggest a rehab center since this has been a problem in your past."

"Not happening," said Gerard matter-of-factly.

"Son," said Andrew. "Don't you want to get over all the crap that has come down the pipe and get on with your life? We saw some real talent yesterday that none of us knew you possessed. And as closely as I have followed your life, I missed the bagpipes and drums completely."

"Bagpipes and drums? Seriously?" Diane clapped her hands before she saw the look given to her by Dr. Jones.

"How about this," said Nick. "You and Ben come and stay with Jill and I in Beaumont until you can shake some of this. Dr. Weir is there if you need extra help. You can stay as long as necessary."

"That's a great idea," said Brenda. "I can help, too. I promise not to fall into the same trap that I did yesterday. I should have been more responsible."

"Ben, you have been quiet. What do you think?" Andrew was looking at him.

Diane spoke up before Ben could answer. "Now Ben, you are Gerard's significant other?"

"Okay, that's it!" Gerard tried to wheel himself out of the room but Andrew stopped him.

"I am putting your second in command in charge of the hotel and The Club. Gwen will assist as well. That is all there is to it." Andrew stood up and went to his son.

"Am I making myself clear? We all love you and want to see you come through this. Nick's offer is a good one. I suggest you take it."

Gerard looked at everyone present. Finally, he spoke. "As much as I hate it, I know you all have my best interest at heart. Ben is not my significant other, Diane, he is my bodyguard." Gerard looked at Nick.

"I will take you up on that offer, Nick, if it still stands. I could use a break from everything that has been going on lately, but only if I hear it from Jill."

"Fair enough," said Nick as he dialed the phone.

"So, Doc, how long before I can blow this pop-sickle stand?" Gerard had a resigned look to his face.

"I would say day after tomorrow, provided you cooperate with testing and agree to some education on your drinking and the possible heart condition," said Dr. Jones.

Gerard sighed and had a terrible grimace on his face. "Okay, let's do this thing."

With that, Rod jumped up, and all but ran out of the room.

Ben went over to Gerard and shook his hand. "It be the best thing, Gerard, and I be there fo' you every step of the way."

"I know, Ben, I know," said Gerard. "What did Jill say, Nick?"

"She said to get your butt back to our house so she can feed you up and get you back on your feet," said Nick. "Oh, and she loves you."

"So, is Jill your significant other?" Diane asked looking at Gerard.

"No, she is not," said Brenda getting up and putting her hand on Gerard's shoulder for good measure. "I am."

"Well, good for you," said Diane in a sarcastic tone.

"Sounds like a plan," said Dr. Jones. "Let's get moving so we can get you out of here as soon as possible."

Brenda manned the wheelchair while the others thanked the hospital staff for stepping in to help.

Gerard spoke softly to Brenda. "They may have won the battle, but they won't win the war."

Twelve

Gerard had followed orders and cooperated with all the testing Dr. Jones put him through. It was determined that he was having a heart arrhythmia called atrial fibrillation and he would have to take medication for the immediate future. The doctor was not totally sure of the underlying cause but he suspected the recent stress Gerard had been through coupled with the return of binge drinking had caused a hidden problem to manifest.

Diane was a major pain in his ass. She wouldn't let him get away with a thing. He could not wait to get away from her.

Brenda had managed to get the time off to stay with Gerard in Chicago. Mamie had been very gracious to take Brenda's classes while she was away, but she made it clear that this can't keep happening.

Gerard was discharged from the hospital two days later. His heart rate and rhythm were back to normal, although he was on medication. He had been forbidden to drink and given information on Alcoholics Anonymous, which he accepted with a smile and when Diane's back was turned, he tore in little pieces.

He was also informed that sex was off limits for the next three weeks or until he saw a doctor in West Virginia and was cleared to return to his normal activities. He was not very happy about this, but he gave Diane a smile and a wink as he signed his discharge paperwork. She left to get a wheelchair to wheel him out while Brenda gathered the rest of the hospital toiletries.

"Bitch." Gerard said as quietly as he could.

"She is only doing her job, Gerard." Brenda also picked up a bag of 'hospital gifts' that she insisted on taking with them. "I don't know why you have been so hard on her."

"I gots a limo waitin' at the front entrance," said Ben entering the room. "Rod is waitin' at the airport with Nick and yo' dad."

Diane returned to the room and wheeled a protesting Gerard to the waiting limo.

"Wow, a limo. Why am I not surprised. You must think you're very important," said Diane with her usual sarcasm.

"You have no idea just how important," Gerard said under his breath as he climbed into the backseat. He pulled Brenda in next to him and proceeded to show her how much he had missed her.

"Thank you for sticking by me, Brenda. That was above and beyond."

"Here you go, Gerard," said Diane handing him a small bag. "You forgot this in the room." Gerard took the bag and looked inside as the limo pulled away. It was the torn- up Alcoholics Anonymous info.

Brenda started to laugh as Gerard stuck his arm out of the window giving Diane 'the bird' as they made their way out of the hospital parking lot and into Chicago traffic.

Later in the day as Gerard was resting at Nick's place, he thought about all he had been through in the last few months.

Had he come to terms with anything he had learned about his family? No, he hadn't.

As he was told by most everyone, he really needed to. Maybe he should think about talking to Dr. Weir. Right now, he was salivating to the smells coming from Jill's kitchen.

She was hosting a small get together for the family to celebrate Gerard's return and his embarking on a new, healthier journey. His parents and Dr. Weir would be there and Brenda, of course. The Dennison's and the old bat. Okay. He had to stop referring to Nana that way.

He hoped Matt wouldn't show up but he didn't think he was that lucky. He wasn't sure why he disliked Matt so much. Maybe it was because he could see Matt was still unable to keep his eyes off Anika's booty. Or maybe that he was so much smarter and insightful than most people. That really irked him.

His thoughts were interrupted as the family began to arrive. His mother and father were the first and he could see they were headed straight for him.

"Son," said Andrew as he shook Gerard's hand. "Don't get up. Your mother doesn't expect it."

"Good. Because she isn't going to get it," he said with a bite.

"Gerard!" He hadn't seen Jill enter the room. "Part of your recovery will be learning some manners, especially here in my home. Is that clear or do you need special education on that?"

Before he could answer, Jill's aunt Shirley and Dr. Weir entered along with Matt. He knew he wasn't that lucky. They were followed by the rest of the Dennison's and Mamie Gray. Bringing up the rear was Ben carrying Mamie's son, Xander, on his shoulders. He had wondered where Ben had gotten to.

His mother had moved to sit near him, but kept her distance and her mouth shut. Dr. Weir and Nana sat beside him on the sofa as well.

Finally, Brenda joined them, but instead of joining him, she went to help Jill in the kitchen. Rats! He was hoping she would break up some of the tension surrounding him right now. His father had retreated as had Ben and Xander.

Nana spoke first, of course. "Gerard, I'm a wondrin' how yer really a doin', son."

Gerard noticed all three of them looked to him for his answer and he had one for them.

"Fine." He looked away and tried to think of a reason to get up and leave. He knew Jill or Nick would stop him before he got halfway to the door. Or Ben, the traitor.

"Are you still having cravings for alcohol?" It was Dr. Weir that asked this question.

"No," he responded. He was pretty sure no one believed him.

Dr. Weir continued. "How about the tremors. Have those stopped?"

"Yes," he said clinching his hands into fists to keep them from doing so. He knew the good doc was trying to see if he was taking his medication.

His mother finally decided to put her two cents in. "Gerard, are you still having bouts of your heart racing?"

"No, thank you for asking. I know what you are all trying to do and it's not going to work. How I am is not really any of your business." He said this as haughty as possible for a down and out drunk.

"I knowed he wouldn't want us a askin' 'bout his health. He's a got too much o' yer sass, Maggie, he does. I knowed it from the start, I did," said Nana looking right at him as she spoke with that lingo he just hated.

Matt wandered over and sat on the arm of the sofa next to Dr. Weir.

"We only want to help you, Gerard, but maybe you still aren't ready for the help you so desperately need." Matt looked him in the eye just like the others.

"Look, Doc..." Gerard ignored Matt's comment and directed his remark to Dr. Weir.

"Please, call me Nathan," said Dr. Weir.

"Look, Doc." Gerard continued. "I am doing just fine..."

Matt interrupted. "No, you're not. Anyone can see that. I know what the problem is."

"Of course you do," said Gerard sarcastically. "Please, enlighten us with your great wisdom."

"Sure thing," said Matt totally missing the sarcasm or ignoring it. "You don't like other people taking care of you, even though you know you need it."

"Is that right." A statement, not a question from Gerard.

"It's like this," said Matt noticing all eyes were upon him, even those who had just entered. "It's like with a pack of wolves when they are on the march. They walk in a line, but have very specific reasons for the order they are in." He paused for dramatic effect just as Anika came in.

"Uncle Gerard," she said. "Listen to him. He knows what he is talking about."

"How would you know, Annie? Can you just keep quiet while I try to get a message into your uncle's head," snapped Matt.

She quickly took offense and ran off to the kitchen in a huff.

"As I was saying," Matt continued. "The first three wolves are old and sick or just sick. That's you, your mother and Nana. They set the pace. If they were in the back, they would be sacrificed to an ambush. The next are five relatively strong ones like Brenda, Jill, Mom, Josie, and Miss Gray. The center is other pack members like my aunts, Shirley and Gladys. Xander, Mark, Uncle Frank. Gwen and Lance. Then, the five strongest. Nick, Rod, Dad, Ben, and myself."

"You?" Gerard rolled his eyes but wanted to see how this played out. "Please, go on."

"Last is the Alpha, watching in all directions for danger." Matt looked around the room. "That's your dad. He's always had your back. Always. You just can't handle that you aren't the Alpha."

"Great analogy, Matt," said Dr. Weir. "I couldn't have put it any better myself."

"Smart ass." Gerard directed this at Matt, got up and went into the kitchen.

"At least I'm not a dumb ass!" Matt yelled after Gerard.

"Watch your mouth, young'n. There's little ears a listenin' in," said Nana looking at Matt. "Maggie, maybe we're a needin' to help in the kitchen. Let's us go take a gander." They got up and followed Gerard to the kitchen.

Man! He couldn't get away from any of them! Here they all were in the kitchen. He caught Ben's eye and nodded toward the door. Ben got the drift and followed Gerard out on the deck.

"Man, this party be fo' you an' you jus' pissin' everyone off." Ben was looking at Gerard. "Why you do that?"

"I'm suffocating in there. They all hover around me like I was a five- year old with polio. What I'd really like to do is get some alone time with Brenda," he said. "Can you get her out of there for at least a few minutes and have her meet me in my room?"

"I can try, man, but they be watchin' me too. I don't think you can disappear long 'cause they be servin' food in 'bout twenty minutes."

Gerard ran his hands through his hair.

"Then quit wasting time and get her up to my room." He turned and stalked off toward the stairs.

Brenda knocked softly on the door to Gerard's room and entered before she was invited. Gerard was lying back on the bed, shirt undone and his shoes off. The usual flask of alcohol next to him on the end table. Brenda paused.

"Gerard, you know better than to be drinking. Nick will throw you out," she said.

"Too damn bad, then," he replied. "I can't deal with all this 'family love' shit."

He got up and walked over to Brenda. He swept her up into his arms and put her on the bed.

"Have a drink on me." He handed her the flask and she drank from it. Then he drank more.

"Come, baby. Lay down here with me. I'll make you feel better." Brenda took her top off and exposed herself to him. He shrugged out of his shirt and loosened his belt.

"Much better," she said and kissed him deeply, pulling him on top of her. "You taste so good. I want more." She egged him on with her body.

"We don't have much time, Brenda. They will miss us soon, but Ben will alert us before trouble starts."

"Then stop wasting time, you fool. I want you. Now. I'm tired of waiting."

Gerard proceeded to kiss her all over her exposed breasts, and she kissed him as well. He removed his clothing and hers and just as he was about to claim her, there was another knock on the door.

"No. This can't be happening again. Every damned time! Yeah? This had better be an emergency!" He yelled at who he figured was Ben.

"Mr. Gerard?" It was Xander. "It is an emergency. My mama has to go save our country and Miss Brenda has to take care of me."

Brenda was immediately on alert. "We'll be there in just a minute, Xander." She got up and started throwing on her clothing. "Gerard, get dressed. This could be serious."

Gerard caught from her tone that she wasn't kidding and began to dress. "I'll be down in a minute. I have to visit the bathroom first." He winked at Brenda.

She winked back and left the room.

When Brenda descended the stairs, she over- heard a strange conversation between Margaret and Mamie.

How do they even know each other? What is that about? She listened a few minutes before making herself known.

"Do you know who the call came from?" Margaret was wringing her hands.

"No. But we both know this is a dangerous situation and I have to be at headquarters to make any kind of difference," said Mamie. "I have to get Xander with Brenda and leave as soon as possible." She looked up and saw Brenda on the stairs.

"Brenda," she said in a too sweet voice. "Have you been listening to our conversation?"

"How could I not? Since when do you and Gerard's mother know each other and what's this about a call?" Brenda continued down the stairs until she reached them.

"Listen, I need you to watch Xander, so I can pursue some military business. Can you do that for me," she asked.

"Of course," said Brenda. "Anything you need, just tell me what is going on."

"I'm not really sure. But Mark got a phone call that had to do with Nancy. You should ask him," said Mamie gathering her jacket and purse. "Here is my key to the house. Get what you need for Xander. If you need help with him, ask Ben. Xander has taken to him. I am not sure how long this will take." And she all but ran out of the house.

Brenda looked at Margaret. Margaret just shrugged her shoulders and left the area. Brenda looked up the stairs and thought, *it can't be taking him that long!* She just shook her head and went to find Xander.

Gerard had taken his time going back down stairs. He finished his alcohol and... the other thing, and he was feeling much better at the moment.

He entered the kitchen to find total chaos. Everyone seemed to be talking at once and it seemed to be directed at Mark.

"What's going on?" Gerard directed this to Nick who was standing closest to him.

"None of us are sure. It was weird. Mark got a phone call from Nancy's phone, but it wasn't Nancy. The guy said something about Mark not having to worry about hooking back up with Nancy, because he had taken care of everything. Then he hung up," said Nick.

Ben joined them. "I was talkin' to Mamie when the call come in an' she gots all upset an' sayin' she gots to leave and go to work right now. She say she be gone for a few days. What she gon' do at school this time of night?" Ben went out of the crowed room to get some air on the deck.

He met Mark standing with his ear to the sliding glass door. "Be quiet, Ben. Something is going on and I don't understand it."

Brenda and Gerard joined them. "Yeah," said Brenda. "I don't get it. I hear Mamie talking with Margaret about something that makes no sense, and she seems upset that I overheard. Then she runs out of here, right after you get a phone call, like a bat out of hell."

"She's not gone anywhere," said Mark. "She's on the back deck talking to Rod and they both seem agitated."

"What the hell is going on here?" Gerard pushed open the glass door just in time to see Mamie put a pistol in her purse.

"Mamie, I thought you had to leave," said Brenda.

"I do, I just had some business with Rod before I take off," she replied.

"Did you just put a gun in your purse?" Gerard made to reach for her purse, but she snatched it away.

"What is in my purse is none of your business. Now I have to leave. I'm behind schedule as it is." She took off at a jog around the back side of the house.

"Is this getting weirder by the minute?" Brenda turned to Rod. "Just what do you and Mamie have going on?"

"And what does any of this have to do with the phone call I just got?" Mark was so upset his face was beet red. "Something isn't right about this whole thing. First Nancy loses the baby, then she refuses to see me, then won't take my calls, now someone else has her phone. What am I supposed to think?"

"Maybe you should see if you can call the number back?" This from Matt who had brought up the rear of the group.

"You're right," said Mark while hitting re-dial.

"Of course he is," said Gerard in his snotty way, prompting a slug in the bicep by Anika.

"Of course," said Brenda. "Anything you need, just tell me what is going on."

"I'm not really sure. But Mark got a phone call that had to do with Nancy. You should ask him," said Mamie gathering her jacket and purse. "Here is my key to the house. Get what you need for Xander. If you need help with him, ask Ben. Xander has taken to him. I am not sure how long this will take." And she all but ran out of the house.

Brenda looked at Margaret. Margaret just shrugged her shoulders and left the area. Brenda looked up the stairs and thought, *it can't be taking him that long!* She just shook her head and went to find Xander.

Gerard had taken his time going back down stairs. He finished his alcohol and... the other thing, and he was feeling much better at the moment.

He entered the kitchen to find total chaos. Everyone seemed to be talking at once and it seemed to be directed at Mark.

"What's going on?" Gerard directed this to Nick who was standing closest to him.

"None of us are sure. It was weird. Mark got a phone call from Nancy's phone, but it wasn't Nancy. The guy said something about Mark not having to worry about hooking back up with Nancy, because he had taken care of everything. Then he hung up," said Nick.

Ben joined them. "I was talkin' to Mamie when the call come in an' she gots all upset an' sayin' she gots to leave and go to work right now. She say she be gone for a few days. What she gon' do at school this time of night?" Ben went out of the crowed room to get some air on the deck.

He met Mark standing with his ear to the sliding glass door. "Be quiet, Ben. Something is going on and I don't understand it."

Brenda and Gerard joined them. "Yeah," said Brenda. "I don't get it. I hear Mamie talking with Margaret about something that makes no sense, and she seems upset that I overheard. Then she runs out of here, right after you get a phone call, like a bat out of hell."

"She's not gone anywhere," said Mark. "She's on the back deck talking to Rod and they both seem agitated."

"What the hell is going on here?" Gerard pushed open the glass door just in time to see Mamie put a pistol in her purse.

"Mamie, I thought you had to leave," said Brenda.

"I do, I just had some business with Rod before I take off," she replied.

"Did you just put a gun in your purse?" Gerard made to reach for her purse, but she snatched it away.

"What is in my purse is none of your business. Now I have to leave. I'm behind schedule as it is." She took off at a jog around the back side of the house.

"Is this getting weirder by the minute?" Brenda turned to Rod. "Just what do you and Mamie have going on?"

"And what does any of this have to do with the phone call I just got?" Mark was so upset his face was beet red. "Something isn't right about this whole thing. First Nancy loses the baby, then she refuses to see me, then won't take my calls, now someone else has her phone. What am I supposed to think?"

"Maybe you should see if you can call the number back?" This from Matt who had brought up the rear of the group.

"You're right," said Mark while hitting re-dial.

"Of course he is," said Gerard in his snotty way, prompting a slug in the bicep by Anika.

"Ouch!" Gerard was rubbing his arm when Mark got an answer on his phone.

"Hello?" said Nancy

"Honey, it's me, Mark. Who was that on your phone earlier?"

"Mark, please don't call me here again." He could hear her sniffling and a male saying something to her in the background.

"Okay, okay. Mark, It's over. I hate to tell you this, but the baby wasn't yours anyway. Please don't contact me again. I'm where I need to be." She hung up.

Mark stood speechless. Brenda helped him to sit down and told Matt to get him something to drink while the others gathered around. Jill brought him a glass of tea and he waved it away.

"Tea? I need something stronger." They all looked at Gerard.

Thirteen

Another week had passed. Mamie had returned to town, collected Xander from Brenda, and had returned to her regular job as the high school principal. But Gerard could tell, something was off. Brenda was irritable, as was Mamie. That caused Ben to be out of sorts, making things more difficult for him and consequently, everyone around him.

He and Ben had taken to spending most afternoons at Mountain Mama's restaurant, eating dinner and just hanging around. The family was practicing for another 'family night' of music and fun, as Jill called it, with the proceeds this time going to Alcoholics Anonymous and the Mothers Against Drunk Driving programs. She had said it was in his honor, but he saw no honor in that. Maybe she should donate the money in honor of Mark. He was drinking more than Gerard. Gerard knew this because Mark was drinking with him.

Ben was coming his way, no doubt to lecture him about his drinking again.

"Don't even start, man," said Gerard before Ben could even speak. "I haven't had anything to drink...yet," he added for emphasis.

"Gerard, you hires me to look out fo' you," said Ben. "But I's learned that you still gon' do what you gon' do. Don't matter none what I say, so I jus' be here when you needs me. So if you don't need me, I'm gonna go watch the family practice."

"No, I don't need anything right now except some of Jill's triple berry cobbler and some ice cream, maybe some of her homemade sweet potato chips," said Gerard who had already eaten more than two people. He just couldn't get enough of Jill's food.

"I'll send Darlene over with yo' order," said Ben and he left to meet the others in the big banquet room upstairs.

Soon Darlene brought his food and remarked that if he kept eating like that, he was going to look like Bam McGee. He just snarled at her and proceeded to eat.

He saw his mother and Nick head to the piano at the back of the room in the studio where he was sitting. Neither one acknowledged him as they passed. They were both in a deep conversation, probably over some music nonsense. He was watching Nick explaining something in detail to her and not paying attention to anything else around him when…

"Hey, Gerard," said an animated Matt. "Mind if I join you?" Matt didn't wait for an answer, but sat his plate of chicken down and grabbed a handful of Gerard's sweet potato chips.

"Oh, good," said Gerard sarcastically. "Help yourself, why don't you. Do you want some of my dessert too?"

"No, thanks," said Matt missing or ignoring the sarcasm once again. "This chicken and chips will hold me until practice is over. I have to hurry. Tonight is dress rehearsal, you know."

"No, I don't know, and I don't care. You just run along and play your little violin like a good boy," sneered Gerard.

Matt looked up and realized that Gerard had never heard their family band before. "You're in for a treat tomorrow night. You've never heard us before." Matt picked up his plate and headed for the stairs.

Gerard turned his attention back to his mother and Nick. They were both playing something simple on the piano. He on the lower register and she on the upper. It vaguely occurred to him that Nick was not at practice, but he didn't let that thought linger too long. He saw the others entering the studio area getting ready to join practice.

"Brenda!" He got up to catch up with her.

"Hey, baby!" Brenda stretched up on her toes to give him a kiss.

"Let's blow this place and go someplace where we can be alone." He started kissing her neck.

"Get a room," said Rod as he headed for the stairs.

Brenda pulled back from him. "Sorry, baby, but I have to be at practice too. How about you wait for me in the studio apartment. Mark won't mind."

"Don't tell me, he's at practice too."

"Okay, I won't tell you, I'll just see you later." She took off at a jog toward the stairs.

He waited until the others had all gone upstairs before he followed, to let himself into the apartment.

He was relaxing watching the tube and thinking about how well this place was insulated. He couldn't hear anything from the practice across the hall. Just then, Mark jerked open the door.

"All I said was I don't like the original version of 'The Sound of Silence'. Not the way we're playing it." Mark was clearly agitated.

"Well, if you don't like the way I sing it, maybe you'd like to sing it yourself," said Jill a little stiffly.

"Yeah, right. I never sing anything but backup. That's for a reason, you know." Mark ran his fingers through his hair.

Jill put her hand on his shoulder. "Mark, you sing just fine. I think it's the song. When did you hear last from Nancy?"

He covered her hand with his. "It's been weeks since that last phone call. I can't help thinking that something isn't right. I can't believe the baby wasn't mine. We were always together."

"Just rest here for a while. When you feel up to it, then come back and join us," said Jill as she kissed his cheek.

Mark sat down across from Gerard just as Brenda barged her way in.

"What's going on? You okay, Mark?" Brenda plopped down on Gerard's lap and gave him a lingering kiss on the lips.

"That song. It gets to me," said Mark. "It reminds me of the silence I hear from Nancy. Jill does a good job singing it, but it sounds so peaceful. The sound, to me, is not peaceful. I know she means it to be for Margaret and her world of mostly silence...it's just hard for me."

Gerard felt the need to put his two cents in. "Maybe you could use that emotion to work for you. Sing the song, that is if you can sing, but put the emotion into it like in the newer version."

"Yes!" Brenda jumped off Gerard's lap. "Mark are you familiar with it?"

"No, I'm not." He stood up. "I know the words."

Gerard pulled the song up on his phone and they all three listened to it.

"Wow!" Mark was overcome with emotion. "That is incredible!"

They played it again and again. Mark began to sing with it. Then he closed his eyes and put all the emotion he had into it. He sounded like the lead singer in the current version.

"Now I have to say," said Brenda. "That is definitely your song. I'm going to tell Jill to change it in the program." She ran out to accomplish this task.

"Damn!" Gerard got up and wandered over to the kitchen cabinet. He poured both he and Mark a drink. "I might just have to see this show, even though I don't really care for the family thing. Here drink this. That wiped you out. I can tell. You look like me after two hours of hot sex."

Mark took the drink and downed the whole thing. He handed the glass to Gerard for another one. They sat and continued to drink and discuss Mark's life with Nancy. Gerard told him a little about different periods in his life as well. When the bottle was finished, so were they.

Ben came in to collect Gerard and was not surprised to find that he was sound asleep, possibly passed out. Mark was in the same condition. Ben decided to leave well enough alone. He reported the situation to Nick and Jill and retired to the third free room in the apartment, shaking his head as he went. He realized, to his knowledge, Gerard had not followed up with a doctor here in West Virginia for his heart problem.

~

The next evening, the restaurant was packed. There was standing room only for family night. The music presented for the night was an eclectic mix. Each family member had chosen a song and they had been taking requests from restaurant customers for the last week. There was quite a mixed bag of music for the night's presentation. The group was dressed in 'normal' clothing for a change. Each to their personal style.

Bonnie and Georgia were in town for the show. Gwen was there and she had brought Victor DeVille along since he had not been to the area and was curious.

Nick and Jill were getting the stage set with help from Ben, Matt, and Andrew. Nana was dressed as Mountain Mama and already entertaining the crowd.

"Nick, what's wrong?" Jill stopped what she was doing having noticed he seemed preoccupied.

"It's nothing, really," he replied. "It's just that I had mentioned to Rich we were having this event and could use his support. He offered to donate quite a bit of money, but I asked him to come see what we do here. He seems to think this is a garage band joke. He thinks I am wasting my time and causing Matt to waste time as well."

"Honey, you know how he is." Jill put her arms around Nick's neck. "He doesn't get out much. He does nothing but write scores of beautiful music, teach the students, conduct the orchestra. When was the last time he even had a date? When was the last time he even saw Anika, his own goddaughter?"

"It's been years. She was about twelve when he saw her last. He sends her cards and gifts for holidays, but he really doesn't know her either." Nick was starting to sound aggravated.

Gerard and Anika wandered over and Ben joined them.

"Are you talking about Uncle Rich?" Anika was looking around for Matt. She was dressed to kill. She had on a silky tan dress with navy blue polka dots and navy-blue mesh around the shoulder area. The dress was shorter in the front and longer in the back. She had on navy heels and her hair was piled on top of her head. Clearly, she had on no bra. She was stunning.

"If you don't mind me sayin' so," Ben stated, "Miss Anika, yo' sho' is fine lookin' tonight!"

"Of course not." She twirled around so they all could see the full effect.

"Well, I mind." Gerard, clearly a little inebriated, pulled Anika to his side and looked like a protective father.

Brenda walked up. "You can thank me for this effect. She is beautiful and she should stand out. I've got to say, I did a great job!"

"I'll get you for this later," said Gerard.

"Is that a threat or a promise?" Brenda gave him a wink and a swat on the rear end.

Nick cleared his throat and looked to Jill for help.

"Anika, honey, come with me. You seem to be missing part of your wardrobe." Jill led Anika upstairs, while Anika protested all the way. Brenda followed.

Margaret entered, escorted by Nana, and was seated at one of the tables reserved for family and special guests. Just then...

"Bam!"

"Guess who is here?" Jill rolled her eyes.

"What the hell was that?" Gerard, clearly startled, quickly got out of the way just as Josie wandered up to join the group.

"I see Bam McGee is here to keep things exciting," she said.

It was ten minutes before show time. "Make way! Make way! Alphonse is in the house!" Alphonse strutted up to them without his usual entourage, but strutting anyway, as was his custom.

Nick glanced his way and broke into a big smile. Behind Alphonse was none other than Dr. Richard Dana. Nick grabbed his friend in a big hug. Then Alphonse grabbed them both in a hug.

"Group hug. Come on everybody." Alphonse was waving the others into the hug.

"I'm good," said Dr. Dana backing away. "Alphonse, you promised not to embarrass me."

Dr. Dana was a man of medium height and build, early forties, with dark hair, graying at the temples, and clear blue eyes. He was dressed in an impeccable suit of good quality, way over dressed for this venue.

"Nick, I decided to take you up on your offer to visit your hometown little band. And to see my goddaughter." He looked around and spotted Josie.

"Sweetheart! My you've grown...wow! Come give Uncle Rich a big hug." He walked over and grabbed Josie in a hug and a kiss on the cheek.

"Um...sir, I'm Josie Dennison. I think you're looking for Anika," said Josie prying herself away from Dr. Dana.

Red in the face, Dr. Dana pulled out a handkerchief and blotted his forehead. "Forgive me, Miss Dennison. I have not seen Anika in a few years."

"No forgiveness needed, Dr. Dana. I am flattered to be mistaken for Anika. She is a real beauty," said Josie shaking Dr. Dana's hand.

"Please, call me Rich, and again, I apologize."

Nana had walked up and saw the exchange. "I'd jest like to call ye an ol' fart, I would, tryin' to sneak up on the young ladies...I declare." She kept on her way to greet the next guests leaving a puzzled Rich to watch her go.

"So, Rich, you obviously know Alphonse from Marcel's?" Nick moved him out of the mainstream of traffic through the restaurant.

Alphonse jumped in before Rich could answer. "We go way back. I cook the food. He eats the food. Enough said. Where is my flower, Marlene?" Alphonse looked around then turned back to Rich.

"Keep your hands off my woman, or no more French food for you. You know you can't handle that." He left, heading for the kitchen.

"Thank God," said Gerard. "So, Dana, are you out slumming tonight?"

"Oh, Gerard. I didn't see you there." Rich gave him a brief nod and turned his attention back to Nick.

"When can I see my goddaughter? Never mind, I see her coming this way. I'd know her anywhere."

He took off toward…Brenda who was coming back down the stairs. He grabbed her in a hug, lifted her off the ground, and spun her around in a circle.

Brenda put her arms around his neck and kissed him on the lips leaving Rich with a shocked look on his face.

"Now that's what I call a real friendly hello! I'm Brenda, by the way. You must be looking for one of my sisters."

Rich put Brenda down and was wiping his forehead again and looking very embarrassed.

"Okay, Nick, you've had your fun. I realize it has been way too long since I have seen your daughter. Miss, I am so sorry. I thought you were Anika."

"Yeah. I get that a lot," said Brenda winking at him.

Gerard stepped up to Rich and grabbed the front of his jacket. "If you ever grab my woman again, Dana, you'll be conducting that orchestra with the baton in your teeth because I'll have to break both your arms. Got it?"

"Got it," said Rich clearly unafraid of Gerard. "Nick, suppose you point her out this time."

"She is a beauty, old friend, and I can see how you mistook Josie and Brenda for Anika. Just wait until you see her," said Nick. "Here she is now, coming down the stairs with Jill."

Rich looked in that direction again. "Holy shit!" He was shocked. He tried to recover before she got to him.

She jogged forward and grabbed him in a hug. "Uncle Rich! I've missed you so much! I can't wait to be at Julliard with you! I love you! I love you!' She was kissing him on both cheeks.

She finally stepped back. "Well, what do you think? I've grown up wouldn't you say?"

Rich glanced at Nick unsure of what to say, but noticed Nick was trying to hide his laughter at the whole thing. Then Ben burst out in loud giggles. Finally, they all started to laugh. Rich continued to mop his forehead.

"I'd have to say, that's an effing understatement," he said to Nick, trying to keep it clean. "What? No pictures to prepare me for this shock? Man, you must have to beat them off with a stick!"

"No, really." Nick leaned in to Rich. "She only has eyes for Matt."

Rich thought for a minute. "Okay, then, that's allowable. I can handle that. But what is it with these beautiful women here? They're all over the place! How did Gerard land such a, pardon the expression, fox? And where can I get me one of those?"

"Oh, Rich, old man, you have got to get out more," said Nick taking Rich by the arm and leading him toward the reserved tables.

Ben leaned over to him. "Dr. Dana, sir, they be plenty mo' o' that. Jus' wait 'til you sees. Hoo wee! Jus' wait 'til you sees."

~

"Welcome, everbidy, to Mountain Mama's fer the best night in music this side 'o th' Blue Ridge Mountains!" Nana was fired up. "We got y'all a mix o' all kinds o' music here tonight. Songs you ain't never hear'ed in this place before. People you ain't never hear'ed sing or play before. So, sit yerself right back and we'll cut one more rusty fer ye!"

The applause was loud and several people were shouting 'Bam' right along with Bam McGee. Gerard was sitting at the table reserved for family, along with Ben, Rod, Gwen, and Rich. There were still two vacant seats there. Gerard looked bored but gave a 'thumbs up' to Mark who was positioned behind the drum set.

The other reserved table had several vacant seats for different band members when they were not on stage. Mamie Gray and Xander were there along with Victor DeVille, Alphonse and Margaret who was quietly talking to Mamie.

Gwen leaned in to say something to Rich, when Matt bounded in pulling Anika with him.

"Dr. Dana! What are you doing here? Awesome! You get to hear Anika play!" He leaped up on the stage and Anika followed.

Just then the blonde gal Rich had picked up and hugged sat next to him. He was a little embarrassed and leaned forward to her.

"Miss, again, I can't apologize enough for what happened in the foyer."

She turned to him. "What happened in the foyer, sir?"

Rich looked confused and Ben started to laugh. "I tol' you so, I tol' you so."

He leaned over to Gerard. "Ain't I tol' him so?"

"Who gives a rat's ass, Ben?' Gerard and Rich looked up and saw Brenda enter at the same time.

Rich looked from Brenda to the woman next to him and then back to Brenda. Then at Nick. Nick was laughing and pointing toward the door. Rich looked up to see a third blonde woman enter. He took out his handkerchief again and started to wipe his forehead.

Brenda came over to him. "Dr. Dana, this is my sister, Georgia, and my sister Bonnie." They shook hands and Bonnie went to sit at the other table next to Victor.

Georgia leaned over to Rich. "I should have known. My sister, Brenda. Nice to meet you Dr. Dana. I am Georgia Montgomery and I live in New York City just in case you were wondering."

The program started with the ever popular 'The Devil Went down to Georgia' which received a standing ovation as usual. Matt and Anika had rocked the Devil's and Johnny's parts, except this time, they had reversed parts, with Anika playing the Devil's part and Matt taking Johnny's. The family had surprised looks on their faces, but didn't miss a beat.

As always, Josie on the bass solo and Jill on the guitar solo was hot. Gerard was no longer looking bored. He was clapping along with everyone else.

Ben stood up and joined the family on the stage, much to Gerard's surprise. He played the harmonica to 'Forty Hour Week' with the whole family singing and to 'Amazing Grace' with Jill singing lead and Nana singing harmony.

It brought tears to most eyes in the audience and Georgia was so overcome, she leaned into Rich's side, using his hankie to dry her eyes. Then she scooted her chair closer to him. Ben joined them back at the table after the song was over. Gerard slapped him on the back and the others shook his hand.

The next few songs were by the Montgomery Triplets. As they were introduced, Gerard noticed Rich sit up straighter. They started with Georgia singing the lead on 'You don't Own Me' followed by Brenda with the lead in 'These Boots Were Made for Walkin'. She flirted with Gerard during the song and kissed him at the end like she had done last fall at another family night.

The three finished with a sexy rendition of 'Hey, Big Spender' pulling Gerard, Rich and Victor out of their seats and flirted with all three. Gerard was loving it as was Victor. Georgia was coming on hot and heavy at Rich and he had broken out in a cold sweat, and was turning pale.

At the end of the song, the girls led the guys back to their seats and sat in their laps. Rich was almost smiling. When Georgia went to get up, Rich tugged her back down, looked her in the eye and gave her a quick kiss. She was shocked at first, but then kissed him back.

As she walked away, he looked at Ben. "I've got to get out more."

The last song of the night would be 'The Sound of Silence' with Mark singing lead.

"Are you sure you're up to this?" Jill was a little worried about her brother. He looked tired and washed out.

"I am very much up to this, Sis. I think you'll be very surprised what I can do."

"Okay, then. Let's do this thing." Jill walked to the front of the stage and made an announcement.

"The last song of the night I would like to dedicate to my mother-in-law, Margaret Wallace. There have been lots of struggles in all of our lives, some of us for many, many years. Some of us have overcome a lot and some of us are just starting out in new uncharted waters, not knowing where it will end. But the difference in all of it is how we choose to handle the hard times. Silence can build to the point of illness, fear, hopelessness and for some, the inability to move forward with their lives. For some, it is only for a short period, but for others of us, it can last a lifetime affecting not only ourselves, but those we hold most dear. Listen to the words as my brother, Mark Dennison, sings them."

Mark moved to the front of the stage and sat on a stool as Nick played the intro to the song. He sat with his head bent and his eyes closed as if he were in prayer.

He began to sing. "Hello darkness, my old friend. I've come to talk with you again. Because a vision softly creeping, left it's seeds while I was sleeping..."

As he started the second verse he stood up and opened his eyes. "In restless dreams I walked alone..." the family could tell something was different. They had never heard Mark sing like this, but they kept up.

He sang on. "When my eyes were stabbed by a flash of a neon light, that split the night, and touched the sound of silence." Mark had his hand over his heart, the emotion starting to build, evident in his tenseness. He stepped out closer to the audience. The same tenseness could be felt in the patrons watching the show.

"And in the naked light I saw, ten thousand people, maybe more. People talking without speaking. People hearing without listening..." He waved his hand toward the audience. The family was as invested as Mark. The violins were beautiful as was the piano and guitars. Margaret was on the edge of her seat.

As Mark got to the next verse, he was almost angry and his voice reflected that emotion.

"Fools, said I, you do not know. Silence like a cancer grows." Mark had both fists clenched and was looking upward. "Hear my words that I might teach you..."

Mark continued pouring his heart and soul into the music. "But my words like silent raindrops fell...and echoed in the wells of silence."

Mark had put everything into the last verse. His voice was almost hoarse with everything he had put into the song.

"And the people bowed and prayed. To the neon god they made..." Mark was bent with the heaviness of the feeling he was trying to convey. He fell to his knees.

"And the sign flashed out it's warning, in the words that it was forming. And the words said the signs of the prophets were written on the subway walls, and tenement halls. And whispered in the sound...of silence."

Mark was spent as the music ended. The room was in total silence. Mark got up and left the room. As one, the audience watched him leave. The family was looking at each other.

Then, Rich stood to his feet, and with incredible emotion on his face, began to clap. One by one the others in the audience and family, including Margaret, joined him in thunderous applause and the longest standing ovation Mountain Mama's had ever seen.

Marianne Waddill Wieland

Fourteen

The aftermath of Family Night was tremendous. The show had been over two hours in length and the customers were wanting more. After Mark's performance, there was noting that could compete. Mark had disappeared upstairs to the apartment. He had been spent and the family had been in awe, as was the audience.

As the customers finally left, the older family members prepared to leave also. The younger group was dispersed in different areas of the restaurant. Brenda was chatting with her sisters and Ben. Mamie was trying to round up an over excited Xander without a lot of success. She finally gave up and left him with Ben. She wandered over to have a few words with Margaret before she left.

"What do you think of this whole thing?" She asked a nervous Margaret while glancing around to see who was in earshot.

"Well, you've got to give the young man credit where credit is due. That was an amazing performance considering what he is going through," Margaret stated reluctantly.

"Yes, it was," replied Mamie. "If he knew the real truth, I don't know what it would do to him. We have got to keep this quiet until we can find out where everything stands. I have to go to headquarters next week again."

Margaret looked unhappy. "You have got to be more discreet about your trips. I think Brenda is getting suspicious."

They continued to talk quietly until Ben and Xander came their way. Xander was riding on Ben's shoulders.

"Evenin', Miz Margaret...Mamie" he said. "I gots yo' boy here. He gots enough energy to power the town o' Beaumont all by hisself, don't ya, boy?" Ben plucked Xander off his shoulders and started tickling him. Xander was laughing and falling in the floor.

Jill and her aunts, Gladys and Shirley, were eyeing Margaret and Mamie.

"Doesn't it seem odd that Mamie and Margaret always seem to be having a discreet conversation when they are in the same vicinity?" Jill was looking pensive at the two.

"I have noticed that," said Shirley.

"I've noticed that Rod and Mamie seem to have some kind of running dialogue as well," said Gladys. "They always look nervous. Like they're up to something."

"Hey! All I said was that Richard Carpenter was the king of the major seven chord." Matt was hurrying behind an angry Anika. "Do you have some kind of problem with that?"

"It is my privilege to disagree," said Anika continuing past Jill and the aunts. "My opinion is of no concern to you."

She stopped abruptly causing Matt to run into her. He grabbed her shoulders to steady himself and her.

"Get your hands off me!" Anika almost yelled, causing Nick and Gerard to take notice.

"What is all the commotion?" Nick was getting upset. "Anika is there a problem?"

"Yes, dad, there is." She made a point of glaring at Matt. "He thinks Richard Carpenter is the king of the major seven chord. I do not agree."

"Matt, you have a lot to learn about girls," said Gerard flippantly. "Just agree with them to shut them up. Does it really matter what they think?"

"Is that right?" Brenda had been within earshot of the conversation and was visibly upset.

"Baby, I didn't mean you. What you have to say is very important." Gerard tried hard to cover his major blunder. "Really, doll. I hang on your every word. Trust me."

Brenda turned slowly around. "I agree with Matt. You can't argue with a song like 'Merry Christmas, Darling'. Are you hanging on those words, Gerard?"

"I agree that the major seven chord is strong in 'Merry Christmas, Darling' but there are other songs that should be considered," stated Gerard like he had a clue.

"Oh, really, Uncle Gerard," said Anika in her snottiest voice. "What would you consider to be another song with a strong major seven chord?"

"Here comes Rich. I know he'll want to weigh in on this one," said Gerard. "He knows everything and never misses a chance to prove it."

Anika explained the discussion to Rich while Brenda's sisters joined the group.

"Well, Matt makes an excellent point," said Rich. "However, there is no more famous major seven chord than Jimmy Pankow's F major seven arpeggio to open the song, 'Color My World.'"

Anika hugged Rich. "I knew you would agree with me Uncle Rich! Come to the piano and we can mess around." She took off toward the piano with Matt following.

"Nick, your daughter is too old to make remarks like that around an old guy like me," said Rich wiping his forehead. "I've been single too long."

Georgia grabbed Rich's arm. "Come on, baby, let's go test out the major seven chord. You play. I'll sing." They went over to the piano to join Matt and Anika.

Rich sat on the bench and began the opening of the song. It was beautiful. Georgia sat next to him on the bench and began to sing. She lightly placed her hand on Rich's shoulder. He gave her a look and smiled. She smiled back. Matt and Anika looked at each other then back at the others.

"I think old Rich might be about to 'get some'." Gerard was laughing at his own statement.

"Well, I know who is not going to 'get some' anytime soon." Brenda stalked off passing Rod and Ben as she went.

"What they be doin' over there?" Ben still had Xander with him since Mamie had disappeared.

"Discussing the differences in the major seven chord," said Nick.

"Major Chord?" Ben scratched his head. "Rod, is that one o' yo' military friends?"

The group started to laugh, even Gerard. Ben was clearly confused. Nick started to explain when Mamie came to collect Xander and head home.

"I'm calling it a night," she said. "I hear you are having an impromptu music night here tomorrow night. Is that true?"

"Yes, for anyone that wants to play or sing. Just kind of an open mic night you could say," said Jill. "Rich will still be here, so we thought, given the response to tonight's performances, it was called for." She and Nick wandered over to the piano with the others.

Gerard and Ben sat down at a table, Gerard with his usual flask of liquor and Ben with some tea. They waved to Mamie as she and Xander left.

"I don't know, Ben. I don't think I can handle Brenda full time. She is ten years younger than me, but it seems like twenty." Gerard was running his hands over his face. "Things go great for a while, then she gets moody or shitty over some small little thing and flies off the handle."

Ben thought for a minute. "She did be gettin' all upset over this Major Chord. I think he should be stayin' his ass in the military 'stead o' comin' out to these parts."

Gerard started to try to explain but just shook his head. "I can't do it, Ben. No matter how good she is with...you know. The age gap is too great."

"Man, the age gap is in yo' hard head." Ben put his hand on Gerard's shoulder. "It don't matter to her. She gots feelin's for you, man. I knows it. I sees it in her eyes, the way she looks at you. She gots it bad, man."

"I don't know what to do," Gerard was watching Rich and Georgia at the piano across the room. He sighed.

"Look at Rich. Flirting with Georgia. No shame. He's got to be fifty if he's a day. It's like child molesting!"

Ben leaned toward Gerard. "Now you need to hush up talk like that, man. He only be forty- one years old. I knows 'cause I heard Mamie ask him."

"It doesn't matter. He's still fifteen years older than Georgia." Gerard was still keeping a close eye on them. "She does look interested, doesn't she? Hmmm...I better have Brenda warn her about the evils of an older man. Especially that one."

"What you gots against him anyhow," asked Ben.

"I've known him a long time and, I don't know, he just rubs me the wrong way. He's too smart. Keeps to himself," said Gerard in a frustrated tone.

"Let me gets this straight," said Ben. "He be too smart and keep to hisself. Okay. I sees now, I does. He need to be put away. Lawd, Lawd. Somebody call in the cops. He be too smart. Lawd, Lawd, Lawd!"

The look on Gerard's face was priceless. He was just staring at Ben with an open mouth. Ben got up and continued his tirade.

"Oh, Lawd have mercy!" Ben walked around the room with his hands in the air. "He keep to hisself! Naw, naw! We can't be havin' none o' that! Next thang you know, he be helpin' strangers! Oh, no. Lawdy!"

Ben saw the others heading their way to see what the commotion was about. He took off to the upstairs apartment leaving Gerard to handle the fallout.

"Problem?" Jill was looking at Ben's retreating back.

"I have no comment," said Gerard. "We were having a conversation about age differences and he just went off. Go figure." Gerard made to get up but Bonnie put her hand on his head pushing him back to the seat.

"Don't be so smug, Gerard. Brenda and I have had the same conversation," said Bonnie. "Whether or not the ten-year age difference will be a problem. We decided if you care about each other and you are compatible, then, no problem."

Nick jumped in to change the subject. "Are you girls coming back to perform tomorrow night?"

"Yes," said Bonnie. "Brenda and I will do a couple of songs and if my guess is correct, Georgia will be performing with Dr. Dana."

"Yes, Georgia will," Georgia replied with a glance at a slightly red- faced Rich.

"I'll collect Brenda and, Dr. Dana, how about you ride with us to Brenda's?" Bonnie was heading toward the stairs as she was talking.

"Sure, but I have to get to Nick's place before too late. I can't stay too long," he replied.

"Don't worry," said Georgia. "You don't have to stay at all. I'll take you back to Nick's place so you can get your beauty rest."

"He needs that for sure," said Gerard. "An old geezer like him, Georgia, you may have to help him up the steps." Gerard got up and headed toward the front door calling Ben on his phone as he did so.

As they all prepared to leave, Ben and Brenda joined them at the front door.

"We'll see you all tomorrow night, then, and for once we will play it by ear," said Jill hugging herself to Nick as Gerard and Ben started out the door headed to Nick's place.

Rich climbed in the backseat of Brenda's SUV with Georgia. She was sitting a little too close to him. Invading his personal space. He was starting to sweat. He had not been on a date in years and was a little concerned about Georgia's expectations.

Soon the car came to a stop at Brenda's place, a cute ranch style house with a big yard. They all got out and Georgia got in the driver's seat, so Rich followed suit and joined her in the front.

"Don't wait up, girls," Georgia shouted as they drove away.

Rich was really starting to sweat now. *Would she be expecting him to make a pass at her? How would he do that? Did he want to? Jesus, did he want to! She was so young! Not that much older than Anika, his goddaughter. Oh, God! She's coming to a stop and it's not at Nick's house. Damn!*

Georgia got out of the car, motioning Rich to follow. He quickly wiped his forehead and followed her saying a silent prayer.

"Baby, you're overthinking it." Georgia led him to a bench in the small park near Nick's house. "Come. Sit." She took his hand and pulled him down beside her.

They sat in silence for a while looking at the stars and listening to the sounds of nature at night. Georgia snuggled closer to him and he put his arm around her.

"I love the way you play," said Georgia. At his stricken look she quickly added to the remark. "The piano, I mean."

"Thank you. Your voice is like velvet. I could listen to it all night," said Rich.

"I would like that, I think. I mean...I don't know what I mean," said Georgia in a breathy voice. "Right now, Rich, I want to feel your touch."

She moved on the bench so that she was looking into his eyes. "I want to feel your breath mixing with mine, your hands almost touching me where they shouldn't, almost...I..." She moved her face just inches from his. Her lips were almost on his...almost...almost.

He had not felt this kind of emotion for a long, long time. "Georgia...I want...to..I..."

"Rich, if you want, I can just take you to Nick's house." Her lips were touching his, just shy of actual kissing.

"Oh, hell, no. Screw formality."

He turned toward her, put his hand behind her head and pulled her to him. Their lips met and Rich unleased ten years of pent up passion. He devoured her lips with his, deepening the kiss until she was across his lap and they were both so breathless, he thought they would drown in his longing.

They were on fire. She began to unbutton his shirt and he lifted her dress over her head just breaking contact long enough for the task to be completed. She looked around and found a table away from the view of anyone passing. She pulled him with her and as the stars blinked overhead, they both knew passion like neither had ever known before in their lives.

Much later, as Georgia walked Rich to Nick's front door, he thought he was going to explode with joy. Never, in his wildest dreams, would he have thought he would lose control like that. He wanted to lose control again. He grabbed Georgia and pushed her up against the door kissing her hard and hot. She was meeting him kiss for kiss when...

"What the hell?" It was Gerard. He had yanked the door open and Georgia would have fallen if Rich hadn't caught her. "What in the blue blazes are you trying to do? You were leaning on the door bell, for Pete's sake."

Gerard took in the scene before him. Rich with his shirt buttoned up wrong and his belt hanging and Georgia with her dress on backwards.

"Damn! Dana got some! I don't get it. I date Brenda for several months and all I get is, well, everyone knows what I get. You meet Georgia for the first time tonight and..." Gerard threw his hands up, turned around and headed up the stairs drinking from a rum bottle as he went.

Rich was having a hard time curtailing his excitement. "I'll see you about five o'clock at Mountain Mama's to go over our songs."

"Yes, yes, yes!" Georgia said as she pulled him to her. "You are damn good. I don't think I can get enough. You are addicting. I'm a Rich addict. I don't know what I'll do when you leave. Wait. We both live in New York City." She smiled as she gave him a quick, hard kiss and then ran down the sidewalk to her sister's SUV.

Fifteen

The next morning, Gerard and Ben were coming down the stairs when they heard a heated debate between Nick and Rich. It was coming from the kitchen and seemed to have something to do with bagpipes.

"I think there is great merit to the skill needed to play the bagpipes," said Rich. "I just prefer the softer, clearer tones of the uilleann pipes."

"I prefer the bagpipes because of the majesty surrounding the instrument," countered Nick. "Nothing beats thirty bagpipes in a parade, all playing together without missing a single note. Words can't describe."

"You are right. Words can't describe." Rich noticed Gerard at the kitchen entrance. He geared up for the offense that Gerard was so good at giving. "You have to be half a mile away to even stand the harsh screech that a group of that size will make. Not to mention whether or not a missed note can be determined."

"Whoa! Time out!" Gerard was all over that remark. "Dana, just because you got some last night doesn't make you an expert on the bagpipes."

"Playing them has not made you one either," Rich replied sipping his coffee and going into his 'I'm bored to death with this conversation' affect, which was the best way he had found to deal with Gerard over the years.

"I beg to differ, Dana. I have been playing most of my life and I play the uilleann pipes as well." Gerard joined them at the table helping himself to a basket of fresh baked carrot muffins.

Jill entered the room followed by Anika. They were listening to the conversation while they began to fix breakfast. Ben offered to assist but was told to sit down and enjoy the muffins while there were still some left.

"I doesn't know much about the bagpipes, but I knows what I likes, and that ain't it," said Ben. "I doesn't know about them other pipes." He grabbed a muffin and added butter to it.

Anika punched something into her phone and started playing the Celtic Woman song, 'Orinoco Flow', explaining to Ben the difference in the uilleann pipes.

Ben agreed that he preferred the softer pipes as well. "I just plays the harmonica and I used to play the sax when I was in school".

"Uncle Rich, can you remember all the way back to when you were in school?" Anika sat down at the table.

"Anika, honey, I am not that old," said Rich. "Why does everyone think I am so old? I am only forty- one for Christ's sake!"

"But you act like eighty-one, Dana," said Gerard causing Ben to laugh. "Although I have got to say, after I saw you with Georgia last night, I might have to re-think my opinion of you."

"I am on the edge of my seat with anticipation for that revelation," said Rich in a bored voice.

"I bets he be, Gerard," said Ben. "I bets he been wild when he in college."

"Yeah Dana. Let's hear some of your wild stories," said Gerard, egging Rich on.

Anika moved closer to Rich and asked with a pleading look on her face. "Uncle Rich, were you wild? Did you get in trouble in college? I bet you didn't. You're too sweet and good to do anything other than study and write."

Rich moved around in an uncomfortable fashion in his chair and looked at Nick, then at Anika. He looked at Gerard and Ben. Finally, he took a deep breath.

"I wasn't wild in college but I did have fun from time to time. There was this one time that I thought it would be fun to grow wheat on the balcony of the apartment I shared with some friends."

"You be growin' wheat? In a 'partment? You be crazy, man!" Ben was slapping Rich on the back nearly knocking him out of his chair.

"Who in they right mind grow wheat in New York City? How you do that, anyway?" Ben was leaning toward Rich waiting for the answer.

"How stupid can you get?" Gerard sneered at Rich, but then started to laugh.

"Okay, I'll bite," said Jill joining in the conversation. "What was the point of that?"

Rich ran his hands through his hair in a surprisingly 'Gerard-like' way. "I got some two by fours and nailed them together to make a square box about six foot by six foot. Then I planted the wheat and watched it grow. End of story."

"But Uncle Rich. What did you do with the wheat when it was fully grown?" Anika was not about to let the subject drop.

Nick caught Jill's eye and gave a slight negative shake of his head in her direction. She winked catching his drift.

"Anika, can you help me carry the food into the dining room? The others will be here for breakfast soon."

Just then the doorbell rang. "I'll get it," Anika shouted and left the room.

"I caught that, Jill." Gerard leaned toward Rich again. "Time to spill it Dana! I know there is more to the story. I can read my brother's face."

"Okay, okay," said Rich looking around to see who was still in earshot. "Actually, we all got high and ate it raw!"

Ben and Gerard just looked at each other, then burst out in laughter so loud, Nick was trying to quiet them down.

"He get high and eat it raw!" Ben could barely get the words out. Nick just rolled his eyes.

"Dana," Gerard just couldn't catch his breath. He stood up. "I want to hear more stories about you later. You might not be quite the stuck up tight ass I thought." He left the room upon hearing Brenda's voice.

~

Later, after breakfast was over, the women were in the kitchen discussing what they would wear tonight since it was an informal musical program. Josie and Rod had separated from the group and were taking a walk toward the park. Matt had asked to speak with Anika privately and they had gone into the study so as not to be disturbed. Ben had gone with Nick over to the restaurant to move some things around upon Jill's instructions.

Gerard was on his own since Brenda was in the kitchen with her sisters and Jill. He decided to sit out on the back deck with his silver flask and relax. Too much food and conversation made him very anxious. That and the fact that Brenda was still very cold to him. His mouth had always been a problem for him. He just couldn't seem to control what came out of it.

He found a chair and lowered his tall frame onto it and began to drink. He finished one flask and started on another. He was feeling very relaxed and his eyes were starting to close when he saw Rich coming around the side of the house.

"Hey, Dana," called Gerard. "Quit skulking around in the back yard hiding from Georgia. Come up here and have a drink. I want to hear more about the wheat!"

"Knock it off, Gerard," Rich replied. "I am not hiding from Georgia. I am just checking out the mountain scenery. I never get to leave the city, so I am trying to enjoy what the country has to offer."

"Keep saying it and maybe you will start to believe it," said Gerard in a slurred voice. "You know you have a problem with Georgia's age just like I have a problem with Brenda's."

Rich sat on the chair next to Gerard and looked at the flask that Gerard was offering.

"Oh, what the hell." He took a big swig and choked. "What do you have in here? Moonshine?"

"Yep. Got it from Bam McGee," said Gerard. "Best in the county, so I'm told."

"You need to lay off that shit. Man, you're going to rot out your guts, not to mention your heart problem," said Rich more intensely than he had planned.

"Nah," said Gerard. "It relaxes me and as long as I don't hurt anyone else, what difference does it make? And the heart problem is no longer a thing."

"Just keep it to yourself, but frankly, you have had substance abuse problems in the past," Rich said in a matter of fact tone. "Maybe you are traveling down another bad road. Anyway, you are an adult so I will leave it at that."

Rich took a few deep breaths of the clear mountain air. "So, you were talking about the age differences with the sisters. I hadn't thought about it until you pointed it out."

"That's me, you know. The voice of reason," Gerard slurred. "I don't think I can do it, Rich. Ten years. That is a big difference. A whole generation. But I want her so much! She can ... I guess you have heard what she can do."

Rich thought for a minute and leaned closer to Gerard. "I haven't heard what she can do, but if she is anything like Georgia...wow! I have never done anything like this in my life, whereas you do it all the time. How do you cope?"

Gerard just held up his flask of moonshine.

"Right," said Rich. "Fifteen years is a lot to swallow. Kind of like the moonshine. What a kick going down, but then comes the after effects."

"Have there been any from Georgia?" Gerard downed the last of his moonshine.

"Not really," said Rich. "If I didn't know what happened, I couldn't tell it by the way she is interacting with me. She isn't ignoring me, but just not acting like I mean anything to her either."

Gerard got up and walked to the rail of the deck. He was feeling shaky in his legs. He leaned on the rail for support.

"Of all the women I have had, why does it have to be her that makes me so crazy?"

Rich walked over to the rail just in time to see Gerard vomit on Jill's rose bushes. "Damn, man! You need to get your shit together." With that, Rich left the deck to join the women in the kitchen.

~

By the time Gerard was able to join the others in Jill's kitchen, Nick and Ben had returned and everyone was laughing at something Rich had said.

"You did not," said Georgia in response to something Rich had said.

"So help me, I did," said Rich.

"Tell him, Rich. Tell Gerard what you done did when you was in college," said Ben trying to control his laughter.

"Yeah, Rich, tell me what you done did," said Gerard mocking Ben.

"Okay, okay. When I had to do senior juries as an undergrad, I did a transcription arrangement of 'I Am the Walrus', you know, by the Beatles." Rich got up and leaned against the counter next to Georgia.

"I conducted it and included people reciting Shakespeare and also had a chorus of people dressed as eggs." He was starting to sweat standing this close to Georgia.

"That never get old," said Ben laughing. "What else you do, man? You be one funny tight ass...I swear, Gerard. He be funnier than you in a skirt wrestlin' with them bagpipes."

Jill broke up the party by saying it was time to get in some practice before the show later in the evening.

~

Mountain Mama's Restaurant was packed once again for the second night of music for charity. The whole family was on hand, as usual, except for Mark. He had headed back to his and Nancy's home to try to find some clue as to her whereabouts.

Nana was working the audience with great finesse that only Nana could pull off.

Each table had an assortment of fresh baked breads with homemade jams, compliments of aunt Gladys. The menu for the night only included appetizers such as mini egg rolls, pepperoni corn muffins, fried pickles, cheese, and vegetables, just to name a few.

"There they is again," said Ben. He was talking to Jill as he was eating most of the plate of appetizers on a platter in the middle of the table.

"Yeah, I see them. It is weird, you know?" Jill was picking at the same food platter. They were both watching Margaret and Mamie in a huddle together and seeming to be in a suspicious conversation once again.

"I wonder what they could be up to. I've got to go. Things are getting ready to start up." Jill quickly left the table and Ben helped himself to the rest of the platter.

Just as Jim was introducing another night of family and friends, Gerard staggered up to the table and plopped into a chair next to Ben.

"Whoa, man. You reeks o' hooch!" Ben stood up to help Gerard sit a little straighter in the chair. He called to Darlene for another plate of appetizers and some coffee. When it was served, Gerard snarled at Ben.

"Get that shit away from me! I won't tell you again!"

Ben had had enough. He stood up and motioned to Rod who was nearby to help him get Gerard out of there. Together they carried him upstairs and put him in a bed. He was out almost as soon as his head hit the pillow.

"I has to go on next," said Ben. "Can you stay with him until I be done?"

"Sure thing, Ben," said Rod. "Knock 'em dead out there. I'll stay here until you get back."

Ben took off at a jog pulling his harmonica out of his pocket. Rod settled down in the living room to stand guard over Gerard.

No sooner than Ben had shut the door than Mamie entered. "Just a quick word, Rod, and I have to get back." She said in a loud whisper.

"You don't have to worry, Gerard is out cold," Rod replied.

"You know what today is, don't you?" Mamie had a reverent look on her face.

"Of course, how could you even think I would forget?" Rod stood, rubbing the back of his neck as he did so. "It is significant in both our lives."

"It changed our lives forever, and linked us together forever," said Mamie with tears in her eyes. 'Neither one of us will ever forget him. It's been four years, but it seems like yesterday."

Rod hugged Mamie tight with tears running down his face as well. "One day I hope to learn of the person who set everything in motion that day. The one who kept me from a life of hell, but in the same instance, caused a life of hell for you."

Mamie brushed the tears from her face and did not meet Rod's eyes. "How about I babysit Gerard while you head on down to do your set?"

"Thanks, Mamie. I owe you once again," said Rod. "He is getting worse. This thing over the age difference with Brenda has him sulking all day as well as drinking all night. He practically passed out when he hit the bed."

"Really sad," she replied. "Now get on down stairs, and raise the roof with that accordion of yours."

Rod gave her a kiss on the cheek and left while Mamie sat in the chair with her head in her hands.

Rod got to the stage right when Ben finished his set. He grabbed his accordion and made it on just as Jim was announcing him. He immediately went into 'In Heaven There is No Beer', followed by 'Beer Barrel Polka'.

As he finished, Josie ran up and gave him a kiss on the cheek. She led him off the stage and into a seat at a reserved table.

Brenda and Bonnie were up next singing some Golden Oldies followed by Andrew playing the guitar and singing 'When You're Hot, You're Hot.' That got a surprisingly loud reaction from the crowd along with several 'Bams'.

Aunt Gladys, Uncle Frank, and cousin, Jean, sang some country songs. Aunt Shirley sang 'How Great Thou Art' accompanied by Nick. Nick and Jill did 'Love Lift Us Up Where We Belong' and 'I Got You Babe'.

Anika and Matt mended fences long enough to sing Pink's 'Just give Me a Reason' and 'Summer Nights' from Grease. Nick accompanied them as did Jill and Josie. They also did a couple of fiddle/violin songs.

But the highlight of the evening was the entertainment by Rich and Georgia. While Rich played, Georgia sang Peggy Lee's 'Fever' and the Pointer Sister's 'I'm So Excited', then Rich surprised everyone, including Georgia, by playing and singing 'Georgia On My Mind'. No one knew Rich could sing.

After the song was over and the Dennison's were taking the stage for the final set as a family, Rich grabbed Georgia's hand and led her quickly from the room. He all but ran out the back door onto the large deck.

"Georgia, I know I must seem to be an old man to you. I am fifteen years your senior, but I feel as young as you. You make me feel young and last night...I have never done anything like that before, just so you know." The words rushed from Rich before he could help it.

Georgia just stared at him. Then very slowly, so slowly Rich broke out into a sweat again, she took his hand and placed it on her breast. She leaned in and kissed him deeply, running her foot up his inner thigh.

He took her lead and ran his hand under her shirt where he could feel her body longing for his touch. They sank down on one of the padded lounge chairs and once again, while everyone else was occupied with the music, Rich made love to Georgia. No heated rush this time. Just sweetness and passion and when it was over, he cradled her to him like she was the most precious thing in his whole world.

Marianne Waddill Wieland

Sixteen

The next morning was filled with mixed emotions. Rod had the jet all ready to fly Rich and Georgia back to New York City. Gerard, Ben, Bonnie and Mamie were there as well. After the stop in New York, Rod was flying the others to Chicago. Ben, Bonnie, and Gerard to return home and Mamie for business she had there. Brenda, Nick, and Jill were there to see them off.

Brenda took Gerard to the side and spoke to him in a soft voice. She could tell he was hung over from last night's ordeal.

"Gerard, I'm sorry you feel the way you do about our age difference," said Brenda. "I don't even notice it most of the time except when you are acting like a five -year old." She had been trying to inject humor into the situation but was failing miserably.

"My mind is made up, Brenda. I can't deal with the drama," said Gerard as he rubbed his head. "If you have any sense at all, you will warn your sister off the good doctor before it is too late."

"My sisters and I stay out of each other's business." Brenda put her hand on Gerard's shoulder and he jerked away like he had been burned.

"Sorry for touching you," she said in an aggravated tone of voice. "I'll make sure it doesn't happen again."

She backed away from Gerard noting he had trouble meeting her gaze. She gave Ben a hug. "Don't be a stranger, you hear," she said as she wiped the tears from her eyes.

"Miss Brenda," said Ben. "You know he don't know what he be sayin' half the time. He be wasted by ten o'clock almost every day. You be better off 'til he get his head out his ass."

"Thanks, Ben," she said. "Take care of him. He needs some help."

Ben gave her a mock salute and turned his attention to what Rod was saying to those getting ready to leave on the jet.

Brenda gave her sister and Rich big hugs and put her hand on Rich's shoulder as he was trying to mount the steps into the plane.

"If you hurt my sister over this 'age difference' crap that Gerard has started, I will hunt you down like the dog you are and have you neutered. I have a friend that is a vet. Don't think for a minute I won't do it."

"Lay off, Brenda. I'm not about to let this one get away. He can run, but he can't hide." Georgia winked at Rich and pulled him close for a kiss.

The final hugs were given and last goodbyes said. Those staying behind backed away from the airstrip near the Grand Wallace Resort currently under construction by Nick and his crew. The noise was deafening as Rod started the engines in the jet and started to taxi to the spot where he would be cleared for takeoff. Brenda noticed that Mamie was seated in the front with Rod and wearing the headgear of a co-pilot.

"Has anyone else noticed that Mamie and Rod seem to have something going on?" Brenda was covering her ears even as she was trying to hear the others response.

Nick, who also had his hands over his ears, tried to answer. "We've been seeing Mamie with her head together with my mother most every day now for some time."

"I have noticed that as well," said Jill. "Now that you mention it, Mamie and Rod do turn up together at times and he has just recently started flying her to her secret meetings that she says are for the school."

"I'm over that excuse," said Brenda as they returned to their vehicles. "I have tried to broach the subject but she either changes it or ignores me altogether."

"Anika got a 'none of your business' crack when she said something to Mamie about how often Xander was at Brenda's," said Nick as he started the engine. "Something is definitely going on and seems to be a big secret."

Brenda, who was sitting in the backseat of Nick's Hummer, leaned up to the front and addressed Nick. "You seem to have mended fences with your mom, Nick."

"Actually, it has been going very well. I have been working with her on her piano skills. She is very talented and wants to get more flexible in her fingers," answered Nick. "She still has problems relating to almost everyone except Nana, but she seems to be trying more since the doctor changed her medication to what she is currently taking. Dad says things are much better than they had been. She paces less and Nana is able to go home at a decent hour most nights."

"Nana has been a real trouper," said Jill. "It has been as much a benefit to her as it has been to Margaret. She has come back to life. Especially being the only one who really could help with the situation. And the problem's she was having with the Alzheimer's have been greatly reduced. Then the magnificent job she does at Mountain Mama's working the dining room...she is better than ever."

They were pulling up at the restaurant when they saw Anika come running out of the front door followed by Matt. Nick jerked the Hummer to a stop and was out the door before Jill could stop him.

Anika was sobbing and Matt was trying to console her. She turned around and slugged Matt in the shoulder and took off running down the sidewalk toward her home.

"Nick! Wait!" Jill was getting out of the hummer to catch Nick before he got to Matt. "I've got this. You stay here with Matt. I will take care of Anika." She went jogging down the sidewalk to catch up to Anika.

Brenda came along side Nick as he was starting to question Matt. She put her hand on Matt's shoulder.

"Twerp! What did you do to her?"

"Knock it off, Brenda," said Nick.

"Matt, you know I love you, but I love my daughter as well. I know she can be headstrong and dramatic, but I suspect something you said or did is driving this." Nick was trying hard to reign it in.

"I felt I had to be honest with her," said Matt almost apologetically. "The prom is coming up and I have asked someone else. We haven't been getting along all that well and I didn't want to precipitate a worse scenario if she finds out from someone else."

"Okay. Out with it," said Brenda. "Who, might I ask, are you taking?"

"I've asked Ginger, you know, I used to go out with her a little," said Matt looking at the ground.

"Are you insane?" Brenda started grabbing for Matt's wallet. "Give me that genius card you wear like a badge, give it to me right now!"

Nick stepped between the two. "Matt, she would not be mine and Jill's first choice for you but having been in your shoes once, there is no doubt in my mind why you asked her."

"Why do you all have to get in the middle of this," Matt was ready to bolt. "It is my business and I was just trying to give Anika a 'heads up' before someone else told her. That would be cruel."

"I am one of the chaperones," said Brenda smugly. "Just remember, I've got my eye on you." Brenda quickly turned and went into the restaurant brushing Matt's shoulder in an angry gesture as she did so.

"Unreal," said Matt watching Brenda's departure.

"What do you mean?" Nick was scratching his head and watching Brenda's departure as well.

"It's unreal how great she is as a teacher in the classroom, but in her personal life she can be a real … well … ass!"

Nick laughed because he and Jill had had this discussion often and how she and Gerard must be soulmates.

~

Gerard sat in his office looking out the window at Chicago in early summer. It had been several weeks since he had spoken to Brenda. He had thought she might call, but there had been no word. Then he had not called her either.

It was ten in the morning and he'd been through almost a whole bottle of rum. But he could handle it. Ben didn't think so. He lectured Gerard and prayed for him and basically was a huge pain in the ass. But Gerard loved him like a brother anyway. Secretly, almost a secret to himself as well, he loved that another person cared enough about his welfare to make his life miserable, and be relentless about it.

He knew his family was worried too. He had it all under control. He never did follow up with a heart specialist but he did not think that was a problem.

He missed Brenda. His feelings were stronger, not weaker as he'd hoped. He knew that she was getting ready to chaperone Matt's prom in a couple of days. He knew because Anika had been burning up his phone getting his opinion on the dresses she was trying to choose from for the event.

The lead singer in a local goth band had asked her to the prom and Gerard suspected she was going just to make Matt jealous. So, he had done what any good uncle would do in this case. He picked out the ugliest dress that covered the most skin and told her that was the one that would drive 'Spike' crazy. Maybe he should rethink that.

The door flew open and Ben filled the doorway like no one else could.

"I knows you been at the hooch, Gerard, but yo' girl out here say that you be missin' that board meetin' you was so fired up to be at."

"I'm fired up, but not about that. I have to see Brenda. Screw the age difference! I have to see her." Gerard stood up and nearly fell over. Ben got to him and sat him back down in the chair.

"You better sober up befo' you tries to do somethin', man," said an aggravated Ben.

"Lottie!" Ben yelled for Gerard's executive assistant. "Can you gets him some strong coffee? A whole pot. He be plum drunk again."

Lottie came in with the coffee and some donuts. Gerard's eyes were rolling back in his head. Ben added sugar and milk to the coffee and spooned some in Gerard's mouth like he had been doing every morning for the last six weeks at least.

"Come on, man, be a good little rich boy and drink this fo' Uncle Ben."

Ben continued to spoon the coffee in. Soon Gerard held his head up straighter. This had become a routine every morning. Gerard started to hold the cup and drink on his own. Eventually he ate a donut. Then another. Then Ben helped him to the bathroom so he could throw up.

"This be gettin' old, man. Same thing every mornin'. Drink the hooch. Can't stand up for yo' self. Spoon in coffee. Eat donuts. Throw up."

Ben was on a roll. Lottie was standing by just in case it took both of them, which on occasion, it did.

"When you be wisin' up, man?"

"Right about now," said Gerard. "I can't keep doing this. I think I have developed an ulcer."

He ate another donut and went to the bathroom to wash his face. "Lottie, get us a plane to Charleston and a rental car. I will be gone for a while. You know who to notify and how to hold down the fort while I am gone."

Ben and Lottie just looked at each other.

"What he be thinkin' now?" Ben just shook his head and went in search of their travel gear.

Seventeen

Brenda was in her classroom explaining the exam process to her students when she saw Gerard looking through the window.

"Quick! Everyone! See that man looking through the window?" Brenda could tell that he couldn't see inside, hence, the pressing of his face into the glass. "Extend your middle finger and give our guest an official Beaumont High welcome."

Thirty- five students did as they were told. Some very apprehensive in the process. Brenda turned the lights out so that Gerard could see the big 'welcome' he was being given.

Brenda could tell the exact moment that Gerard saw he was being given the 'bird' by all the students. His lower jaw dropped and he took a step backwards. Brenda decided to go one better and she turned her back to the window, lifted the skirt portion of her sundress, and having on a thong, mooned Gerard.

She heard the collective gasp from her students about the same time she realized she had crossed the line. She had never done that in her entire teaching career. She would so do that in her personal life, but she had worked hard to keep 'personal' and 'professional' life separate. This would get back to the school board. She could apologize to the students and she could ask them not to tell, but that would be worse than what she had just done.

"I am so sorry you all had to witness that total lack of professionalism." Brenda straightened her skirt and faced her class.

"I think I have explained the rules to next week's exam thoroughly and with clarity. If you have any questions, please refer to these handouts."

She proceeded to pass out the papers in a dignified manner and when she was finished, faced the classroom once again. She noticed Gerard was no longer at the window.

"Class, I wish you the best of luck on the exam and I suggest you use this weekend to study hard. I feel certain that, come next week, I will not be the one issuing it. I know you have the prom tomorrow night, but remember, especially you seniors. Don't ruin the chance of a real future for a piece of ass."

Brenda held her head high, gave a short nod to the room full of shocked students, and softly closed the door behind her as she left the room. She walked at a moderate pace all the way to the other side of the school straight to Mamie Gray's office. She figured she had better put her 'big girl panties' on and confess before Mamie heard the version that was sure to circulate throughout the school by the time the next period started.

~

Gerard stood by the rental car, next to Ben, who was looking at him and scratching his head.

"What be wrong wit you, man?" Ben kept looking from Gerard to the school. "You be lucky she ain't call the cops on yo' self. Lookin' in the school window like that. Did she see you lookin' in, man?"

"Yep." Gerard looked at Ben and then started to laugh. He was laughing so hard he doubled over with his hands on his knees.

"What you be seein' in there. What she do, man?"

Gerard told Ben what had happened between more peals of laughter until Ben heard the whole story. Ben was laughing by the end of the tale so hard he was pounding his fist on the hood of the rental car making a small dent.

Both men stopped laughing as they saw Brenda and Mamie exit the building and head in their direction.

"Awww…man… Gerard!" Ben started to shuffle around nervously. "Look what you done did. We be in fo' it now. She done gone an' got Miss Mamie. She be bringin' out the big guns! We be goin' down now fo' sho'!"

"Shut up Ben," said Gerard in his irritated way. "I got this."

He stood up straight and tugged a little on his tie like he was fixing his appearance for a job interview. Which, in his mind, it just might be. He was hoping to convince Brenda to let him escort her to the prom tomorrow night as a co-chaperone. Ben was sweating and wringing his hands.

"Ladies," said Gerard with a smirk on his face.

"Asshole," said Brenda with a smirk of equal arrogance on her face. Her comment was directed only at Gerard causing Ben to relax a little.

"Brenda!" Mamie snapped and put her hands on her hips staring down both Gerard and Ben. "I cannot tell you how ashamed I am at the three of you."

"Now, wait a minute," said Ben. "I be mindin' my own biz'ness . How I know Gerard gonna make Miss Brenda…"

"I would just shut my mouth right now, Ben, if I were you." Mamie took a step toward him and pointed her finger at Ben's chest. "Guilt by association. You are with him. Isn't it your job to keep him out of trouble?"

Ben dropped his head and stared at is feet. "Yes'm. It be my job."

"It is my job," corrected Mamie.

"Yo' job?" Ben was confused. "How it be yo' job?"

Mamie started to respond and then shook her head. She noticed Brenda and Gerard were shooting daggers at each other with their eyes.

"So, what have the two of you got to say for yourselves," asked Mamie in as calm a voice as she could.

"Yeah," said Brenda with a cocky little flip of her shoulder. "What have you got to say for yourself, slick?"

Gerard was aghast. "My…myself? What have I got to say for myself?" He started to gesture toward the school windows.

"I was just looking in the window to see if you were even in class and received a whole flock of 'birds' and a pretty moon looking back at me. Not what I expected."

"Not what you expected?" Brenda stepped forward and Ben jumped out of the way. "What did you think you would see? You have treated me like shit for over two months and you thought you would see me welcome you with open arms? What was I supposed to say to the class?"

"Well, after what you did, I hope it was something like 'Hey class. Excuse me. I'm a moron.'" Gerard was imitating Brenda.

Ben made to get in the middle of what was turning into a very nasty fight, but Mamie stared him down. He turned and went to stand by the car.

"Now, I have a pretty good tolerance level for immaturity, but I have had about enough of you two."

Mamie put a hand on Brenda's shoulder and on Gerard's arm. "The truce starts now."

"What do you mean by that crack?" Gerard said this to the heavens.

"Brenda," said Mamie. "You have to know this is going to get to the school board as soon as Monday. It will be out of my hands when it does. In the meantime, you are to still chaperone the prom tomorrow night. And Gerard will be your date."

"Now hold on, sister," said Gerard holding out his hands and backing up.

"Ohhh...Gerard...you done done it now, man," said Ben with a worried look at Mamie.

Mamie stepped toward Ben. "And you will be my date." She said this with a finality that neither of the three dared argue with. Then she stalked away.

"Lawd, Lawd!" Ben started to pace. "That jest goes to show you what my granny said be true. 'If you can't stay outta sumbody elses biz'ness, yo' sure get into biz'ness.' Now we gots to go to a high school prom. Gerard, what you go an' do that fo' anyhow?"

Gerard ignored Ben and put both hands on Brenda's shoulders. "Brenda. I just wanted to apologize to you for the way I treated you back in the spring. I have so many hang-ups and twisted thoughts going through my head, I took a lot out on you. You are young, but in so many ways, much wiser than I."

Brenda stared back at him. "You know you have probably cost me my job." She hesitated. Took a deep breath.

"Let me re-phrase that. I made the poor choice to react in a childish manner to your looking into my classroom window. And I made the conscious choice to involve my students in the game, as well as expose myself to the public. I am sorry too."

"Where do we go from here?" Gerard ran his finger down Brenda's cheek.

Brenda shut her eyes and leaned into Gerard's touch. "We go to the prom tomorrow night."

"How long we gotta be in these monkey suits, man!" Ben was complaining before they even got out of the door.

"Let's just say it's going to be a long night," said Gerard as he headed out to Nick's Hummer. They would be using it for the night. "Did you see Anika leave? I wanted to see the guy escorting her to the prom."

"Nana said she be gettin' ready at her friend's house and I don't like it, man." Ben kept tugging on his bow tie.

Gerard stood still for a few minutes then shrugged his shoulders. "Nothing we can do about it now." He reached inside his jacket and checked to make sure he had everything he needed. He had three flasks of alcohol. The best moonshine in the county.

Ben started to say something, but changed his mind. "We be needin' to git on down the road. Last thang I wanna do is piss off Miss Mamie."

The two of them climbed into Nick's Hummer and started down the road. Ben had Mamie's address and Gerard programmed it into the GPS. Brenda lived a little farther outside of town, so she was going to drive herself to the school. When they pulled up to Mamie's house, Gerard issued a long whistle.

"Would you look at that!" Gerard opened the door and jumped out. "How much money does a high school principal make?" The house was two stories, natural stone, with split log exterior. Beautifully landscaped with a pool and what appeared to be a tennis and basketball court in the back.

"Do she live wit her folks?" Ben had gotten out as well and the two started up the muted lantern sidewalk.

"I don't think so." Gerard pulled out a flask and took a long drink. He wiped his mouth on his sleeve. "Let's do this."

The door opened before they had a chance to knock. Xander came running out and hugged Ben around the waist.

"I've been waiting all day to see you, Ben. When are you going to take me fishing like you promised?"

"Soon, little man, soon," said Ben picking Xander up.

Mamie came out locking the door behind her. She turned around and sized up the two men before her.

"Well, well, well," she said. "You two clean up quite nicely. I wasn't sure what you would turn up looking like."

Gerard was looking Mamie up and down. "May I be the first to say how stunning you look."

She had on a floor length strapless gown of pink lace. Her hair was in ringlets on top of her head and she had a hair piece of silk roses pinned to one side.

Ben was having a hard time looking her in the eye. "Uh...what he say, Miss Mamie."

She just shook her head and all three climbed into the Hummer and left to meet Brenda who was probably already at the school waiting for them.

Eighteen

When the threesome arrived at the prom, only a few people were there, and as they figured Brenda was one of them. Being chaperones, they needed to be on top of everything that was going on and know where every child was at all times. Ben's presence alone would keep a lot of trouble makers from starting anything.

Gerard was having a hard time keeping his eyes off Brenda. She was wearing a short, silver sequined dress with red spiked heels, blood red lips, and continuing the red theme, red nails. Damn! She was hot! That definitely called for a shot of Bam McGee's moonshine. He took three swigs and saw Ben's face.

"What?" Gerard put the flask away and continued his thorough inspection of Brenda's attributes.

Ben just shook his head, as he did all too often these days at Gerard, then returned his attention to Mamie. She was having a difficult time answering questions of students and staff as to Brenda's behavior at school yesterday.

She had confided in him earlier that maybe it was not such a smart idea for Brenda to have attended the prom. It seemed to have spiked quite the rumor mill. Unfortunately, most of it was true. Ben noted that Brenda, resilient as ever, held her head high and ignored the less than complimentary stares.

"I did not do it to piss you off!" Anika was almost jogging to get away from Matt who was hot on her heels.

"I think everything you have done lately has been to piss me off. Why don't you just grow up and admit it!"

Matt grabbed her arm as she stopped abruptly and turned on him. She nearly knocked Gerard over as she did so.

"I tried out to be a cheerleader because I wanted an extra- curricular activity that wasn't a musical activity, if you must know," said Anika in a loud voice.

"Like hell, you did!" Matt was red in the face. "You are willing to let your music suffer just to make a point. And who is that...that...person you came here with? No wonder you dressed at your friend's house. Nick would never have let you leave the house with that guy or looking like a hooker."

Anika drew her hand back to slug Matt, but Ben caught her before she could make contact.

"Hold on there, Miss Anika," said Ben. "Matt, he got's a point. You be lookin' like you be standin' out front advertisin' fo' some cat house."

They all looked at Anika. She had managed to stay out of site for most of the evening so far. She was dressed in a very short spandex, black dress, five- inch black spike heels, black nails and dark gray eye makeup, bright red lips, and safety pins through her ear lobes.

Gerard didn't say it, but he was pretty sure she had no underwear on. "Okay, this has gone far enough. Anika, I am taking you home to change or calling Jill to bring you some proper clothing."

"I don't think so, Uncle." She emphasized 'Uncle'. "For one, you are almost drunk as a skunk or will be soon and for another, Dad is working on the piano with grandmother. Every. Single. Night."

"So, this is a way to get back at Matt and your dad?" Brenda had been quiet up until this time.

"Oh, don't you even say anything to me, *Miss Montgomery!*" Anika squared off at Brenda.

Mamie had been observing up until now. She took a step between Brenda and Anika. She turned to address the group as a whole.

"Matt, you did not come to the prom with Anika. I would suggest you keep your thoughts to yourself." Mamie put her arm around Matt's shoulders and guided him away from the group.

"And as far as looking like a hooker? Take a good look at your date." Mamie turned Matt in the direction of Ginger, who was falling all over one of the band members.

"Excuse me," said Matt. He nodded to the group and stalked away toward Ginger.

Mamie turned her attention toward Anika who had a smug look on her face. It turned into a stare down until finally, Anika broke eye contact first.

"You, young lady," said Mamie. "I am very disappointed in your behavior tonight. There is nothing wrong with trying out and making the cheerleading squad, but not at the expense of your studies. Or to 'get back' at someone."

Anika had the good grace to look chastised. "I am sorry Mrs. Gray. I had better get back to my date before he finds someone not dressed like a clown. I guess I was trying to get Matt's attention and I know I look ridiculous. I might just call it an evening."

Gerard winked at Brenda. "Mamie, how about if Brenda and I bug out too and take Anika home? We seem to be creating quite a stir in the midst of all these young men and women."

"We be ridin' together," said Ben. "How bout we all leave?" Ben was still tugging at his collar.

"Not a chance," said Mamie. "You will be staying here to finish this night out just as was intended."

"Lawd, Miss Mamie," whined Ben. "You be killin' me. I gots to get outta dis fancy suit."

Mamie addressed Gerard and Brenda. "That might be best for all concerned. Take Anika home and I suggest that Brenda, you drive."

Mamie addressed Gerard. "You need to cut out the drinking. Take Brenda's car and Ben can drive the hummer." She looked at Ben. "You drive, right?"

"Yes'm," was all Ben said.

Matt was coming across the school yard again heading toward Anika. He stopped just short.

"Good. Someone has the good sense to get you out of here before the male population starts offering you money for sex." Matt all but stomped his foot after the statement.

He looked from Brenda to Gerard. "Let me be the first to thank you on behalf of the male population." He grabbed Gerard's hand and shook it, then turned on his heel and marched back into the school.

Brenda, Mamie and Anika stood there with their mouths hanging open. Gerard had his hands both in fists at his side. Ben just shook his head.

Anika looked at Gerard. "Get me a bat!"

"We'll make it look like an accident." Gerard said in an angry voice.

"I did not hear that." Mamie grabbed Ben by the hand and lead him back into the school.

"Okay, then," said Brenda. "On that note, let's just get the hell out of here."

She proceeded to get in the car as Gerard opened the back door for Anika. Brenda could see that Anika had tears ready to fall from her eyes.

"Baby, girl. You know he didn't mean it."

"Right now, I hate him." Anika put her face in her hands and sobbed.

Gerard looked at Brenda with a helpless look on his face. Brenda just shook her head slightly and pointed to Gerard's pocket. He pulled out one of the flasks and handed it to her. They looked at each other and started to drink. Clearly, Brenda was having a hard time getting the moonshine down. But she hung in there as Anika continued to cry.

Soon, Gerard started Brenda's car, and they left the school grounds. Both noticed at the same time that the flasks were empty. Brenda started to giggle causing Anika to look up.

Her sobs had turned into quiet sniffles. "Are you both drunk?"

"Now, sweetie, Gerard and I can handle a few snorts. We are both adults and we will have you home in a few minutes."

Brenda fished around in her purse and pulled out her red lipstick. She began to look in the visor mirror trying to put it on while Gerard was driving on a bumpy road. She had it all over her cheeks and chin.

Gerard looked at Brenda and started laughing. Then Brenda started laughing. Anika looked scared.

"Uncle Gerard," said Anika. "How about you just drop me off here? I can walk the rest of the way." She had her hand on the door handle.

"Nonsense, Sweetie," said Gerard in a slurred voice. "I want to make sure you get home safely. Now buckle up, buttercup!"

Brenda turned the radio up very loudly and started trying to sing with it. She was way off key, but obviously didn't care. She stuck her head out of the window and yelled as loud as she could, obscenities about Matt and the school board. Gerard started in on the singing and tapping the brakes in time with the music.

"Please, Uncle Gerard," cried Anika who was on the verge of panic. "Let me out here. See? There is my house and Dad is in the yard." They were two blocks from her home.

Gerard pulled to the side of the road and let Anika get out. "This is a good idea, Sweetie. I don't want your uptight father to lecture us right now. You get on home then and I will see you in the morning."

Anika was barely out of the car when Gerard squealed tires pulling back out on to the road. All she could do was stare after him. Then she saw Nick try to flag Gerard down and she took her heels off and ran to her front yard.

Nick took one look at her. He was speechless. Jill came out of the house and slowed her walk upon seeing Anika.

"Anika," she said. "What is with this new look? Are you planning on modeling the new fall 'Halloween' look?"

Nick stomped over to where Anika was standing holding her spiked heels in her hand, mascara running down her face, and runs in her panty hose. He looked her up and down.

"Halloween? Is that what you call it? I'd call it the 'main street harlot' look myself," said Nick a little too brusque.

Anika looked from Nick to Jill and burst into tears again. "Uncle..Gerard..Brenda...very ...drunk..." She could not get anymore out.

Jill put her arms around Anika and let her cry it out until she finally lapsed into quiet sniffles again.

"How about we all go into the kitchen for some hot chocolate and have a discussion about what happened at the prom."

Anika just nodded her head and the three of them slowly walked into the house.

Nineteen

Gerard was driving very fast down poorly maintained mountain roads. Brenda was hanging out the window with her back resting where the window rolls down. Her arms were outstretched and she had exposed her bare breasts to the night air. She was screaming at the top of her lungs each vowel sound, over and over.

"Brenda, give it a rest!" Gerard was trying to get Brenda to hear him but without much success. He started pulling at her legs causing one of her shoes to fly out his window. He started to laugh and the car swerved violently.

This got Brenda's attention and she pulled herself back into the interior of the car. Gerard mimed Brenda's shoe flying out the window. Brenda started to laugh as well and took her other shoe off, throwing it out Gerard's window, hitting him in the eye with the heel.

"Damn it, Brenda!" Gerard was rubbing is eye. "You could have put my eye out! Have you no shame, woman?" He looked sideways at Brenda who was marking her bare breasts with her lipstick to look like two eyes.

"No. I guess you don't". Gerard began to laugh all over again and the car was swerving dangerously over the pot hole filled road.

Gerard was laughing so hard, the car ran into the ditch. They were both doubled over laughing. Laughing so hard they had tears running down their faces.

"I guess you had better get out and push," said Gerard to Brenda between fits of laughter.

"Me? You asshole! How am I going to push us out of the ditch?" Brenda was putting her arms back into the sleeves of her dress, getting lipstick all over the fabric.

"At least get out and see if we are stuck," whined Gerard.

"Oh, okay, you wuss." Brenda stomped out of the car. When she reached the back end, she stepped knee-deep in muddy water. She started to curse and then doubled over in laughter again.

"Brenda!" Gerard was looking out the window now. "What does it look like?"

"Baby, you need to see this for yourself," yelled Brenda trying to coax Gerard out of the car. She clapped her hands when she saw him open the car door.

Gerard stepped out of the car and sunk to his knees in the muddy water just like Brenda.

"Damn it, Brenda! Holy shit!" Gerard was trying to pull his feet out of the mud without any luck. He looked to the rear of the car and saw Brenda in much the same predicament as himself. He started to laugh as hard as Brenda.

Slowly they each made their way out of the mud, with Brenda falling face first into it. Gerard got to her, but lost his shoes in the process. He helped Brenda back to her feet and back on solid ground. They sat there staring at the car.

"You know," said Gerard. "The car itself doesn't look stuck. Just part of that back tire." He was pointing in the direction he wanted Brenda to look.

"You know, you could be right. The car has front wheel drive and I think if you push, I can drive us back onto the road." Brenda got to her feet and tried to brush the mud off her face.

Gerard looked at Brenda, covered from head to toe in black mud. He started to sing.

"Ol' man river, that ol' man river. You must know somethin', but don't say nothin'. Just keeps on rollin' just keeps on rollin' along..."

Brenda looked like she was going to hit him but instead, she started laughing. She pulled her dress off and left it on the bank by the mud. Gerard shed his jacket and gave Brenda his dress shirt to cover herself with. Brenda got in the driver's seat and Gerard positioned himself behind the car.

"Floor it, Brenda!" Gerard shoved the back of the car with his shoulder, but since he was still knee deep in the mud and drunk, he slipped as the car moved forward. He fell to the side and the back tire sprayed him with mud, covering the few areas that had not been previously mud covered.

Brenda had the car back on the road. She stopped and jumped out onto the road laughing so hard she fell to her knees.

"Ouch!" Brenda stood and tried to make her way toward Gerard. One knee was bleeding and when she noticed, she spread some mud on the area.

"And that fixes that," she said. Her gait was very unsteady but she made it to the edge of the ditch. When they saw each other, the laughter began all over again.

Finally, the laughter died down and they tried to figure out what to do next. Gerard sat up. Brenda lay down, half in the road, half on the muddy grass.

"What do we do now?" Gerard was wiping mud off his chest. He was sobering up more quickly than Brenda.

"Look, Gerard," she said. "I can swim across the field. I'm doing the backstroke."

Gerard started to laugh, then got to his feet. "Let's get in the car. We aren't far from your place, so let's go there and get cleaned up. I could use a nap." He hauled Brenda to her feet.

"Nap? It must be midnight." Brenda was scraping mud off her face. "We go to my place and take a shower together, and then both sleep in my bed, after you ravage my body, of course."

Gerard smiled and pulled Brenda to him. "Of course. I like the way you think." He helped Brenda into the passenger side of the car and went to the driver's side.

Brenda was leaning her head back with her eyes closed, but she was not asleep.

"Gerard, I don't have my seatbelt on. I can't find it." She sat up and turned toward Gerard. "I think I am drunk," she stated. "You will have to drive."

"I know that, gorgeous, that is why I am in the driver's seat." Gerard started to laugh at Brenda. "Your shirt, or rather, my shirt, is wide open. I can see everything you've got."

"Is that right?" Brenda looked at Gerard and made no move to cover herself. "Ain't nothin' you ain't seen before. Besides, your fly is open."

"Easy access, baby, easy access." Gerard laughed at Brenda.

"Well?" He gave Brenda a wink as he started the car and pulled away.

Brenda crawled over to Gerard and ran her nails over his mud- covered chest prompting a moan out of Gerard.

"I'm glad you like it, baby. There is more where that came from." Brenda proceeded to help herself to Gerard's body, like she had several times before.

Neither noticed that they were driving on the wrong side of the road. The car was swerving as Gerard worked to avoid the pot holes. Brenda's head was wedged between his abdomen and the steering wheel. Gerard was moaning loudly.

"Baby, you're the best." Gerard took one hand off the steering wheel to hold the back of Brenda's head just where he wanted it. "Oh, yes, yes…"

Gerard saw the deer leap out in front of the car just as he was trying to make the ninety- degree turn that would lead to Brenda's house. The car hit the deer and it bounced onto the hood and into the windshield. The car swerved off the road, down the short embankment, and smashed into a huge elm tree.

The front of the car folded like an accordion. The horn was blaring. Gerard could hear someone screaming. He couldn't move. He couldn't see. After a few minutes, he realized the screams were his own. It was so dark. He could feel Brenda still on his lap but she was no longer moving. His head was spinning and his hands were covered in a sticky substance. He raised his hand to his face and smelled the metallic smell that could only be blood.

He couldn't feel his feet. Brenda, was still not moving. So still. So sticky. The blood mixed with the mud that covered them both. Realization hit and he started to panic.

His heart began to race. He could feel the skipping beats and vaguely realized he had never seen the heart specialist. He was barely able to hold onto consciousness. He could feel himself slipping away. He felt his head. It was still there and had a gash across is forehead.

He had to get them out of the car. He could smell gas. He could feel his irregular heart continue to race. He couldn't see Brenda but he could feel that she was at an odd angle. She had not been that way earlier. He tried to feel for a pulse but couldn't find her arms and her head was so covered in a mushy, sticky substance that...

My God, he thought. Her skull must have cracked open and her brains were spilling out!

He tried to move as the panic continued to rise. He began to scream for help.

"Nooo! Brenda! Wake up, dammit! Wake up!" Brenda did not move.

"God, help us." He cried. Panic was overtaking him. His head began to spin. He tried to remain conscious but he felt the blackness closing in. He could feel death. He could no longer hang on. The blackness overtook him. And then nothing.

Twenty

It was eleven o'clock at night, yet Mountain Mama's restaurant was still brightly lit. Jill and Nick were busy making breakfast food for those who wanted to keep celebrating after the prom had ended. Josie and Lorraine were on hand setting up tables with condiments, silverware, and water glasses. Jill chose to do this every year as an alternative for those who wanted to stay away from the more 'popular' after parties.

Over the last couple of years, there had been more and more kids coming to this party than had been going to the beer parties or the cheap motels on the outskirts of the town. Nana and Margaret had left a couple of hours ago, saying they were way too old to horn in on the younger generations all night mischief. Andrew and Jim were rearranging some tables to fit the large groups that were expected.

The door opened, and Anika came into the room. She was dressed in jeans and a tee shirt. All of the make-up had been washed off her face and for all intents and purposes, she looked to be back to normal.

"Hey, Dad, Jill," she said nodding at each of them. "Thought I would come by and help instead of sitting at home licking my wounds. After all, I can't make someone want or love me that is determined not to do so. Did Uncle Gerard and Brenda stop by?"

"We haven't seen them and to be honest, I'm a little worried. I've been trying to call Brenda, but it just goes straight to voice mail. Same with Gerard," said Jill wiping her hands on her apron. "Brenda almost never has her messages go to voice mail unless she is teaching."

Jim's phone rang and he answered it at once. "Matt, son, I was getting worried." He paused and a look of great concern crossed his face causing the others to take notice. "Matt, could you repeat that? I'm putting you on speaker phone."

"Dad, I am on the side of the road, near the old grist mill, you know, on Rambling Road," said Matt in an urgent tone. "It looks like someone slid off the road into the ditch, but was able to pull themselves out without being permanently stuck. There are tire tracks like they were in a big hurry when they took off."

"Matt," said Lorraine in a worried tone. She took a deep breath before speaking again. "Do you see any signs of foul play or any items that might have been left behind?"

"Let me look around," said Matt. "I will call you right back."

The family just stood there looking at each other. Finally, Andrew spoke. "No reason to believe it has anything to do with Gerard and Brenda. They have level heads, well at least Brenda does, and so does Gerard when he isn't drinking."

"That's the problem, now isn't it?" Anika looked around the room.

She hadn't said anything to Nick and Jill about Brenda and Gerard being as drunk as they were. She had thought it would be better to down-play it, but now she wasn't so sure. She was getting ready to say something when the door opened again and Ben and Mamie came walking in.

"I gots to get outta dis monkey suit fo' it kills me," said Ben pulling off his bow tie and jacket while he was speaking.

"Gear up," said Mamie. "The troops will be showing up shortly. The band stopped playing an hour ago, and most of the kids are getting ready to head this way." She looked around at the faces staring at her.

"What?" Mamie quickly put down her purse and shawl. "Something is wrong, I can feel it."

"We are just waiting for Matt to call us back. He passed a place on Rambling Road where someone went in the ditch and we can't get in touch with either Gerard or Brenda," said Jill.

"We know they have better sense than to drive drunk," said Josie.

"Well, I don't know 'bout that Miss Josie," said Ben. "Gerard, he get a burr up his butt and he don't care what he do or who he do it with."

Anika raised her hand like she was in a classroom. All eyes turned toward her. "Gerard and Brenda were very drunk when they left me a couple of blocks from home earlier."

"Anika," said Nick urgently. "Why didn't you tell us?"

"I didn't want to get Brenda in any more trouble than she's already in," whined Anika.

"What trouble is she in?" Jill took off her apron and walked swiftly to Mamie. All eyes turned toward them.

"We had an incident yesterday at school when Gerard showed up and looked through the window at Brenda teaching her class." Mamie looked at each of the others and looked at Ben and Anika before continuing her story.

"Brenda had her class flip Gerard the bird and then she..." Mamie closed her eyes and took another deep breath. "Then she lifted her dress and mooned him."

"No," said Jill. "Please tell me she did not do that!"

Lorraine was aghast. "The school board...they will not take this lightly. She will probably lose her job."

"She was pretty drunk," said Anika.

Jim's phone rang again. "This is not good," said Matt. "I found what looks like Brenda's dress she was wearing at the prom. It was on the side of the road in the grass covered with mud. I backtracked a little and found one of her shoes in the road."

"Lawd, Lawd," said Ben. "She be runnin' 'round naked in the dark. Both of 'em be drunk as skunks."

"It looks like they left the area in the car. Maybe I will drive a little ways down the road in the direction it looks like they went," said Matt in a worried tone.

"Do that, son," said Jim. "But be careful. If they are still on the road, they could be dangerous. At least drive as far as Brenda's house. They probably won't go any farther than that."

"Okay, dad." Matt could be heard getting back into his car. "I will let you know what I find."

Andrew was rubbing his face with his hands. "I think we all need to pray. I have a bad feeling about this. Gerard has been sinking further and further down the rabbit hole. I am not sure he can crawl out this time."

The group formed a circle and held hands. Andrew led them in prayer and each, in turn, added to the prayer. They were still praying when Jim's phone rang again.

The circle broke but most still held hands. "Matt!" This was all Jim could get out before Matt interrupted.

"Dad." Matt was trying to hold it together. "It is bad. I have called 911. Brenda's car is wrapped around a tree on Rambling Road at the sharp turn."

Jim was visibly upset. "Son, stay where you are to flag the emergency vehicles. Your mom and Josie will be right there and Andrew and I right behind."

Josie grabbed the phone and put it on speaker while she grabbed a large duffel bag from under the counter. Lorraine was running from the room and up the stairs as fast as she could.

"Josie," she yelled over her shoulder. "You take off with the guys and I will have Nick bring me. I am going to collect some blankets and other supplies." She disappeared out of sight.

"Oh, Lawd! I be so sorry!" Ben was pacing and running his hands over his head. "I be the one that 'sposed to keep him outta trouble."

"No, Ben," said Mamie as she touched his arm. "You wanted to go and I stopped you. It's all my fault."

Anika wailed. "If I hadn't acted an ass, none of this would have happened."

Josie rounded on them all while Nick and Jill looked on in shock. "No one is to blame but Brenda and Gerard. Now all of you, shut up while I help Matt assess the situation." She was looking through the bag while she was talking.

Nick stepped out to help Josie carry the duffel bag. Andrew grabbed it from him while Jim grabbed large spot lights and headed to the door.

"I don't understand what is happening here," said Nick looking at Jill.

"Nick," she replied "Josie and mom are going to get to the scene to help and dad is a First Responder."

"How in Heaven's name are your mom and Josie going to help?" Nick was almost angry as Anika was becoming hysterical. Mamie went to her to try to calm her down.

Jill looked at him like he had three heads and was getting angry herself. "Why the hell wouldn't they help, Nick? Josie is a Paramedic and Mom is a critical care nurse."

"What?" Nick yelled. "Whenever did that happen? We've been married for five months and this is the first I have heard of that. They work here at the restaurant."

"If it make you feel any better," said Ben, "I never heard dat either."

Nick looked around at Ben. "No. It does not make me feel any better. Jill…"

"Nick, I guess it just never came up," said Jill as she faced Nick with her hands on her hips. "Josie only works part time and mom only works now on an as needed basis. But she does handle the school records for immunizations. Most of the time they are here and neither one talks about their work."

Lorraine ran past Nick. "Come on, Nick." She grabbed his arm and pulled him along. "Time could mean lives."

Twenty-One

Matt made his way carefully down to the site of the wreak. He could hear voices so he knew his family was close. He could smell gas so he knew time was of the essence. He looked in the window, or what was left of it, and what he saw turned his stomach.

He walked a few paces away and would have thrown up if there had been anything in his stomach. After the bout passed, he went back to the site to find his father and Andrew setting up spot lights and carrying other equipment.

"Matt," yelled Jim. "Are they alive?"

"I was just getting ready to check when…when…I will check now." Matt felt for Gerard's pulse in his neck, the closest thing he could reach.

"I feel a weak pulse in Gerard. Brenda is a little harder to reach, but I don't have a lot of hope." His voice broke as he was speaking. He grabbed his stomach and gagged again just as Josie arrived at the scene.

"Get the hell out of the way!" She pushed Matt and he fell to his knees still gagging.

"Dad!" Josie was on the side of the car closest to Brenda. "Oh, God!" She was pulling on the door and Andrew was aiming a spot on the scene.

"My son," he wept. "My poor son! What has he done. Brenda…she can't be alive." He dropped the spot light and buried his face in his hands and dropped to his knees. "Oh, precious Lord and Savior! Please let them live! Please" He dissolved into sobs.

"Dad, help me!" Josie got the back door open and climbed in to try to feel for a pulse on Brenda, but her body was at such an angle that she could not find a spot that she could check.

"Brenda...I can't tell. So much blood! Throw me some blankets. Matt! Get Andy out of here! Mom! Hurry!"

Sirens could be heard in the background. Nick was on the side of the road waving them down.

"Over here! Down this ravine! Hurry!" After the vehicles saw the area, Nick ran down the slight hill. Ambulance personnel and firefighters following with professional equipment.

"I am going to have to ask you all to vacate the immediate area. Thank you, First Responders. Josie, we need your help." The team leader for the paramedic crew was inside the car assessing the best way to get Brenda and Gerard out of the vehicle.

"John, you know I will do what I can, but you have to know these people are like family to me." Josie wiped the tears on her face and was back in professional mode.

Nick felt he was in the way, but that was his brother. He couldn't leave. He watched as the professionals did their jobs along with Josie and Lorraine. He went to his father who was sitting on the side of the ravine with his head on his knees, still praying.

"Andy," said Nick as he put his arm around Andrew's shoulders. "It will be okay. These people do this every day. They will get them out alive."

Even as Nick said it, he had some doubt inside. He felt guilty for having the doubt. One thought was leading to another and he couldn't do what he needed to do, which was pray.

Jim came with Matt to sit down by Nick and Andrew. They could hear shouts and commands being issued from the paramedic and firefighting teams. They were having to bring in the jaws of life.

"The girl is alive too!" John, the team lead for the paramedics, shouted toward the others. "Both alive, thank God!"

Jim got on the phone to the others back at the restaurant. He gave them a run- down of what was going on. Jill promised to call Rod and Gwen to come as soon as possible. Then she promised they would all pray. She informed them that Mark was on the way as well to help in any way he could at the restaurant. Jim thanked them all and promised to keep them informed.

As the professionals worked to free Gerard and Brenda from the vehicle, Andrew realized he would have to tell Margaret. He honestly did not know what she would do.

"Maybe you should call Nana and have her break the news to Margaret," said Jim.

"Might be the best thing. She can handle her far better than any of us," said Nick.

Andrew nodded giving his consent.

It was nearing midnight, but Nick knew Nana well enough to know that she would sense something was wrong long before she was notified. He made the call.

"I knowed you was a gonna call, Nick, I just knowed it, I did." Nana sounded almost frantic.

"Nana, something terrible has happened and I don't know what to say except we need you to pray and pray hard." Nick's voice caught in his throat and he had trouble getting the words out.

"Son, just say it. This ole' gal can take it. Like I said, I knowed it was a comin'"

Nick tried to speak but words failed him. Jim took the phone and proceeded to tell Nana what had taken place.

"We need you to break the news to Margaret. Andrew is in no shape to do it and we have no idea how she will react. She may not care or she may go ballistic. Please, Nana. Do what you can. We'll keep you updated."

Jim hung up the phone just as a loud, shrill screech sounded as the jaws of life cut into the side of the car. Two more cuts and they were able to reach Gerard. The paramedics had him strapped to a stretcher in no time. As they started up the hill, Gerard's eyes opened.

"Brenda," he groaned. "Brenda...where is...". Gerard had passed out again.

Josie was holding his arm and helping to move him up the hill. "Gerard, she is alive. I know God will let you know that in your heart." She helped load Gerard into the first ambulance as the second ambulance pulled in.

Lorraine met the second ambulance and explained what had happened and what still needed to be done.

"I think we are going to have to transport her to Charleston by Air Ambulance after she is stabilized. I am not sure the hospital here has the means to help her, but we will have to see. First things first." She marched back down the hill like she was the one in charge.

Andrew jumped into the back of the first ambulance with Josie to ride to the hospital with Gerard. He sat on the bench seat and tried to hold Gerard's hand but Josie had to move him so she and the EMT could do their jobs.

Josie started an IV while the EMT got oxygen hooked up and a mask placed on Gerard's face. Gerard tried to fight those working on him. The EMT got on the phone with the doctor standing by at the hospital emergency room.

"Josie, Dr. Emmons wants Ativan, one milligram IV push to hopefully sedate him," said Dan, the EMT.

"Can I give another milligram in ten minutes if the first doesn't work?" Josie was busy administering the medication.

"Affirmative," said Dan as he continued to relay information to Dr. Emmons.

Andrew began to pray over his son and after a while Josie joined him. Gerard slowly settled down after the second dose of the sedative. Andrew sat silently after that and the rest of the ride to the hospital was quiet.

~

Back at the scene of the wreak, the firefighters were finally able to extract Brenda from the totaled car. They carefully splinted her left arm and applied a neck brace, but she was clearly having trouble breathing.

John quickly got on the phone with the Emergency Room for help. The decision was made to intubate Brenda on the spot before transport to ease her struggle to breathe. John quickly inserted the tube and connected the portable respirator. Lorraine assisted with the resuscitation effort. Together they were able to load Brenda into the second ambulance.

Jim, Nick and Matt watched from the side of the road ready to follow in their cars. Jim stated what they were all thinking.

"It never ceases to amaze me at how scatterbrained Lorraine is at the restaurant, but put her in a situation like this and she is calm and collected. Like night and day."

Nick was brushing the dirt off his clothing and preparing to get in the jeep with Matt.

"I am shocked. If I hadn't seen it with my own eyes, I would not have believed it."

Matt jumped in the driver's seat as Jim got in his vehicle waiting for the ambulance to pull away. Lorraine would ride with him to the hospital. Jim knew Lorraine so well in situations such as this. She would break down once she was in the car, until she got to the hospital and then she would have her mask firmly back in place.

~

By the next morning, there was quite the gathering in the intensive care waiting room at Raleigh General. The Dennison's were still there keeping vigil with the Wallace family.

Brenda's parents were at her bedside. She had not stabilized enough to be moved and was on a ventilator. Her sisters had not yet arrived but were on the way. The word was, she was not going to make it.

Nana and Margaret were huddled together in a corner sipping coffee. Margaret had a blank look on her face, void of all emotion, but the family had heard from Nana that she'd had a meltdown when Nana told her the news.

Andrew sat not far away with Nick waiting for the arrival of Rod who was flying in from New York with Gwen and Georgia. There had been a delay during the night and Rod had not been cleared for takeoff until early this morning. He would be landing any time now and would call as soon as his feet were on solid ground.

Gerard was in surgery to repair his left arm that had been broken in three places, but other than that, he had survived the crash without major damage.

Ben had been pacing the floor, waiting on those who might need food or coffee, and praying loudly over the protests of the intensive care staff.

All eyes turned to Andrew when his phone rang. "Son," cried Andrew. "Are you on the ground yet?"

"Not exactly, Dad," Rod replied. "Bonnie can't get a flight out of Chicago until later today and since Gerard is not critical, I thought it best to go and pick up Bonnie, you know, just in case."

"I think that is a grand idea, son, but hurry here as soon as possible. I will let the others know." Andrew explained Rod's situation and then went to inform the Montgomery's that both daughters would be at the hospital soon.

"Thank you all for the prayers and company through the night." Liza Montgomery, Brenda's mother, said before she burst into tears again.

Hank Montgomery, Brenda's father, put his arms around his wife and guided her back to the bedside. When she was settled, he returned to where Andrew was standing near the nurse's station asking if there was any word on Gerard as of yet.

"No word yet, Mr. Wallace," said the unit clerk. "The doctor will be out just as soon as he is finished and sure that your son is doing well in recovery."

"Thank you, miss," said Andrew as he turned his attention back to Hank.

Andrew noted how bad Hank looked. He knew the man had a heart condition and this could not be helping him any.

"Andy, I know what you're thinking and you can stop it right now," said Hank in a stern tone. "You think I need rest.

You think I need to eat. What I need is the strength to do the right thing for my daughter." Tears were flowing down Hank's face.

Andrew looked in the room where Brenda was hooked up to at least five IV bags, the ventilator tube taped securely in place, and her body swollen almost beyond recognition. Andrew was at a loss for words. He tried to speak and nothing came out. He turned to see Nana and Margaret approaching.

"Andy, ye been gone so long we got to worryin' what might be a happenin' down to this end of the hall." Nana was holding Margaret by the hand.

Margaret looked toward the room and could see Brenda through the glass. "Oh!"

She backed up until she felt the nurse's station touch her back. Her mask was still in place, but there was a subtle hint of alarm present that had not been there before.

"Maggie, I think you and Nana should go back to the waiting room. It is not good for you to be here." Andrew put his arm on her shoulder to guide her.

"Absolutely not," she said. "Nana came down here to pray and I am here to support her as she has supported me all these weeks."

At Hank's and Liza's okay, Nana and Margaret entered the room. The three women joined hands as Nana spoke a heartfelt prayer for Brenda's recovery.

Hank cleared his throat and full of emotion, spoke to Andy again.

"As soon as the girls get here, the doctors and social workers want to have a family meeting about Brenda's condition. I don't think I can handle it if they suggest the worst. Taking her off life support. They don't think she will stabilize, so they can't move her. She is running a high fever.

The mud she was in was from old man Simmon's hog farm. No tellin' what got into her system."

"Hank, I don't know what to say. My son was driving the car that caused your daughter to be in this condition. We knew he had a drinking problem. But we couldn't control him. He made his own choices, just like we all have to do. I wish I could say I raised him better, but the truth is, I didn't raise him at all. I'm the cause of all of this. And now your daughter might pay the ultimate price for what I failed to do." Andrew wiped his hand over his eyes just as a loud racket could be heard coming down the hall.

Hank and Andrew turned and the women came out of the room to see what was going on. Bonnie and Georgia were running down the hall with Bonnie in near hysterics. Rich was bringing up the rear and trying to be of some support for Georgia.

When they reached the others, Nana and the nurse were quick to close the curtain to Brenda's room so that the girls could be prepared for what they would encounter when they came face to face with Brenda.

The parents engulfed their daughters in hugs as they all cried together. Rich stood to the side with Andrew and Margaret quietly waiting to see if they were still needed. Nana walked over to the group.

"I'm a tellin' ye that this is the awfulest thing we've had happen in these here parts in many a moon." Nana wrung her hands, then began a softer prayer for strength for the Montgomery family to be able to do what needed to be done for the sake of their daughter.

One of the doctor's approached the group accompanied by two social workers. Hank briefly explained to the girls that they all had to discuss Brenda's possible fate and it couldn't be put off any longer.

"Can we see her first?" Georgia was reaching for Rich's hand as she spoke. Bonnie took her mother's hand. Both parents looked at each other and to the nurse for guidance.

The nurse explained what they were about to see, but before she was finished, Bonnie broke loose and ran into the room. The others heard a loud scream and a thud. The doctor and nurse went into the room and immediately called for help. Bonnie had fainted.

Another two nurses joined them in the room and had Bonnie back up and sitting in a chair. She was unable to look at the bed of her sister.

Georgia looked at Rich and he gave her hand a squeeze.

"Let's do this," she said.

They slowly entered the room taking in the pitiful sight Brenda made in the huge bed with all the equipment.

Rich gasped. "Oh, dear Lord!"

It came out without his conscious thought. He could feel Georgia's death grip on his hand as she silently stared at her sister. She said nothing, but leaned over the trash can and threw up. Rich held her shoulders until she was done, then with the nurse, led her to another chair near Bonnie. The nurse closed the curtain around Brenda's bed. Rich couldn't help but think they had closed the curtain on Brenda's life.

Twenty-Two

The group left in the waiting room were almost deathly silent as they waited to hear some news of Gerard. Andrew, Margaret and Nana had joined Jim and Lorraine at the small card table where they sat silently, each with their own thoughts. Matt and Anika sat on opposite ends of the sofa, each reading magazines. Josie and Rod sat in stiff backed chairs quietly talking and praying.

Ben sat in a chair by himself with his hands over his face. Every now and then his shoulders could be seen shaking as he silently cried out his grief. Gwen and Nick had gone in search of any news they could find. Jill and Mark discussed how they could best keep the restaurant going in the midst of all this chaos. Rich had not returned to the group.

Just then Nick and Gwen came through the automated doors with all eyes upon them and Nick addressed the group as a whole.

"We have been told that Gerard is out of surgery and currently in recovery. He is doing as well as can be expected considering his alcohol level was three times over the legal limit." He went to join Jill and Mark.

Gwen was headed to sit with Josie when her phone rang. She looked at the name on the caller ID. She made a face.

"Gwen here. Make it quick."

"Sorry to bother you, but I need to give you a 'heads up'," said Victor Deville. "I couldn't stop him when he saw you rush from the hotel. He didn't stop until he found out what was going on. He finally overheard a conversation between Oscar and Henri about the accident. I am so sorry, but I just wasn't able to stop him."

"Of course, you couldn't," said Gwen with a resigned sigh. "No one could have. That man needs a keeper."

"Which brings me to my next piece of info." Victor coughed a couple of times. "I am with him. I couldn't let him loose on his own with the tragedy at hand. No telling what he might get into. I will keep him out of the way and under control."

"Like you really could, Victor, but thanks for the warning. What time should we expect…" Gwen spun around at the sound of a door being thrown open.

"Make way, oh people of misery, make way," said Alphonse loudly as he burst through the door in his most pompous fashion. "Alphonse is in the house of pain to bring you a bit of sunshine on your cloudy day."

"Please kill me now," said Gwen as Alphonse grabbed her and gave her a big hug. He moved on to the table where the Wallace's and the Dennison's were seated. He made to reach for Margaret's hand, but she stopped him cold.

"Touch me, you idiot, and I will make sure you never use that hand again," said Margaret standing to her full height of almost five-feet.

"I would be willing to bet my right hand that yours gets quite the workout, if you get my drift." She stalked across the room and sat down near Ben with a stony look on her face.

The others in the room stared after her, shocked at what she had said. Nana stood and slapped her hand down on the table causing Lorraine to jump nearly out of her seat.

"That's a tellin' him, Maggie." Nana felt the muscle on Alphonse' forearm.

"I do declare, Alphonse, ye got yerself quite a muscle there. A big 'un fer a big 'un if ye knowed what I'm a meanin.'" She laughed at her own joke, as Nana tended to do. She went to sit on the other side of Ben.

Alphonse brushed his hand down the front of his shirt, for lack of anything else to do and turned his red face toward Nick and Jill.

Nick stood up, his six- foot, five -inch frame towering over the five -foot, four- inch frame of Alphonse. They shook hands. Alphonse took Jill's hand and kissed the back as he bowed in her direction.

"I know you all think I am just a joke, but Alphonse has feelings. Maybe not like most of you, but he has feelings." He turned and stalked out of the room.

"I better go see where he thinks he is going," said Victor. "No telling what kind of trouble he can get into here." Victor started to follow Alphonse out the door when Nana stopped him.

"Just a minute, now, he ain't a gonna get in no more trouble here than anywhere else." She stood up and slowly walked around Victor.

"My, my, my," she said as she looked him up and down.

"Nana!" Jill put her arm around Nana and guided her back to her seat next to Ben. "That is no way to behave."

"All I was a gonna do, honey chile, was interduce myself and ask if he has a wife."

Nana extricated herself from Jill and moved back to a confused Victor. "Son, ye can call me Nana like everbidy else, ye can."

Victor took her outstretched hand and lightly shook it. "You can call me Victor and, no, I do not have a wife. I had one once and that was enough. Now, if you all will excuse me, I need to find 'his highness' before he gets us all kicked out of here."

As Victor was exiting, he stopped to speak with Rich as Rich was entering the room wiping his brow. Rich nodded and came fully into the seating area. All turned in his direction.

He was pale and slowly looked around the room before he spoke. When he did, it was with much emotion.

"The Montgomery family has asked me to update you on the situation with Brenda."

Lorraine was on her feet in a minute, in full nurse mode. "Rich, I know it isn't good but how bad is it?"

"I..." Rich cleared his throat and tried again. "Well, you see..." He loosened his tie and mopped his forehead again.

"Please just tell us," said Andy. "My son is responsible for this and I would like to know exactly how much damage he is responsible for."

"Brenda is not expected to make it beyond twenty-four hours. She has pressure on the brain and fluid in her lungs." Rich stopped to gather his strength on what else he had to say.

"She is bruised inside and out and the doctor said he had never seen an alcohol level as high as hers on admission."

Anika began to cry and Matt tried to go to her but she swatted him away. She ran to her father instead and buried her face in his shoulder.

Ben stood and was weeping as well. "Lawd God a'mighty," he cried. "It be all my fault."

Before Ben could continue, Rich interrupted. "The family made the decision to keep her here and to terminate the life support given the grave state of Brenda's life. Even if she were to make it, she would probably be a vegetable." He walked over near Rod and sat down, rubbing his hands through his hair.

"Now we can't have that," said Lorraine. "Brenda is like another daughter to me. Nana, Jim, Andy we need to pray now and pray hard. Any of you who would like to join us, please do."

The two families moved to the center of the room, some holding hands, while others raised their hands toward Heaven. Each took turns adding something to the prayer until they all drew in closer with their arms around each other and prayed silently.

"Victor, look!" Alphonse entered the room with Victor on his heels. "Group hug!"

Victor managed to stop him from interrupting. "You moron," he said. "They are praying. Silently. Something you know nothing about. Now either join the praying or keep your trap shut!"

Alphonse moved closer to the group as did Victor. A few eyes opened and looked toward him. No one said a word. Alphonse bowed his head and spoke.

"Great God of all things holy. I stand here before you as a humble man seeking your magic touch for our friend, Brenda Montgomery. Oh, and for the second of the three wishes..."

Many heads turned at that statement. Alphonse had his hands lifted upward and his eyes closed tight. He was unaware the group had turned to watch him.

He continued after a slight pause. "Help Gerard Wallace, asshole as he may be to all who know him, but I am sure some here wish for his recovery. I will have to think about my third wish. Amen"

The room was silent until...

"Oh, Lawd have mercy on us and this po' ignorant soul!" Ben was shouting to the heavens with his arms outstretched.

"He done unleashed all dem demons from hell on us all. Lawd God! Please spare us dis unholy bastard come to bring harm to Miss Brenda and Mr. Gerard! Oh...Land o' Goshen!" Ben dropped to his knees. "I be sorry Lawd. Dis be all my fault. I 'posed to keep Mr. Gerard out 'o trouble..."

Jill and Nana went down on their knees next to Ben as he dissolved in tears. Both began to pray over Ben. When they had finished, the others had returned to their seats to talk among themselves about this turn of events and the drama that had been brought upon them by Alphonse.

Alphonse was sitting with Victor to themselves in the corner and Alphonse had the good grace to look ashamed of himself.

Jim and Mark cautiously approached him but it was Mark that spoke.

"Alphonse, we understand that you meant no harm. In your own way, you were trying to help."

"That is all Alphonse wants to do. To help. To help his mountain family. I am sorry I do not know how to pray. I am sure your God does not hear me anyway."

"That is not true," said Matt. "God hears the prayers of all of his children, and you are one of his children, Alphonse. Even if you do not know him, he knows you,"

The doors opened again and Georgia and Bonnie joined the group. Georgia ran to Rich and he held her while she cried until she was spent. He cried with her.

The others tried to console Bonnie, but it was hard. Of all the Montgomery triplets, Bonnie was the quietest and hardest to get to know. Each one hugged her in turn and she went over to sit in a chair near the windows by herself.

They knew her well enough to know she preferred it that way.

Jill, Nick and the parents had been in a huddle trying to figure out some of the logistics of keeping Mountain Mama's restaurant running while they tried to be a network of support for the Montgomery family and also remain near Gerard.

Matt crossed the room as he spoke. "With Mark here and Lance at our other site, we could use Alphonse to help with the kitchen work, at least while he is here. If he is willing."

"That is a wonderful idea, Matt," said Jill and Nick together.

"That could be a godsend," said Jim. "With Mark, Jean, and Alphonse doing the chef work, and Shirley, Gladys and the twins doing prep, I think we will be fine. It will allow the rest of us to concentrate on Gerard and help the Montgomery's through this terrible time."

Gwen spoke to Victor before she spoke with Alphonse. "What do you think? Will he take direction? He is not used to this kind of cooking. Henri can handle Marcel's."

"We can ask. I know he will jump on it, but how he will fit in? All we can do is let him try." Victor ran his hands through his hair. "Do you want to ask him or should I?"

"Let's let Jim and Jill talk to him. They will get a good feel for the situation," said Gwen and she went to discuss it further with the Dennison family.

The room was full of sorrow and it was reflected in the faces of all who were present. Tears and prayers were going up for the strength to move forward into another day.

Twenty-Three

The next morning found the Raleigh General waiting room with a few people from the Dennison and Montgomery families still present.

The surgeon had pronounced Gerard fine and expected to make a full recovery. Jim and Nick had persuaded some of the family to leave. Josie and Gwen had taken Matt and Anika home and remained with Anika while she was in such a state of anxiety.

Lorraine had taken Nana and Margaret home, but Andy had refused to leave. Rod and Mark had taken Alphonse and Victor back to the guest quarters at Mountain Mama's and the two of them went to stay at Jill and Nick's home. Rod stated he would rather sleep with a colony of red fire ants than to share quarters with Alphonse. Mark echoed the sentiment.

The Montgomery's were camped out in Brenda's room with the parents sleeping off and on in the stiff chairs while Bonnie and Georgia shared the recliner. Rich, who had refused to leave as Georgia might need him, was sitting in the waiting room with Nick and Jill. Ben had taken up watch over Gerard, along with Andy in Gerard's room.

"Ben," said Andy, "You should try to get some sleep. You have been up all night and frankly, you look like hell. Gerard is going to be fine."

"I can't rest 'till I knows he be awake and okay," said Ben in his pitiful voice. "He don't know 'bout Miss Brenda and I be right here by his side fo' when he find out. Dis whole thing be my fault. Lawd have mercy!" He dropped to his knees beside the bed just as Mamie and Margaret walked in followed by Matt. Bringing up the rear was Nana and Anika.

Ben continued to cry out while the others just stared at him.

"My fault, my fault. Miss Brenda be leaving this world today 'cuz I didn't stop him from leavin' that school house."

Mamie stepped toward Ben and put her hand on his shoulder.

"Ben, the blame lies with me. You wanted to go with him to drive and I made you stay with me. I knew he had been drinking. I was even the one that suggested they leave in the first place."

Ben stood up and started to speak when Anika interrupted him.

"No Ms. Gray. It's my fault. If I hadn't dressed like a hooker and behaved like an idiot, no one would have had to leave the prom early."

"No," said Matt. "You can't take all the credit for being an idiot. It's my fault for starting trouble with your date and criticizing you in the first place. You would not have been upset if I had behaved like a gentleman. And I never should have taken Ginger to the prom. I knew better and I am sorry."

"This has to stop. Seriously, this has to stop." Andrew walked to the foot of the bed and looked at his son.

"I am the one that caused Gerard's problems in the first place. I should have stepped forward and been a real father to him from the beginning. I might have been present at his milestones, but he never knew it. It would not have made any difference if I had not bothered to be there at all. What good did it do? He's been into drugs, alcohol, rehab, more drugs and alcohol. I never once stepped up to the plate and even told him I was proud of him. And now this..."

He put his hands over his face and his shoulders shook as he cried for all the misfortune that he felt he had caused.

They felt Margaret's presence in the room before they saw or heard her. She held her head high.

"I know you all blame me for this whole mess and you are right to do so. Because of my past, I have made some decisions that should never have been made, and allowed...no...forced Andrew to do the same. And because of his background, he gave me very little opposition. So, the blame is all mine."

"What a bunch of whining losers!"

Everyone whipped around to see Gerard propped up on one elbow in the bed with a look of disgust on his face. A look typical of Gerard.

"Oh, Lawd, God! Thank you, Lawd!" Ben was in Gerard's face before any of the others had a chance to react.

"Get the hell off me, you big ass!" Gerard was struggling to sit up straighter and fend off Ben at the same time.

"All of you, shut up right now!" He managed to operate the button to raise the head of his bed. Everyone took a step back at the sheer audacity of Gerard's comments to those who had been at his bedside caring for him.

Gerard looked at each one of them in turn. "The fault lies with no one but myself."

Gerard was pale and had lost that look of being so much better than everyone else. He had been reduced to looking up at everyone, instead of looking down his nose at them.

"What the hell are you all looking so miserable for?" Gerard took a deep breath and winced.

"I know I have a lot to answer for, but we survived. We are alive. It could have been so much worse." He continued to look around the room as all eyes failed to meet his searching ones.

"Right?"

When no one answered, Gerard made to try to sit up on the side of the bed like he was going to get up and walk. His head started spinning and he was forced to rest back against the raised head of the bed. He closed his eyes and took calming breaths over and over. Finally, he spoke.

"What are you all trying so hard not to tell me? I want to see Brenda. I want to see her right now! Either someone go get her or take me to her and I am not even close to kidding!" He began to try to pull off the cast on his arm and pull his IV out.

Ben tried to calm Gerard as Andrew pushed the nurses call bell.

"I think everyone should return to the waiting room and let me have a few moments alone with my son."

Andrew poured a cup of water and tried to get Gerard to drink as the others left the room. Gerard took his good hand and smacked the water cup in the floor.

"Ben," said Andrew. "Maybe you should hang around within earshot if you don't mind."

Gerard's eyes flew open at this as he looked hard from Andrew to Ben. The nurse came in and checked the IV for signs of infiltration. When she was satisfied that all was okay, she left the room but not before telling Gerard in a stern voice that he was to remain in bed and leave his IV alone.

Andrew geared up to tell Gerard what he knew he had to about Brenda's condition and probable eminent death. He took a deep breath and...

'I'm glad you are here, Andrew,' said Dr. Weir, Margaret's psychiatrist as he entered the room.

"I am sorry it took so long and I am glad to see Gerard is awake so I can explain his regimen of medication that will be started soon." He pulled a chair next to the bed.

"Father, why is this quack here? You are all acting like I have a disease or something. Is that why you sent everyone away?"

Gerard was trying to sit up again. He looked at both men and noticed how uncomfortable they both looked. Andrew's foot was tapping a mile a minute and Dr. Weir was shuffling his chair back and forth which was really getting on Gerard's nerves.

"Oh, for God's sake, just spit it out!" Gerard punched the side rail with his good hand.

Dr. Weir looked at Andrew. "Okay, Gerard, the gist of the matter is that you are an alcoholic. I know you will dispute that, but it doesn't change the truth. You will be going into D. T.'s soon without medication. That stands for delirium tremens..."

Gerard rudely interrupted him. "I know what the hell it stands for, you over priced buffoon. I've been in rehab enough to know what comes next. Probably Librium or some new assed drug that will make some drug company rich. Now is that what all the fuss is about?"

Andrew stood up and began to walk a few paces back and forth in the room. He rubbed his hands down his face, scratched his head, and cleared his throat.

"This is ridiculous! What could be worse than going through that again?" Gerard raised the head of the bed higher and readjusted his pillow.

"I'm a New Yorker, born and bred. Whatever it is, I can take it."

Andrew, seeing a way to prolong the inevitable, took a different tactic.

"Well, son, that is not entirely true. You were not born in New York like the rest of your siblings."

"Is that right?" Gerard was turning red in the face. "Then where was I born, Timbuctu?"

All of a sudden, the answer dawned on him and he looked at his father. "No. No, no, no. Don't say it. Don't you dare say it."

"Son, haven't you ever looked at your birth certificate? It says right on there that you were born in Beckley, West Virginia," said Andrew. "You have had to get passports. You must have had to show it before."

Gerard put the pillow over his face. "I never read the shit."

Ben chose that moment to look around the corner into the room.

"I see you told him."

"Told me what, Ben? That I'm nothing but a damn hillbilly?" Gerard was getting more and more dramatic. "Come here Ben and press this pillow as hard as you can over my face and don't let go until I stop kicking."

"So, he don't know 'bout Miss Brenda yet?" Ben came into the room.

"What about Brenda? Nothing could possibly be worse than this news."

Ben removed the pillow from Gerard's face and looked at him straight in the eye. This was unusual for Ben and Gerard took notice.

They all stared at each other for a few minutes and, finally, Andrew spoke.

"Gerard, Brenda is here in the hospital too." He went back to the foot of the bed and sat down.

"Damn! Haven't I been trying to get someone to take me to her? I bet she is so mad at me she just might cut my balls off. Ben, go make sure she doesn't have access to a knife." Gerard made to get out of the bed again.

"No, son," said Andrew in a sorrowful tone. Ben put his hand on Gerard's shoulder to try to keep him in bed. "Brenda didn't fare as well as you did in the accident. She has remained unconscious."

"Oh," said Gerard looking a little shaken. "Probably a concussion and, well, we were pretty drunk."

He looked hopefully at Andrew, then Dr. Weir, and finally, at Ben. He saw Ben had tears on his face.

"What..." Gerard began but was interrupted by Rich coming into the room.

"Just wanted to let you all know that they are getting ready to disconnect Brenda from the ventilator."

He noticed that Gerard was awake. "Sorry, man. It's just a matter of time now."

Marianne Waddill Wieland

Twenty-Four

Those of the Dennison and Wallace families that were still present in the waiting room were talking quietly about the events of the last few days. Nana stopped talking and stood with a look of severe concentration.

"I have a bad feelin', I do," she said. "Mark my words...somethin'..."

She didn't get anything else out when they all heard it coming from beyond the doors into the patient area. A blood curdling wail so loud and long it caused staff and security alike to run toward Gerard's room.

Nick and Jim took off at a dead run, followed closely by Lorraine who was yelling as she ran.

"Matt! Anika! Stay here and help Nana!"

Margaret got up to follow but Nana laid a hand on her. "Maggie, ye best stay here. Ye don't know how he's a gonna react when he sees everone. We need to mind our Ps and Qs right now and just pray for that poor boy o' you'rn."

Jill had remained behind to look after the others and keep a check on how things were going for Brenda. She went over and put her arms around Nana. Jill was softly crying.

"It's okay honey chile," said Nana in a soothing voice. "God hasn't abandoned either one o' them there children. He loves each o' them like they was his only child."

Jill just cried harder. Anika came over and joined in the hug leaving Matt to sit alone on the chair near the window. Margaret wandered over and sat near him.

"Young man," she began. "I can see how close you are to your parents. That is the way it should be. Not like I raised, or failed to raise, my own children. There is no excuse for what I have done."

Matt looked at her and took her hand.

"The time for blame is passed. Now we have to concentrate on what we can do to help Gerard. He will have to face life without Brenda and I know he loved her. Sadly, I do not believe he ever told her and he will have to live with that." He looked over at Anika as he said the words.

"Yes, he will. He will also have to face the fact that because of this whole mess, he contributed to her death." Margaret let go of Matt's hand and returned to where she had been.

Jim came back through the door followed by Rich. He sat down near Margaret. Rich went to sit near Matt. Jim spoke first.

"They were getting ready to remove life support from Brenda but Gerard went hysterical. He wants to see her before…well…" Jim shifted in his chair clearly shaken.

"Well, anyway, they are going to let him see her. I'm not sure it is for the best."

"Jimmy," said Nana. "Where is everbidy? Maggie would like to see her son."

"Not a good idea, Nana. Ben had to restrain him and I think they are going to have to recast that arm. He is nearly insane right now." Jim got up and walked to the window.

"Lorraine is with Brenda's family and Andy is with Gerard. I think the only thing the rest of us can do is pray." Jim went back to sit by Margaret.

"I would like to be with my son," said Maggie.

Jim took a deep breath. "Margaret, he hit Andy and Ben pretty hard. Blacked an eye of one of the nurses as she tried to sedate him. No good can come of it."

"I understand. Is Andrew alright?" Margaret quickly amended her statement to include the others.

"They are all fine. Just minor injuries, really," said Jim.

Jill jumped up and went to her father. "What about Nick? Is he okay? Where was he in all this?"

Rich came to her and put a hand on her arm. "He was talking with me in the hall at the time. Security would not let him back in the room."

Jill gave Rich a hug and he hugged her back. "I am sorry for those that were injured but thank you for being out of the way and having Nick with you."

"It just worked out that way. I really had no hand in it," said Rich. Jill went over to where Rich had been sitting and sat with he and Matt.

~

Gerard was back in the bed staring at the ceiling. He had been given a sedative and was warned he could not see Brenda until he settled down. He was told he would be allowed in to see Brenda for five minutes only before life support was terminated. He was not taking it well. Andrew, Nick and Ben were standing by the windows talking quietly.

"He should have been knocked out by now with the dose of Ativan they gave him," said Andrew.

"I think he has an excess of adrenaline flowing through him right now," said Nick. "When he finally crashes, he is going to sleep for a long time."

"He need it too," said Ben. "He sho' do need it."

The nurse came into the room to see if Gerard felt he could conduct himself in a manner that would not cause a problem for the Montgomery family.

"Yes, I would like to see her."

"I want you to understand that she does not look like the last time you saw her."

The nurse had brought in a wheelchair to cut down the risk of injury if Gerard lost it again. She assisted him into the chair.

"Do you mind if we take him?" Nick was assisting the nurse with Gerard.

"That is not a problem if you can handle him," stated the nurse.

"It ain't gon' be no problem," said Ben. "Is it, Mr. Gerard?"

"No, it isn't," said Gerard with his head down. "Let's do this."

Ben pushed the wheelchair to Brenda's room. Gerard kept his head down the whole way. When they entered the room, Lorraine came to stand at the end of the bed to explain what all the tubes were for. Bonnie and Georgia stood on the opposite side of the bed, Bonnie with her hand on Brenda's shoulder and Georgia holding her hand.

Gerard slowly looked up as Lorraine began her explanation. The others heard the gasp and Ben put his hands on Gerard's shoulders as he tried to get up.

"You knows you gots to stay in yo' chair or they will make you go back to yo' room. You heard what dat nurse say." Ben was softly patting Gerard's shoulders.

Gerard eased back down. "Can you push me closer?"

Ben did as he said and Gerard put his hand over Brenda's. He quickly pulled it back and put his head in both of his hands. His shoulders began to shake.

"Would it be okay with everyone if Gerard had a moment alone with Brenda?" Lorraine directed her comments to the Montgomery family. They all agreed and silently left the room, but Ben remained just outside the door.

Gerard rubbed his hands across is eyes a few times, then ran them through his hair. He leaned forward and put his hand on Brenda's hand again. Then he moved it to touch her upper arm and the calf of her leg. He finally moved it back to her hand. He could hardly bear to look at her swollen face with all the tubes on which Lorraine had given instruction. He knew what he had to say.

"Brenda," he started but had to clear his throat. "I don't even know how to begin to say how sorry I am, for everything. I don't know if you can hear me, but I have to let you know how much I love you. I have loved you almost from the start. No woman has ever affected me like you have. I let this happen. I knew better. I caused problems for you at your job, cost you your dignity, and now, your life. All in the name of fun. Of getting drunk. Of being an ass to everyone who cares about me. I have never been good at life. Only the easy parts."

He put his head down on the edge of the bed and sobbed again. After a few minutes, he gained control and continued.

"I made the choice for both of us. If it hadn't been for you, my niece would have been here too, or worse. I have never been able to handle life when the going gets tough and now I have dragged you into it. If you were going to recover, and I am not sold on the fact that you aren't, I would love to pursue a normal relationship with you, free of any substance abuse, free of any sarcasm, and free of any danger. Except the danger of losing my heart to someone who may never want to see me again. But, I can handle that if only you would live to beat the shit out of me, because we both know that is what you would do. I love you, Brenda, with all my heart."

The nurse came back into the room followed by the Montgomery family.

Lorraine was the one to speak. "Ben please take Gerard back to his room. The family is ready to terminate life support."

"Please," Gerard begged. "I want to stay."

"We would like everyone to be with us that would like to be," said Mrs. Montgomery. The rest of the family agreed. The nurse left to get the others who would like to be present.

When she returned, Nana and Margaret were the first to enter the room. Rich went to stand behind Georgia and Jill joined Nick. Josie and Rod joined Bonnie, but Matt and Anika had elected to stay in the waiting room. Jim was the last to enter and he took Lorraine's hand.

The nurse began the process of removing the tubes and IVs. When everything was out she explained that Brenda would probably be gone within a half hour. She explained her breathing would be sporadic until she passed away. Soft crying could be heard from several of those gathered in the room.

"I'd like us to lay hands on Brenda, at least those of ye that are okay with that," said Nana. "The rest o' you'uns hold each other's hands"

Nana began to pray loud and strong for Brenda, her family, her friends and for her to be received into the hands of God and his glory if that was His will. When she hesitated, Jill continued the prayer and each one in turn had a few words to say about what Brenda meant to them.

It ended with Ben starting to sing 'Amazing Grace' and soon, the others joined in. No one mentioned the fact that Gerard said nothing nor did he join in with the singing.

They all watched as Brenda's breathing began to slow and one by one they touched her or hugged and kissed her goodbye as they filed out of the room. The only ones remaining in the end were the immediate family.

Twenty-Five

Matt and Anika were asleep in the waiting room when the others returned. Most of the family said their goodbyes and left. Anika wanted to say goodbye to her uncle Gerard, so Matt left with his parents while Anika went down the hall to Gerard's room.

Ben was standing outside the door when she arrived and he stopped her from going in.

"Miss Anika, best you not be goin' in there right now. He not in his right mind." Ben moved her out of the area of the door.

"You best be goin' on home wit yo' folks and give him time to get hisself together. He'd have my head if I let you in there."

"Has Brenda passed away?" Anika braced for the answer.

"No," said Ben sadly. "She be hangin' on. Her family be with her fo' when that time comes, but Mr. Gerard, he not able to accept her passin'. He blamin' hisself fo' everything."

Both were surprised when Gerard looked out his door and motioned Anika into the room. She looked at Ben and when he shrugged his shoulders, she went on into the room not sure what to expect. She was shocked when Gerard pulled her into a tight hug with his good arm.

"Anika, Anika…" Gerard kept saying her name over and over and holding her in a rocking motion. He finally let her go.

"Anika, I am so sorry. If you hadn't begged to be let out of the car, you could have been here too or even worse. I have a lot to answer for with causing this tragedy, but I am so thankful you were not with us when this happened." Gerard sat on the side of his bed and motioned for her to sit with him.

"Uncle Gerard," said Anika. "I am very grateful I was not in the car too, but more than that, I am glad you are not suffering from a worse injury. You could have…"

Anika wiped at her eyes and walked to the windows. Gerard followed and put his arms around her, resting his chin on her head. They stood there for a long time, neither speaking. Finally, Gerard backed away as he wiped sweat from his forehead.

"I think you had better go, Anika. I am not feeling well and I think I need to lie down for a while. I am still pretty weak." He walked with an unsteady gait to the bed and collapsed down on it with his arm across is eyes.

Anika laid her hand on his shoulder for a few seconds and then left the room. She stopped to speak with Ben.

"He scares me, Ben. He will be okay and then just have a total change in his demeanor. Do you think he has a personality disorder?"

"I be sho' he do," said Ben. "But the problem here is he be comin' down off all that hooch he drink all day long. His body crave mo' hooch and when he don't get it, he have a reaction. It get ugly. That be why he axed you to go."

Just then the nurse went in and gave Gerard an injection. His doctor had switched him from oral medication to injectable due to his alcohol withdrawal and his grief over

Brenda. She told Ben that Gerard would be asleep soon and he should get some rest as well. Anika gave him a hug and left. Ben went to the recliner in Gerard's room to keep tabs on the situation and to get some rest if he could.

~

    An hour after the life support had been removed from Brenda, she was still hanging on. The family was exhausted but no one wanted to leave the bedside lest she die when they were not there. The nurses had brought the family coffee, water and crackers.
    "We are going to have to get something to eat soon or we will be sick and no use to Brenda at all," said Hank Montgomery.
    "One of us will have to go to the cafeteria." They were debating this issue when Rich entered the room carrying several bags and two pizza boxes.
    Georgia jumped up to help him. "Rich, you are a life saver! We were just discussing how we could get some food without leaving Brenda."
    "I figured as much, so I decided to bring an assortment. I don't know what any of you like to eat. I have burgers and fries, subs and chips, and two pizzas. Help yourselves. I am just going to go down to the cafeteria for some drinks for all of you," said Rich in one breath trying not to look at Brenda. He quickly left the room almost at a jog.
    When he returned with a variety of drinks, Georgia pulled him to her and began kissing him with renewed energy. The others tried not to watch but curiosity got the best of them.
    "Hey," said Bonnie. "Knock it off. I'm trying to eat. You two need to give it a rest."

"Sorry," said Rich. "Please, everyone. Eat." He sat down by Georgia and helped himself to some of the pizza.

Liza Montgomery came over and gave him a hug. "Thank you, son. You have been very helpful to us and we are very grateful."

Rich stood and hugged her back and shook Hank's hand. Bonnie came over and gave him a hug as well. He began to blush and wipe his forehead.

"You do for friends," he said. "And family."

~

Nick and Jill were standing in the kitchen of Mountain Mama's restaurant admiring the great job that Mark, Alphonse, and Jean had done organizing and running the kitchen. The food prep was excellent, the timing was perfect, and all seemed to be working together to make it happen.

Jill looked at Nick. "Honey, this kitchen looks amazing."

"Thank you, Sweetie," said Alphonse before Nick could answer. He kept right on working without realizing he had not been spoken to.

Nick laughed and Jill elbowed him in the ribs. "Thank you, everyone. You don't know what this means by having things go so well in our absence."

"You're welcome," said Mark. "I think this has helped in more ways than you know."

Jill went over and gave him a kiss on the cheek before joining Nick to check in with the rest of the family.

Jean was arranging baskets of the homemade bread and jam made by aunt Gladys. It had proven to be very popular with the guests. She was setting things in order to make serving easier for the wait staff and she noticed how tired Mark looked.

"Hey cuz." She put her hand on his shoulder as he turned toward her. "Are you getting any sleep? Any at all?"

Mark hesitated. "I sleep better here than I do at home. It helps to have family nearby. Lance is doing such a great job running the place that I may stay here longer than I originally intended."

"Hey, I won't complain," said Jean turning back to her work.

"I want you all to know that Alphonse will stay too, however long he is needed. I am enjoying being roommates with my mountain brother, Mark," said Alphonse without any interruption in the food he was preparing.

"I have to say, Alphonse," said Mark. "You keep things interesting. And you have been a great help here. I was almost afraid to see Victor go back to New York."

"Alphonse is to helping others as a duck is to biting or a goat is to dinner," he responded being perfectly serious.

Jean and Mark looked at each other trying to keep a straight face, but knowing if they asked for an explanation that there would be one. They also knew it would be funnier than the original statement, so they kept quiet.

"Mark, is there any news from Nancy?" Jean tried to ask as normal as possible since Mark's wife had left him, lost their baby, and told him it was not his a few months ago.

"Not a word. Her phone is inactive, I can't reach her parents." He took a deep breath. "I went by several times to their home but it doesn't look like they even live there anymore. Lance drives by once in a while and he hasn't seen anyone there either. I think they have moved."

"What is this?" Alphonse stopped what he was doing and turned his attention onto Mark. "Alphonse does not understand."

"It is a long story, Alphonse. Another time, maybe." Mark took his apron off and threw it in the bin to be laundered.

"I think I am done. The twins will be here in fifteen and so will Frank. Everything is prepped, precooked and ready to go thanks to both of you. I need a break." He turned and headed out the door toward the stairway.

Alphonse turned to Jean with a question on his face. She sighed and shook her head. She opened her mouth to say something when Marlene entered the kitchen.

"Marlene, ma Cheri, come to Alphonse. He has missed you with all his heart." Alphonse pulled her in for a kiss which ended when Frank entered the room right behind her.

"Enough, you two. We have work to do." He looked around to see the perfectly organized kitchen.

"My apologies. Y'all have been busy. I can get right to the pastries and desserts." He grabbed an apron and went farther into the kitchen where he usually worked alone.

Alphonse gave Marlene a quick kiss and said they would meet later after the dinner crowd was over. All went on about their duties.

~

Nick and Jill were sitting drinking tea at one of the back tables away from where Darlene was seating the early dinner crowd. Jill was texting on her phone and Nick was looking through his messages.

"I haven't heard anything from Rich," said Nick in a worried tone. "He promised to let me know as soon as Brenda passed away. It's been over two hours, even three. Not a word."

"I am trying to get Georgia to answer my text. Maybe I will try Bonnie." Jill continued to work on her phone.

"Dad," said Anika as she came up to their table carrying a bread basket and a dish of fried okra, her favorite.

"Gerard is acting weird. Before I left the hospital, he pulled me into the room and kept hugging me and telling me how sorry he was about everything. How he could have easily killed me too if I hadn't demanded to be let out of the car. It's just not like him to give a shit."

"Anika," said Jill a little too harshly. "Watch your mouth, young lady. But, yes, that is unusual for him. But then he has had to realize that because of his drinking, he has caused much anguish in the lives of some very special people to us all. And Brenda…" Jill stopped, unable to keep talking. She put her face in her hands and sobbed.

Nick was quick to get to his feet and kneel down beside her. He pulled her into his arms and let her cry it out.

Anika was wiping tears from her face as well. She pushed the bread and okra away from her and held her head back to keep the tears from causing mascara to run down her face.

After a few minutes, Jill's phone chimed. She was quick to grab it and saw it was Bonnie. She quickly read out loud that Brenda was still hanging on. She was breathing on her own but the doctors still did not hold out much hope.

"Not holding out much hope," said Anika. "Well, that's better than the 'no hope at all' that has been told to us since the accident. So, I will take it." She stood up, grabbed the okra and left the room.

Nick and Jill watched as she retreated and noticed that Matt had been within hearing distance as well. He walked over to their table and looked at them both.

"You have raised a very, very wise and intelligent daughter, Nick. She has pointed out what none of the rest of us have considered. Brenda is still alive and she was not supposed to be. I wonder if anyone else has realized what this could mean?"

He turned on his heel and strode out of the room, out of the restaurant and got into is Jeep. They heard tires squeal as he pulled out onto the main road.

Both stood up and looked at each other. "We had better follow," said Nick.

"Yeah," said Jill. "They are both way too smart for their own good."

Twenty-Six

When Gerard woke up later in the afternoon, he felt like he had a slight hangover. But it did beat the crawling skin, muscle aches and pains, sweats and vomiting of alcohol withdrawal. He'd been there more times than he would like to admit. Everyone thought he did not realize the depth of his problem.

He was clearly an alcoholic. He had been since his early college days. He had also had a problem with other recreational drugs when he was in high school and college. How could he not be with a mother like Margaret and a father like Andrew? That was always his excuse. He always had a ready excuse. He had always known what he was. The problem was that he didn't care and, what the hell. He enjoyed it.

He lay back with his good arm behind his head and after a few minutes everything came rushing back into his brain. What had happened. What he had done. Whose life he had ended and what that meant to his life. He had always been afraid of losing those things that were important to him. The problem was that he had never had anything really important in his life before. At least not a person. Not even family. The truth, as he had to accept, was that the most important thing he had ever had in his life was taken away and it was his fault. He loved Brenda. He had not even admitted that to himself, much less to her. He suspected that she might have loved him as well.

He covered his eyes with his good hand. Tears started leaking out of both. He could not stop the flow, nor did he want to. He cried until he had nothing left. He was wiping his face when the nurse entered the room.

"Gerard," she warily began, having been on his bad side before. "I have some news about Brenda Montgomery. The family asked me to tell you."

Gerard sat up quickly and threw back the covers.

"Shut it, right now!" He stood up and grabbed his wallet and robe. He stalked to the door and then turned on the nurse.

"I don't want any of you lame ass medical people to mention her name to me again. You have no idea what she meant to me and what a great loss this is to everyone that loved her. Besides, I already know."

He stalked through the door and turned in the opposite direction from where Brenda's room was located. He got on the elevator and punched in a random number. When he stepped out of the open elevator door, he was facing the hospital chapel. He stood still, clenching and unclenching his hands. He took some deep breaths. He took a couple of steps in that direction then turned around, but the elevator doors had closed. He rocked back on his heels, then turned back around to face the chapel again.

"Okay, God. I think it's time you and I had a little talk," he said in his snottiest tone.

He threw back the chapel doors and when they quickly rebounded on him, he kicked them open again earning him shocked looks from the two women sitting in the front pew.

He quickly recognized Mamie Gray and his mother.

"Well, speak of the devil and there she is."

He looked at Margaret with a look that would have frightened a lesser woman, but she was unfazed. He did not like that.

Mamie stood up, hands on hips. "I am sorry for all that has happened, Gerard, but that display was uncalled for."

"It is okay, Mamie. I think we are done here." She held her head high and nodded her head at Gerard as she passed. She stopped at the door and turned to face him.

"Contrary to what you might think, we do need to have a discussion at some time about our relationship. I made a terrible mistake with my children. Sometimes you have to make a decision between the easy path and the right path. I chose the easy one and set some things in motion that I could not take back. I have lived my life in regret. I would like the chance to explain myself. Let me know when you are ready."

Gerard was red in the face.

"When Hell freezes over you piece of shit!"

His mother had already gone through the door and he figured she had not heard him. He turned to Mamie.

'You can tell your *friend* that I said for her to 'Go to hell'. I will never speak with her about anything personal. Only business as long as we are both alive."

He turned and walked up to the front of the chapel and stood looking at the candles that had been lit in remembrance of many loved ones.

Mamie took a few steps toward him. "I will just say this. Gerard, you do not know what you are talking about. There is much you don't know and I thought you were a smarter man than to refuse to get all the facts. I guess I was wrong." She turned and went through the chapel doors much the same as Margaret.

Gerard sat for a short while with his head in his hands. Finally, he stood. He faced the cross on the wall.

"Why?" Gerard scratched his head. "God, it's just you and me and I want answers, not silence. Do you hear me God? Why take Brenda? Why not me?" He was almost yelling.

"Brenda was kind and good and had friends and family and love and...and..." He wondered if he could get one more 'and' into the sentence.

"No one would give a shit if I bit the dust. I don't have any love in my life. Never did. Until Brenda...and you took her from me!" He was shaking his fist at the cross now.

"I never got the chance to tell her. All because of you!" He was screaming. He turned and started throwing song books across the room.

"All because of you!" He flung more books at the cross. "You!"

He shook his fist at the cross again, then bounded across the room and tried to pull it off the wall. It was fastened tightly. He could not budge it. But then, he was using his good arm and also trying to use his bad arm which had not been re-casted yet from his earlier tirade.

He felt stitches rip and saw blood stains forming on the sleeve of his bathrobe. It hurt like hell but he relished the feeling. He felt some of his wrath at God leaving his body as the blood left his arm.

He turned and grabbed his bad arm with his good one and turned to sit back down on the front pew, much as he had started.

"Bravo."

Gerard turned enough to see Matt walking up the aisle clapping his hands slowly.

"This just keeps getting better and better," sneered Gerard. "How long have you been spying on me you little son of a bitch?"

"I have been in the chapel in the very back corner since before Margaret and Mamie came in."

Matt took a seat next to Gerard. "You are bleeding through your bathrobe."

"Well, aren't you the master of the fucking obvious!"

"And you remain the biggest moron I have ever met." Matt was not fazed by Gerard's outburst. "I can't believe anyone as smart as you could make such an ass of himself time and time again. Tell me, does being a total ass come easy to you or do you have to work at it? Frankly it's hard to tell because you are doing it so often."

"Why you little... you piece of...how dare you...God why are you doing this to me?"

Gerard got to his feet but the exhaustion was getting to him, not to mention the blood loss, and he had to sit back down.

"Keep it up, Gerard. You might as well get it all out. You can't possibly be a bigger jerk in my eyes than you are right now, so go ahead, get it out. You have hated me since the day we met. Don't bother to deny it." Matt crossed his arms and sat back against the pew.

"Why in the hell would I deny it? Listen shithead," said Gerard opening his wallet and removing a twenty-dollar bill. As he did a small piece of paper fell to the floor unnoticed by Gerard.

"Take this and go get yourself a candy bar for your candy ass, and don't bother bringing me the change."

"I'll pass, you piss kisser. I am going to sit right here until you get it all out so you can get the help you need." Matt reached to the floor and picked up the piece of paper and dropped it on the pew between them.

"Did you just call me a piss kisser? What the hell is that?"

"You know, a piss kisser," said Matt looking uncomfortable. "One who kisses…piss, or something like that."

"You just made that up, didn't you? You didn't have a decent comeback." Gerard was putting the twenty back in his wallet.

"So, I made it up. Not that big a deal." Matt turned sideways to see Gerard better. "You had already used shit, damn, ass, son of a bitch, and hell and you even said fuck once. I don't like to say fuck if I can help it, if that is okay with you, you fucker."

Gerard stared at Matt for a minute and then burst into laughter that only served to make his arm hurt and bleed more.

Matt stared back at Gerard like he had lost his mind. Gerard just laughed harder.

After a few minutes, Gerard stopped and took a couple of deep breaths. He looked at Matt with a hint of a smile on his face.

Matt just looked at the floor with a disgruntled look on his face.

"Matt," Gerard began. "Would you like to know why you get on my nerves so damn much?"

"If it's not too much of a stretch for your pea brain," Matt responded.

Gerard started to make another snide remark, but looked at all the lit candles and seemed to change his mind.

"You remind me so much of Nick when he was younger." Gerard stretched his legs out in front of him and leaned his head back against the pew.

"When he was sent to boarding school in England to live and study there with me, I couldn't handle it. He excelled at all subjects. He was the master of the keyboard. The teachers loved him. The other students loved him. He was accepted right away by almost everyone." Gerard sat up a little straighter, still holding his arm.

"I had been doing quite well until he showed up. I was an excellent athlete. I played soccer, lacrosse, tennis, polo, track...you name it, I played it. Not only did I play it, I excelled at it. But I struggled with my book work. I had a hard time with every subject. Then Nick comes along and I look like a total idiot. I began to start trouble and blame it on Nick. I was good at it. He never made a scene even though he knew I was to blame. He sucked it up. Always had words of wisdom to say. Never ratted me out. I hated him."

Gerard got up again and again had to sit back down. Matt continued to listen without interrupting.

"Nick finally realized he had stolen my thunder and made enough trouble of his own to be sent home. He was a damn martyr. Always the 'pretty boy'. Everybody's pet."

"Is that how you see me?" Matt stood up and walked toward the cross and began to pick up the song books.

"Yes, I do. Look what you're doing now. You're fixing the mess I made even though I have treated you like shit."

"Sorry, dude, but I don't see you being able to do it. You need to get back to your room and get your arm taken care of." Matt continued his chore. "Is that when you started drinking?"

"Yes, among other things," Gerard stated bluntly.

"I can't go back to the room. I don't want to face any of the Montgomery's if they are still hanging around. I can't face the fact that I killed their daughter. The only love I have ever known all because I couldn't control myself."

"They're still there in her room, Gerard. She is still living." Matt went over and sat back down on the pew and turned to Gerard. "She has been off life support for six hours now and she is still with us. Struggling but still alive."

Gerard's mouth dropped open. "No one told me. The last I heard was that there was no hope."

"Thanks to a very smart niece of yours, I realized I had to come here to give you a small bit of hope. Jill got a call from Bonnie stating Brenda is still alive but they are not holding out much hope. Anika made the remark that this is far better than no hope at all."

Matt picked up the piece of paper that had fallen out of Gerard's wallet and handed it to him. Gerard took the paper and ran his fingers over it.

"You are right. That is much better. I need to get to her room I have to tell her again how I feel. Do you think she can hear?"

"It's hard to say." Matt took the paper from Gerard and read it. "Where did you get this?"

Gerard took it back from Matt and looked at it. "Jill gave this to me right after she and Nick were married. I never understood it's meaning."

He looked at Matt. "But I bet you do,' he said a little more sarcastically than he meant.

"Greater is He that is in you, than He who is in the world." Matt sat silently for a few minutes. "What do you think it means?"

"Hell, I don't know," said Gerard. "Maybe that I am greater than anyone else in the world? I thought for a while that it was some kind of code from Jill that she had a crush on me even though she married my brother."

"Oh, no, Gerard," Matt began but was interrupted.

"Then I thought she was trying to say that the world is all mine for the taking. All I had to do was to reach out and grab it." Gerard made a grabbing motion with his good hand.

"That's not..." Matt tried again, but Gerard had more to say.

"Then I realized that it was probably some Bible crap and for some reason, I put it in my wallet instead of throwing it away like I should have."

"Would you like to know what it means?" Matt leaned back and crossed his ankle over his knee in typical teenage fashion.

"Not really, but I'm sure you won't let that stop you," Gerard said in a bored voice.

"Gerard, we all have to make choices in our lives every day from small inconsequential things to major life changing decisions."

"Well, shit on me for missing that one all my life. Where was I when that logic was passed out?" Gerard was being as sarcastic as he could.

Matt waited for him to finish. When he did, Matt continued.

"One of the most important decisions you will ever make is the decision to accept Christ as your Lord and Savior. Once you have done that, then Christ lives within your heart. He guides and directs you. Satan is of the world, but Christ defeated him at the cross. Does that make any kind of sense to you?"

"I think you are saying that if accepting Christ has taken place, then greater is He that is in my heart than Satan who is in the world."

"Well, that didn't take quite as long as I had thought it would," said Matt getting to his feet.

Gerard stood up as well. The sleeve of his bathrobe was soaked in blood.

"Okay, pipsqueak, I acknowledge that you are smarter than the rest of us, but I am bored with this discussion and I want to talk to Brenda." He started slowly walking toward the chapel doors but stopped before he went through.

"Are you coming with me or going to stand there picking your nose?" He looked at Matt with a half-smile.

Matt gave a smile back and jogged to join Gerard. Together they made their way to Brenda's room.

The family stepped out so that Gerard could say his piece to Brenda. He bared his heart and soul again on a more serious note and felt much better for it. When he was finished, he kissed her on the forehead and turned to join Matt and Ben, who had come just in case Gerard needed any help back to bed.

Gerard cooperated while the staff resident stitched him back up and contained the bleeding. He cooperated when his arm was re-cast. He cooperated when the nurse came to give him his withdrawal medications and issue him a warning about leaving the floor without telling anyone where he was planning to go. He apologized and said it would not happen again.

As Gerard drifted off to sleep, Ben looked at Matt with many questions in his eyes.

"Matt, I don't know what you done did to turn him 'round like this, but you is some kinda miracle worker. He done never give in this easy."

"Ben, all I did was turn it all over to the Lord," said Matt.

"You knows, Matt, that He who is in you is greater than He who is in the world," said Ben putting his arm around Matt as they left the room.

"I think I heard that somewhere recently, Ben, my man. Very recently as a matter of fact," Matt said with a smile as the two of them left the building in search of food that had not been prepared by a hospital.

Marianne Waddill Wieland

Twenty-Seven

Gerard slept through until the next morning. When he opened his eyes, his brain came alert and his first thought was of Brenda. He sat up quickly and looked at the clock.

"Ten o'clock? Really?"

He started to get out of the bed but pain shot through his newly stitched arm causing him to remember the events of the previous evening. He took a deep breath instead of yelling for the nurse or making a scene. He slowly eased his way off the bed and put his robe on.

He didn't see Ben anywhere so he made his way out into the hall. He still didn't see anyone so he decided to go to Brenda's room on his own. He was in a lot of pain, but in some new way, he felt better. Not angry like he almost always was. He wasn't craving 'hooch' either as Ben would say. This was a new and strange feeling for him.

He looked into Brenda's room and saw only Liza Montgomery putting Brenda's personal items in a small duffle bag with the hospital's logo on it. Brenda's bed was empty. Gerard grabbed the wall and felt blackness closing in. He must have made a sound because Liza looked up from her task to greet him.

"Oh, Gerard," she began. "It's nice to see you this morning."

He felt he couldn't speak. He just looked at the bed with his mouth hanging open. He felt the world had tilted, but he was still being held in place by gravity.

Liza noticed his distress and came over to him. She laid her hand on his good arm and explained that Brenda had made it through the night breathing on her own. It was still touch and go but they made the decision to move her to a care facility in Richmond, Virginia that the doctor had said might offer her a fighting chance. She was still in a coma, but her vital signs were stable enough to transport her with a flight team by helicopter. Since this area had no helicopter and the hospital to which she was going had a helicopter for emergencies only, the Wallace family had offered Rod's service to fly Brenda there earlier this morning.

"So, you're saying that my little brother took Brenda and a flight team in a real helicopter to a new hospital in Virginia this morning?"

"Richmond, yes. About seven o'clock." She went back to her packing.

"I imagine she is there by now. Georgia and Bonnie went with her and her father and I are driving in very soon."

"So, she is going to be okay," said Gerard looking at the floor.

Liza moved to sit on the bed next to him and gave him a one-armed hug.

"Son, we know you love her, but we can't get our hopes too high. She is still critical. I hate to say this, but even if she comes out of this, she may never be the same. Her brain activity may be abnormal. We aren't blaming you, really, we aren't. Of all the girls, Brenda was the free spirit. She always did what she wanted. We could never talk sense into her. She always leaped before she looked. I promise to keep you updated on her condition. We are going to put it in the Father's hands and I hope you will too."

Gerard nodded his head and kept his mouth shut. He wanted to yell at her mother because he didn't get to say goodbye to Brenda and see her off. He nodded once again and made his way back to his room.

"There you is!" Ben was standing by the bed holding coffee from the local coffee shop because he didn't feel like listening to Gerard bitch about the hospital brew.

"I went to see Brenda, but she's been transported to another facility. I almost passed out when I saw the empty bed. And Rod took her in his helicopter. I really thought he was kidding about that." Gerard was looking at Ben with a questioning look.

"It be quite the machine, Gerard. You needs to have him take you up in it 'fo he go home," said Ben.

"Wow," said Gerard. "I have been here but I really haven't been here, for months, years, maybe a lifetime. I have never cared before. Never thought of anyone but myself. I figured I just wasn't wired like most people. Do you know what I mean?"

Ben looked at Gerard and sighed. "I does know what you mean, but I also knows you is wrong. Very, very wrong."

"How so, Ben?" Gerard had a look of hope on his face.

"You cared fo' me, Gerard. You met me when we was in jail. You talked to me like I was somebody. You paid my bail and paid fo' a funeral fo' a man you didn't know. Then you looked fo' me. Nobody ever done nothin' like that 'cept my granny. Nobody."

"You helped me think straight that night, Ben, even though I was a bastard to you and the others. I didn't deserve any kindness," said Gerard like he meant it.

"Then you took me in. Give me shelter, a job, clothed me. Nobody do that if he don't care fo' other people. Only think o' hisself."

"I don't know, Ben…"

"Man, you done had a heart all yo' rich ass life. You just be coverin' it up with all that hooch and shit. Now, yo' doctor came by earlier and he be sendin' you home today, so we gots to get you cleaned up and ready fo' when he come back."

"Yeah. Home. Where is that? I don't even know anymore," said Gerard with a great heaviness.

"It is with us. All of us," said Andrew.

Gerard looked up to see his father and brothers as well as Jill, Anika and Matt. Even Alphonse.

Alphonse? Really?

"Alphonse is here with breakfast pastries I made for my mountain family. Enough for all."

He laid the food out on the table in the room and added the coffee Ben had brought in. The family talked about the situation and it was decided that Gerard would stay with Nick and Jill for as long as it was necessary and as long as Gerard was willing.

Gerard did notice that one person was missing and that was his mother and for that he was grateful. He didn't think he had come far enough in his mindset to include her in his life. He wasn't sure if he would be able to ever make that transition in his mind and in his heart.

The family helped him get his things together and they left as a family unit. His hope was to find his true self in the land in which he was born.

God help him! He didn't think he would ever get over that turn of events!

~

Summer was coming to a close. There was much activity in Mountain Mama's with the changes to the fall menu, Jill's cooking show going into it's third season and the changes taking place within the Dennison and Wallace families themselves.

Anika had decided to continue with her endeavor to be part of the cheerleading squad during her senior year and had been in regular practice for that as well as the orchestra. Matt had been working on music and recording with Nick and was preparing to take off to Julliard in a few days. Nick and Margaret had been working on her piano playing skills to help with the physical therapy on her hands and arms. Alphonse had returned to New York and so far, had caused no more problems allowing Gerard to remain with Nick and Jill.

Brenda was still living. She was still at the care facility in Virginia and all anyone heard anymore was that her vital signs were stable and nothing else had changed. Gerard thanked God every day that she was alive and not on life support. The family had requested no visitors and the others had respected that.

It had been very hard for Gerard, but he was trying to learn boundaries and respect for himself and others. He had managed to stay sober. He had not had a drink since the accident.

His arm had healed and he was thinking of trying a short trip back to Chicago to see how he handled being away from the family. He had assumed a role in the building of Nick's Mountain Resort and was handling the legal issues since the resort was three quarters finished.

"Okay, Dale. Give it to me straight," Gerard said to Nick's site foreman as they had lunch at Mountain Mama's. "What seems to be the real problem with the property lines?"

Dale flexed his muscles as he tended to do often, especially if there happened to be pretty ladies in the area.

"Farmer Brown, that owns the property to the west, says the lines are incorrect. His goats and cattle need the creek that is just on our side of the property line. He says his animals will suffer without it."

Dale shoved a piece of paper at Gerard and Gerard noted that in the 'name' space, Dale had written 'Farmer Brown'.

"Dale, for crying out loud. You can't just write in "Farmer Brown'. You have to put the man's real name. You should know better than that."

"Just what are you saying, Gerard," said Dale. "Are you insinuating that I don't know what I am doing and that I am not as smart as you?"

"Hell, no, Dale." Gerard picked up the paper. "You can't just write in 'farmer' for his first name because that is what everyone calls him."

"For God's sake, Gerard," said Dale grabbing the paper. "The man's first name happens to be 'Farmer'. The fact that his occupation is also a farmer is purely coincidental."

"Oh," was all Gerard cold come up with.

"Man, you need a woman," said Dale. "You are way too uptight. If you died today, they would have to screw you into the ground."

Neither noticed Margaret had approached their table.

"Young man," she began. "I don't know who you are per se except you work for my son, Nick. But I would thank you to keep your remarks to yourself when it comes to my son, Gerard's personal life. You know not of which you speak." She turned and nodded to Gerard before walking off in the direction of the dining room.

"Gerard, I meant no harm, and now that your mother said what she did, I remember what happened a few months ago. I am so sorry, man."

Dale stood, stretching and flexing hoping to be noticed by any newcomers.

Gerard rolled his eyes and told Dale he would look into the situation and get back with both he and Nick about the property dispute.

Dale headed into the dining area to pick up more food to go while he was in the area and looking for any of the local single ladies while he was at it..

Gerard stayed put looking at the document. His mind wandered to Brenda and some of the good times they had shared. However, he realized he had never had a sober moment with Brenda. He had always had alcohol on board. So had Brenda a good majority of the time. He wondered would she have even liked him when he was sober. He knew he was not as much fun. But time ran out. He would never be with Brenda again, but his heart refused to accept that.

He got up and stretched, and looked around for Ben. He found him coming down the stairs with Jim and Lorraine. They were talking excitedly. When they got to him, they immediately closed down the discussion.

Lorraine gave him a kiss on the cheek, Jim patted him on the shoulder and Ben just stood there grinning.

"Did I miss something?" Gerard was rubbing his old arm injury that still bothered him on occasion.

"Naw," said Ben. "You not be missin' a thang. Let's get somethin' to eat then maybe sees if Mamie be lettin' us take Xander to the carnival over in Beckley fo' a couple o' hours."

"Why not? I already ate some lunch but I can always eat a little more. And I didn't have desert yet."

Gerard realized that four months ago he would have made a nasty remark about a statement such as that, but he had changed. He had changed for the better.

Twenty-Eight

September was at a close. Another month had passed and Gerard had noticed something strange seemed to be going on and he seemed to be left out of whatever it was. He had been working hard on the problems of property lines at the resort. He had been going to local high school football games to watch Anika cheer, and he had to say, she was as good at that as she was at everything else.

He had done a segment of Jill's show with Ben and it had received rave reviews. It had been funny as well as instructive with Ben trying to help Gerard learn how to cook food that might be eaten if one lived on the street. No one clued Gerard in as to the content of the show so the reactions on Gerard's face were natural.

He had wanted a drink really bad that day, but he managed to kill the feeling by deciding that this must be what all the secrecy had been about. He figured he would just relax now and enjoy the beauty of the changing colors of the surrounding areas that he had been forced to call his birth place. Damn! He didn't think he would ever get used to that!

~

Nick and Jill were loading their suitcases into the Hummer to meet Rod at the airstrip. They were heading to New York early to practice for the beginning of the fall concert series. Rich had been visiting at Mountain Mama's for the last week, making plans with Nick as well as intense conversations with other family members.

Gerard wandered out on the pretense of lending a hand. "Well, Rich, did you accomplish what you came here for?"

"Yes, Gerard, I believe I did. Thank you for asking." Rich gave him a strange look and climbed into the back seat rolling the window down. "Nick, are the others coming soon, we're on a tight schedule."

"Yes, they will be right behind us. Mother is helping Nana pack some snacks to eat on the plane." Nick continued what he was doing in the rear of the vehicle.

"Wait," said Gerard. "Mother and Nana are going? Why are they going now? Can't they come with the rest of us this weekend? The concert isn't until Saturday."

"Sorry Gerard," said Nick impatiently. "I don't have time to explain now but just plan on coming back up this Saturday morning. Rod will be here for you and Ben. And Xander. And the rest."

"Xander?"

Ben wandered out just as Mamie pulled into the parking lot. Xander jumped out of the car and ran to Ben who scooped him up sitting him on his shoulder. Mamie followed with a small duffle bag handing it to Gerard.

"Thanks again, Gerard, for you and Ben volunteering to watch Xander while I go to New York early."

Gerard looked at Ben who was trying hard to look anywhere but at Gerard.

"You're welcome," he said in an almost sarcastic tone.

Mamie gave them all kisses on the cheek which Xander wiped off quickly.

"See you all Saturday!" She climbed into the Hummer with Rich as Jill and Nick took their places in the front.

Andrew came out with Margaret and Nana getting them settled in his car while Lorraine jogged out with Josie on her heels. They threw their bags in the trunk and quickly got into the car. Josie, however, threw her bags into her own car and waved to Anika to hurry as Nick took off out of the parking lot.

Anika and Mark joined Josie and began to get in the car when Gerard, having had enough, stopped them.

"What the hell is going on? What am I missing here? Who is left to even run the place?"

Lance wandered up next to Gerard and Gerard, startled, jumped a foot and would have fallen if not for Ben.

"When did you get here? I haven't seen you in months." Gerard saw Jim join Lance.

"Don't get riled up, Gerard," said Jim. "We are going to man the place while the others are gone and we will all meet in New York on Saturday. Rod is going to come back for us on Saturday morning."

"But why is everyone going now. This is almost everyone that works here," said Gerard testily.

"I ain't said nothin'," said Ben carrying Xander into the restaurant.

"Gerard, somebody has to watch Xander so he doesn't miss school. You and Ben do a great job with him, so Mamie thought that was the best solution." Jim started back into the restaurant.

"But that doesn't explain why everyone is going up now," whined Gerard.

Lance looked at him. "Gerard, you know there are some things that just can't be explained." He turned and went inside as well.

"Whatever." Gerard gave up and just decided that things looked and sounded really strange since he was sober. He wasn't so sure it was that much of an improvement.

~

Saturday morning, as scheduled, Gerard, Ben, Xander, and the rest of the troupe were assembled out at the airstrip waiting for Rod's final check to finish so they could board the plane. Ben was playing with Xander, running with him on his shoulders while making airplane noises. He had played like this all week. It had been left to Gerard to help with homework and read the bedtime story. He found that he had enjoyed that and looked forward to it each night. He was finding there was a lot more to life than he realized. Life was not a full- time party.

Jim came over to him and explained that he had spoken to the Montgomery's and that Brenda had started to show some improvement.

"What does that mean for her life, Jim?"

"To be honest, I have no idea. They didn't elaborate, but she has been there quite a while now and this place is known to work miracles on these types of cases," Jim replied.

"Is everyone all set?" Rod was by the door to help everyone board.

Lance moved to help with the luggage, making sure Xander's duffle bag with his flight entertainment was in the cabin of the jet. He helped the boy into his seat while Gerard and Ben got the rest of the luggage loaded and secured so as not to slide around on the flight.

Jim sat in the cockpit with Rod after Gerard declined. He was growing more used to his brother being a pilot but not so secure that he wanted to see a problem, should it develop, first hand. He had been there and done that all too recently.

During the flight, Jim and Rod discussed how Rod had started working with Andrew and Margaret to take over the company business as Chief Financial Officer as had been announced earlier in the year.

Margaret had retired from that position in order to get her life and mental status back in order. She was still only really comfortable when she was with Nana and was undergoing psychotherapy and medication changes with Dr. Weir on a weekly basis now instead of daily. She had mended her relationship with Nick and was doing much better accepting Jill as her daughter in law. Her relationship was still strained with her other children, but Dr. Weir told her not to stress and that each would be repaired or built when the time was right.

Lance spent the time talking to Gerard about Gerard's sister, Gwen, and how beautiful and fun she was while Ben watched Xander play his electronic games.

"I just don't see it, man," stated Gerard. "She has just been a big pain in the ass as far as I can see. Never has been nice to me. I have had to deal a lot with her and that asshole agent, Victor DeVille, over the years thanks to Alphonse."

"Gerard, do you think things might be different now that you are clean? You haven't seen much of her since your life has changed." Lance took a drink of tea and started raiding the snack basket that had been put together by his sister, Jean.

"To tell the truth, I had not considered that," said Gerard. "I have been seeing some things differently for sure, but I guess time will tell on that one. In the meantime, I will just say to you, good luck with that."

He turned his attention out the window as they approached New York City. This would be the first time he had been away from Beaumont since the accident. His thoughts rested on Brenda and how he would have loved to share this time with her.

~

After settling in at the Grand Wallace New York, they had been greeted by Gwen and ushered into Marcel's to meet with the rest of the group for lunch. Gerard had to say it was somewhat pleasant. He was able to converse with the others without feeling he wanted to cut his own throat as he had felt like in the past. He had always hated conversations that did not have himself as the center of attention.

He had a little difficulty seeing Georgia for the first time since being in the hospital a few months back. She was identical to Brenda and he felt more than a little jealousy when Rich put his arm around her or kissed her. This was immediately followed by guilt about the whole thing being his fault in the first place.

"Are you two ready to go?" Lorraine had come into Gerard's and Ben's room as she had made it her duty to make sure everyone was assembled in their seats for the opening of the symphony's new season.

"We is, Ms. Lorraine," said Ben puling at his tie as he did when he had to wear his tux.

"Yep, this is as good as it gets, Lorraine, and thank you for making sure we get there. I am almost looking forward to it," said Gerard.

"Trust me, Gerard, you're going to love it." She left to move on to her next victim.

They left the room to join the others already seated in the front rows near the orchestra. Gerard was wondering why they weren't seated in their family box as they usually were. He finally chalked it up to one more thing that he couldn't quite make sense out of.

"Let it go," said Ben in his usual intuitive fashion.

"Let it go, let it go," said Gerard, mocking him.

"Hush, you two," said Lorraine. "You don't want to miss a minute of this. Ben, you know what you need to do. Do you know when?"

"Yes'm, I does," replied Ben not looking at Gerard.

"What are you going to do?" Gerard was getting testy now. Something was going on and he was not privy to the information. He started to get up.

"Sit down and shut up!" Lorraine stood up and bent over Gerard. "You need to pay attention. Am I making myself clear?"

"Uh...yes you are," was all Gerard could get out. What the hell was going on?

Lorraine resumed her seat just when Rich walked out onto the stage.

"Good evening ladies and gentlemen. I would like to welcome you to the opening night of the New York Symphony Orchestra's fall season."

Loud applause has heard all through the house and when it died down, Rich began to speak again.

"Tonight, our opening number will feature members of two very special families that are close to my heart. Our featured pianist, Nicolai Wallace, will be playing the first number accompanied by some of his family members and friends. Our newest symphony member Matt Dennison will be playing the violin and will have some of his family members and friends on the stage as well. So please give a warm welcome to Nicolai Wallace and Margaret Wallace to explain this opening number further. Thank you." Rich left the stage and joined the orchestra that he would be conducting.

"What the hell?" Gerard was starting to realize most of his family and friends were in on this, but his mother? What could she have to do with anything? He wasn't sure he wanted to know.

Nick came onto the stage with his mother holding onto his arm. "Good evening everyone. We have a few surprises for you tonight. This first song we will be doing will be played by most of our two families as Dr. Dana explained. My wife, Jillian Dennison Wallace will be singing the solo parts in the beginning of the song 'Silence and I' that was made famous many years ago by the Alan Parson's Project. I am sure many of you will recognize it. The last part of the song will be sung by a special guest who some may have heard of, but most of you will not know her. My mother will explain the rest." Nick stepped to the side and handed the mic to Margaret.

"I am here tonight for a very special reason close to my heart," she began.

"What? She has one?" Gerard said a little too loudly and Lorraine swatted his arm.

Margaret continued. "This song was brought to my attention by Dr. Dana and my son, Nick, a few weeks ago while Nick was helping me to strengthen my fingers so that I might play the piano once again. I have spent my life in silence to my family and children. I have alienated them and because of this, they grew up thinking I didn't love them or have any use for them. I have suffered a kind of mental illness most of my life stemming from abuse in my younger years. I must admit I used it as a crutch. I refused to see reason and take any responsibility of the fact that my family did not even know each other. I have a long way to go and I will not make any more excuses. I have spent the last year getting to know my son, Nicolai, and the family of his wife. My life is changing little by little and I am trying to connect with my own family members and this song is dedicated to another one of my children that I have much love for and with this song I am asking that he accept my apology and break our silence so that we might mend this family just a little more. Because of me and my silence, he has much silence in his own life that I hope will end to a small degree tonight. Gerard Wallace, please accept my apology and know that I always loved you. This is for you and I think before the song ends you will understand." She and Nick walked off the stage to thunderous applause.

"Shit!" Gerard made to get up and leave but Ben held him in place. "Of course, this is your part." Gerard spoke in his old snotty tone, but he sat backdown and slid down in the seat.

The curtain raised to reveal Nick on the grand piano and Margaret on the baby grand next to him with their backs to each other. Jill was off to the right with a guitar on a stand near her. Gwen was seated in front of the pianos with a flute and an oboe on stands. Matt and Anika were on the left with their violins with Josie on a viola. Behind them was Mamie on a marimba and Mark on a drum set.

Rich raised his baton and directed the music to start. Nick began the piano solo in his beautiful style while Margaret appeared to be playing only a few chords. Gwen joined in with an oboe solo in a haunting style.

Jill began to sing. "If I cried out loud over sorrows I've known and secrets I've heard. It would ease my mind someone sharing the load, but I won't breathe a word." She walked over as she started the chorus and laid a hand on Margaret's shoulder. Margaret briefly patted her hand as she was not playing much at this time. The strings had joined the song.

Jill continued. "We're two of a kind, silence and I. We need a chance to talk things over. We'll find a way to work it out." The oboe began again and Margaret was playing more chords now. Jill walked to the front of the stage and looked directly at Gerard.

Gerard was feeling an emotion he had not felt much in his life. Humility, and he bowed his head not meeting Jill's eyes. When he did look up she was smiling.

She sang beautifully, he noted, as she continued. "When the children laughed, I was always afraid...So I close my eyes 'til I can't see the light and I hide from the sound."

She continued with the chorus again as the drums joined in. The orchestra was playing very softly so as not to over shadow the family. As the chorus ended again Jill went back to her spot by the guitar and the strings became louder as did the pianos.

Gerard was stunned that his mother could play like that. He had no idea. He sat in stunned silence almost overcome with emotion.

"You hasn't seen nothin yet," said Ben in Gerard's ear. Gerard looked over at him to find Ben with the biggest smile Gerard had ever seen on Ben's face.

Then Gwen switched to the flute and Nick began a more complicated piano routine. Margaret began to hammer out a contrast to Nick's playing with loud staccato notes showing she still had quite a bit of skill while Mamie joined in on the marimba showing that she, too, had great skill. The horn section of the orchestra picked up the melody and became louder as Rich continued to direct in his own special elaborate style.

The brass section continued to increase in volume until Jill picked up the electric guitar and began a guitar solo that had most on the edge of their seats.

As Jill finished her solo, Gerard noticed a couple of people step into the wing of the stage like they were coming out, but he could not see who it was. Something inside said this was very important. Well, that and Ben nudging him in the arm.

The music slowed and someone came walking out onto the stage taking over the singing. Gerard noticed the limp before he saw…Brenda. She was coming onto the stage continuing the song where Jill left off. She walked to Margaret who took her arm while Georgia came out and took Margaret's place at the piano.

Margaret held her arm while she sang the verse. As the chorus started again Brenda held her arm out to Gerard as did Margaret.

Gerard realized this was the moment of truth and it was his guess that his mother had somehow assisted in getting Brenda to this place in her recovery. He didn't know what to do.

As the song continued, Ben stood up and pulled Gerard out of his seat and up onto the stage. He was so overcome with emotion, he felt his legs give way as he reached Brenda. He dropped to one knee as he felt the sting of tears flowing from both of his eyes. She put her hand under his chin and raised his face to look at him. His mother put her hand on his shoulder and he was so overcome, he began to sob. Brenda dropped to her knee as well assisted by

Margaret and Gerard grabbed her in a tight hold like he would never let her go. They both cried out as much emotion as their hearts and souls could handle.

The song was winding to a close as he pulled away to look at Brenda's face. She looked at Margaret and smiled.

"Thank you," she said. Then she looked at him.

"I heard every word you said, felt every touch. And I want you to know that I am in love with you too. I love you Gerard. I love you. I love you so very much."

Gerard's tears began to fall again as he looked at his mother. She had tears on her face as well.

"Thank you, mother," he said.

As the song drew to a close, the three embraced each other tightly as they laughed and cried and began to live life in the real world maybe for the very first time.

The Mountain Mama Series

Epilogue

It was a month later and most of the family was gathered around the living room of Nick and Jill's place getting ready for Sunday dinner. They were discussing final changes to plans for the opening of the Grand Wallace Mountain Resort that would take place the following spring. Matt was not present as he was at Julliard and Lance had returned to Mountain Mama's in Blacksburg, Virginia.

Mark had remained with his family after the concert. His mood had become more and more despondent as the months had passed without any word from Nancy. He had even hired a private investigator to try and find her. Her family was still adamant that they had heard nothing either. Most of the family continued to worry about him.

"I think it might be time for me to return to Blacksburg and let Lance come back home," said Mark. "I think it is about time I faced facts and call it a day. She's not coming home. Nancy has gone her own way and is not coming back. She probably has a new husband by now."

"Mark," said Jill. "You and Nancy are still legally married. She has to file for divorce, or you do, before either of you can marry anyone else."

Just then the door flew open and Gerard and Brenda entered with Xander and Ben close on their heels. Rod had flown them in from Chicago where Brenda was on an intense physical therapy program and staying with her sister, Bonnie. Gerard and Ben had returned to Gerard's place in the Gold Coast area of the city. Gerard was doing very well and had remained sober.

"Look what I got!" Xander was holding a replica of Rod's helicopter that Gerard had a friend make for him. He ran in to show the others his treasure. Mamie was off again on one of her continuing mystery trips.

Gerard went over and gave his mother and Jill a kiss on the cheek and a hug to Nick. He grabbed Anika up and spun her around giving her a kiss on the cheek as he set her down.

"So, why the long faces on all of you on this fine day?" Gerard was glowing.

"Mark is thinking of giving up the search for Nancy and going back to Blacksburg." Jill was filling glasses with tea and handing them out as she spoke.

"You can't give up," said Brenda. "I am living proof of that." She went to give Margaret a hug and kiss as well as one for Andrew. It had come to light that they had paid for specialists to work on Brenda's case while she was at the Richmond facility.

"We have news we want to share," said Gerard. Before he could say another word, Brenda held out her ring finger to reveal a huge diamond.

Anika squealed in delight as she grabbed Brenda's hand. "Oh...my...God!" She squealed again. Everyone got up to admire Brenda's ring.

"When is this happy event taking place," said Margaret.

"We can't set a date yet," said Brenda. "I have one more surgery to get through so we can have a real honeymoon, if you know what I mean."

Jill put her hands over Xander's ears. "We know what you mean!"

Brenda joined Jill at the counter where she was assembling appetizers that would precede the dinner that she and Margaret had prepared. Margaret had expressed an interest in learning some simple cooking skills.

The men sat at the table and tried to say anything to offer Mark some hope about his situation. They were still waiting for Jim, Lorraine and Nana to get there and Rod to finish with the jet and pick up Josie.

As they discussed options that Mark might not have thought of, the door opened and the rest of the group came into the huge kitchen to join those already there.

They were quickly brought up to speed on Gerard and Brenda's engagement as well as Marks dilemma. As they were talking, Mark's phone rang.

He walked out of the room to take the call. After a minute, the others heard him yell.

"Nancy! Nancy! Where are you...what??" He dropped the phone and slowly walked back into the kitchen having the attention of the entire group.

"What? What is it, son," said Jim. When Mark's pale face just stared into space, Lorraine went to her son and felt for his pulse. Josie came to his side as well.

"What happened? Was that really Nancy?" Lorraine guided him to a chair and Jill got him some water.

"Yes, it was Nancy," Mark said slowly as he looked at each one around the room. "She has been kidnapped."

"Kidnapped!" This word rumbled around the room.

"Did she say where she is or who has her?" Josie was the first to voice their thoughts.

"She just said that she had been kidnapped, was okay, and she loves me. Then the phone went dead." Mark was clearly in shock. "How are we going to find out where she is?"

"How can we find out who has her. All this time and no one has demanded anything."

No one noticed Mamie enter the kitchen behind the others. "I know," she said as she exchanged a look with Margaret and Rod. "I know who has her."

Acknowledgements

I would like to mention a few people that assisted me in the writing of this second book in the 'Mountain Mama' series. Paula Hawkins has stuck by me throughout the writing of all my books and has read every word of each one. She has given me good editing notes and storyline feedback and has been with me at almost every book event to which I have been. She is a big advocate of my writing and I can't thank her enough. I could not have done this without her.

Gini Hawkins and Gladys Barrington have also been beta readers of my novels. Both have given me much support in continuing to write the sequels to this series and I thank them with all my heart.

Richard Diakun also played a big part in this book and you can read his contribution in the dedication page.

Marianne Waddill Wieland

The only constant in this world is change and in my life, there has been more than enough with more looming on the horizon. I am currently working on more than one book at a time and enjoying writing short stories more than I can tell you.

I am still living in Michigan, but I am sad to say my mother passed away in January 2017, peacefully, may I add. I feel like a part of me left with her but at the same time part of her lives on within me. I miss her with every breath. She lived to be ninety-six years old.

As I am writing this, I am thinking about all the author friends I have met over the past year. I have also reconnected with some old friends in my hometown of Williamsburg, Virginia, and am considering this town as a possible place to relocate as well as the Washington DC area. Although I am sure I will miss my boys, Scott and Steven, as well as my grandson, Liam, I am continuing to live life to the fullest as much as possible. And I wish the same for all of my readers!

Other Books By
Marianne Waddill Wieland

Moments in Time
Mountain Momma Series book one: My Heart for Jill

Coming in 2018:

Meeting Henry

Made in the USA
Columbia, SC
28 June 2018